almost definitely never

LUCY DAY

Blue Crow Books

Publisher's Cataloging-in-Publication Data
Day, Lucy 1978-.
Almost Definitely Never: Jasmine Falls Love Stories/ Lucy Day.
p.____ cm.____
ISBN 978-1-947834-70-5 (Pbk) | ISBN 978-1-947834-69-9 (eBook)
1. Women—Fiction. 2. Love—Fiction. I. Title.
813'.6—dc23

Blue Crow Books

Published by Blue Crow Books
an imprint of Blue Crow Publishing, LLC
Chapel Hill, NC
www.bluecrowpublishing.com
Cover Design and Cover Illustration by Lauren Faulkenberry

Also by Lucy Day

The Almost Lovebirds

Chapter One

SADIE

MY LIFE WAS OFFICIALLY a dumpster fire.

You wouldn't think so if you saw me here today, standing in the kitchen of this lovingly restored Victorian house with a to-die-for wraparound porch. Nestled on a tree-lined block in the small town of Jasmine Falls, it was the prettiest house in the whole county. My parents had bought this house decades before and turned it into a bed and breakfast that had been featured in dozens of regional magazines and was a favorite spot for tourists.

It was a beautiful house. A historic landmark. A beloved piece of Lowcountry architecture. Today, though, it just reminded me of how I'd failed. Again.

"I can't believe I agreed to this," I said, adjusting the apron Mom had loaned me. "What was I thinking?" As of last week, I'd lost my job, my housing, and now my last scrap of pride. For me, being here at the inn felt like the worst kind of humiliation—the kind that knocks you flat on your back and then sends you home licking your wounds. It was bad enough to lose my job and my home in one fell swoop, but to be back here, taking money from my parents at age twenty-nine?

Epic failure.

Dumpster fire.

My mother huffed. "Probably that you owe me for last summer when I babysat that wretched snake for you."

"That was an emergency situation," I said. "And Elvis was completely friendly."

Elvis the Education Snake was a lazy king snake who spent most of his time being petted by children during ranger programs at Congaree National Park. When the visitor center flooded, we had to evacuate Elvis for a few days, which unfortunately coincided with my time off. In short, Mom had done me a favor by watching him.

I'd forgotten to tell her that Elvis was a champion escape artist.

"It nearly gave me a heart attack when it hid under my pillow," she said. "That monster took ten years off my life." She frowned as she arranged her signature blueberry scones in a perfect little sunburst shape on the silver serving tray. "So now, I'm calling in the favor."

Truth be told, my mom had a lot of favors that she could call in. She'd helped me more times than I could count.

She turned and put her hand on her hip, and I realized with a shudder that we were standing in identical postures. We probably looked like the mirror image of each other in that moment—though she was heavier and shorter, and her hair was threaded with gray. We had the same blue-gray eyes, the same deep brown hair, the same narrow shoulders, and the same stubborn resolve that came from relentlessly clawing your way toward your goals. As she stared me down by the breakfast buffet, I felt like I was looking at my future self, and that sent a chill straight through my heart.

I did not want to be in this house, in this town, when I was her age. I had bigger plans for myself—much to her chagrin.

Not that there was anything wrong with this house and this town—they were quaint and sweet, the epitome of Southern charm. But they were my mother's dream, and not mine. My goals were different, and being back here was just a reminder that I'd failed to reach them.

"You do realize that the *breakfast* in *bed and breakfast* is like fifty percent of the appeal," I groaned. "And you know I can barely make toaster waffles."

The last time I'd tried, the fire department had showed up as thick black smoke poured out of my tiny kitchen window. Because I lived in park housing, it was extra embarrassing. Having your emergency blasted across all radio channels by park dispatch— followed by its humiliating conclusion that a toaster pastry was to blame—was not something one could easily live down.

For weeks, the other rangers had called me Julia Wild Child and left toaster waffles in my office. One of the law enforcement rangers had even given me a pair of fireproof pants and two fire extinguishers (which I kept, of course, because I like to be prepared for any kind of emergency). But even that debacle was not as humiliating as being back here at the inn that my parents owned, doing a job that meant I'd officially failed at life. Again.

"Sadie Anne, I'm not asking for the moon here." Using my middle name meant she was deadly serious, and it always made me bristle. "I'm asking you to check in a few guests, change some towels, and turn over a few rooms. You could do that in your sleep. And you can order food from Gwen's. I'm not expecting a miracle." She paused and took a deep calming breath, and then moved on to re-arranging the fruit platter I'd just assembled. "This is fortuitous for both of us."

"Is it, though?"

She huffed. "Since you no longer have a job or a place to live, I thought that solving both those problems for you was fortuitous, yes."

Her words stung, even though I knew she wasn't trying to hurt my feelings. Being here now felt like the worst failure of my life. For the last three years, I'd felt like I'd finally found my purpose—that sweet spot where conservation and education overlapped. Working for the park service here in Jasmine Falls wasn't just something I was good at, but something that gave me instant community. Between my colleagues and the steady stream of visitors eager to see our programs, I finally felt like I belonged—and that people appreciated my skills.

The job was fun, too: canoe trips in the wetlands, junior ranger talks with kids, birding walks with cute little old couples who carried field notebooks to record their sightings. Getting people more curious and excited about the nature in their own backyard was more rewarding than any other job I'd ever done—and I'd tested a lot of jobs to see if they fit.

My mother had been trying for years to get me to work at the inn—ever since I'd been in college. Now that my job with the park service had ended abruptly, this was her sneaky way of doing it again. My parents were delightful innkeepers—everyone loved them. They'd poured their hearts into restoring this house and building a business they were proud of. They relished making people happy, whereas I'd worked hard to break my people-pleasing habits. The last thing I wanted to focus on was making everyone else around me happy when I felt like my whole world was falling apart.

Losing my job hurt, but the worst part was feeling like I'd

been kicked out of the club. I'd stumbled into a job that came easy to me, and let myself believe I was good at it. Based on how easily District Ranger Mike had let me go, I'd been wrong.

Dating his son hadn't been my most brilliant move. But I hadn't thought either of them were vindictive people. I'd been wrong about that, too.

"I thought you'd enjoy being here," Mom said sweetly. "It's so quiet this time of year."

"Could you really not get Sean to come here and cover for the week?" I said. "He's so much better at this than I am."

My older brother Sean was naturally charming and had worked here the whole time he was in college—he'd been our parents' first choice for taking over the inn one day. Now he was married to a full-time novelist who supported them both, and his job was basically managing his wife Jacqueline's social media accounts and book tours. Because he'd found success, he was off the hook.

Mom folded her arms over her chest. "Sean's busy this week and is hundreds of miles away. You, however, are right here at my fingertips and have nothing to do."

Except job hunt. And try not to die from humiliation.

I rolled my eyes. Sean lived on some distant Florida key that sounded like paradise. Distance was almost always his excuse for not coming back here, but I knew he'd felt suffocated, too.

"It's just a week," she said, arching her brow. "You can do anything for seven days, dear."

"Easy for you to say. You're spending seven days in Hawai'i."

Last night, when Mom had called and talked me into being her stand-in, she'd explained that she and Dad had, on a whim, signed up on a waitlist for some kind of woo-woo couples' retreat on the Big Island last winter. Another couple had cancelled at the last minute, and she'd gotten the call inviting them to come instead. Airfare was included, so it was a no-brainer—especially since I couldn't remember the last time my parents took a vacation. When I'd offered to go in Mom's place ("It'll be a great way to get over suddenly losing my home and career," I'd said), she didn't find that so amusing.

I didn't find her counteroffer all that amusing, yet here I was.

"Sadie, this will be good for you. I'm paying you twice what I'd pay anyone else." Mom sighed, and her voice softened. "I just thought this would take your mind off the park business and give you a little extra money. And you know you can stay in the carriage house as long as you'd like."

At least I wasn't staying under the same roof with them—Mom had offered to let me move back into their house, but I'd sooner eat my ranger hat. They lived a few blocks away, in another historic house they'd restored. These days, guests could just text them if they had any kind of late-night needs, so there was no reason for my parents to be onsite all night long. This week, though, I'd be staying in the carriage house behind the inn to make sure everything ran smoothly while they were away.

"I know, Mom. I appreciate the help."

She patted my arm and said, "See? It's win-win."

I bit my lip. It was hard to be irritated with her when she put it that way—she was only trying to help me, but it still felt like she was poking a wound. My last paycheck from the park service would come in two weeks, and I needed to save every penny until I figured out my next move. No other parks were hiring right now, and there weren't many in the area to begin with. Congaree was the biggest in a two hundred-mile radius, and it was the main attraction here. District Ranger Mike had terminated my position because he said they needed more wildlife biologists than they needed interpretive rangers. (That, of course, was a lie.) Probably this week was Mom's way of easing me into working here full time and then taking over when she retired…but I was going to bury that thought as deep as I could and focus on just surviving the next seven days.

This is temporary, I thought. *You can do this. You take children on swamp tours. You relocate lost alligators and move rattlesnakes out of campgrounds. This is a cake walk.*

If I said it enough, I might believe it.

"Plus, this week is important," she said. "We have special guests and I need someone here that I trust."

Oh no. *No.*

"Mom, please tell me it's not a wedding party." My heart sank at the thought. Nothing was harder than managing a rowdy bunch of bridesmaids and groomsmen. They were worse than ornery alligators.

"No, it's better!" She clasped her hands together and said, "A film crew is staying for the whole week. They're shooting a travel show and want to feature Jasmine Falls. And maybe even the inn!"

She squealed so loud I thought a window would crack. No wonder she was paying me double—it was hazard pay.

"Mom," I said, pressing my fingers into my temples. "Why are you just now telling me this?"

"It'll be so much fun, Sadie. And you'll be perfect. Just show them around and tell them all the things that make our town amazing. And make them feel at home. They mentioned doing an interview, so if you're lucky, they might even ask you a few questions and include it in the show. Wouldn't that be something? I always wanted to be on TV." Before I could even register all of her words, she grabbed the tray of scones. "Let's get these out. Your father's in charge of omelets and coffee, but you know how he gets once he starts telling people one of his stories. He'll keep everyone here until lunch time."

An hour later, my head was spinning from the detail overload —not to mention what having a film crew here meant. My mother was Type A all the way, and had a particular way of doing—well, everything. Mom and Dad had painstakingly restored the huge Victorian from its pressed tin ceiling tiles down to the baseboards. Now it was one of the crown jewels of Jasmine Falls—and really, the whole Lowcountry of South Carolina. The upstairs held five bedrooms and bathrooms that were tastefully updated to showcase features original to the house. The front rooms downstairs were for the guests—a sitting room, a library, and a dining room, all furnished with stunning antique furniture. In back were the office, the kitchen, and the laundry. That area was separated by a lovely set of pocket doors that they hadn't even realized were in the house until a year after they bought it.

The last time I'd helped Mom at the inn, I'd been a freshman in college—home for the summer with "nothing to do" (her words, not mine) and some half-formed ideas of what I wanted to do with my life. After a whole summer of helping with check-ins and doing more laundry than I thought possible, I'd been certain that running the inn was not my calling. It had felt dull and meaningless, but that was something I could never say to my parents because they loved this work. Though my mom had insisted she wasn't disappointed by my decision to quit my hospitality-track degree and opt instead for parks and recreation, I had my doubts. Deep down I knew that she had hoped her love of this place would rub off on me and inspire me to run the inn when she and Dad retired.

Now, the way Mom got all excited explaining her check-in protocols, I wondered if it would be harder to step away this time around. I loved my mom, but there was no way I was working for her. Hard pass.

"I've put together a check-in list for you to follow," she said. "It'll make things easy." She pulled out a binder that was as thick as the dictionary and thrust it into my arms. "You'll need to freshen up the rooms before the film crew arrives. They should be here today between four and six."

"Got it."

"Have I forgotten anything?" she said, crossing her arms over her chest. She wore a floral blouse and tan cropped pants, like she was already halfway into vacation mode.

"I can manage," I said. "Don't worry. Go have fun and pet a dolphin for me."

She straightened a framed print on the wall by the desk and said, "Just remember to be twice as friendly as you think you need to be. Everyone's here for an escape, and your job is to help them relax and enjoy this place."

"It'll be fine," I said, with a little extra gusto just for her.

"Of course, it'll be fine," Dad said. He stepped into the office, still wearing one of mom's chef aprons. "You got this, Monkey." He turned to Mom and said, "We should head to the airport, hon. Wheels up in two hours."

"I'll have my cell phone with me at all times, so you just call if there's any trouble," she said. "Just remember the time difference."

"I'm not going to call you on your vacation," I said.

Dad groaned, steering Mom toward the kitchen. "Let's go get the last few things packed," he said. "I'm ready to drink fruity drinks with umbrellas and feel sand between my toes."

She smiled and said, "Sadie, we'll let you know when we land."

Dad gave me a big hug and said, "Have a good week, kiddo. Thanks for standing in."

"Of course. Safe travels."

After about a hundred more reminders from Mom, they were out the door, and I was left in silence. Our current guests (two retirees from Florida) would check out in two more days. This was the shoulder season, when you could take a breath—the Labor Day rush was past, and the next big wave of visitors wouldn't come until October, for the Fall Festival. The film crew had booked four of our five rooms, but I expected to barely see them at all. With any luck, this week would be completely uneventful.

After the last couple of weeks, uneventful was exactly what I needed.

It was easy enough to handle a couple of nice old people from Florida. A few muffins and scones and tales from my park service days would keep them entertained, and there would be nothing for me to do after dinner time each night, except stream movies and eat ice cream from the carton as I mourned the death of yet another career path.

Easy.

AFTER MAKING myself a fresh coffee and setting up my laptop in the library, I called my friend Gwen to see about ordering breakfast for our guests. She owned the Sentient Bean, which was just a few blocks from here on Main Street. It had the best coffee and pastries on the whole planet because Gwen was a culinary wizard. We'd been friends forever and were the same age—but somehow, she made twenty-nine look a lot more adult. Unlike me, Gwen owned her own business, had her life in order, and had plans for her future that didn't get upended nearly as often as mine.

"Did you manage to get Sabrina Harper on an airplane?" Gwen asked, teasing. There was a clatter in the background, the whir of a coffee grinder. Gwen was a workaholic, too, though she'd never admit it.

"They should be cruising somewhere over the Midwest right about now," I said. "I've been directed to hire a pro to handle breakfast."

Gwen laughed. "You don't want to whip up some eggs Benedict every day?"

"You and I both know that would end badly. I'm trying to keep Mom's perfect five-star online rating, and it seems that the discerning traveler wants more than Pop-Tarts."

"No problem, babe. I've got you covered. I'll text you some options and you can let me know if the head count changes."

"Super. You're a lifesaver."

"Does this mean you won't need my guest room?" she said.

Gwen had offered to let me stay with her when the park service had yanked the rug out from under me (along with the rest of the furnished apartment). I'd had to move out after my last full day of work last week.

"Mom wants me to stay on site in the carriage house. Just in case of nighttime needs or emergencies. Even though I think our current guests will be in bed by seven o'clock."

She snorted. "Movie night at your place, then. I'll bring the wine."

The front door opened and the tiny string of bells on the doorknob tinkled. Our Florida guests must have forgotten something.

"Can you bring some day-old cupcakes?" I said. "Cupcakes make everything better."

"Absolutely."

"Hello?" a voice called. Footsteps echoed on the hardwood floor of the entryway.

"Let me call you back," I said, standing. When I stepped out of the library, I walked right into what felt like a brick wall but was almost certainly a human. After bouncing off, I saw that it was not one of our retiree guests.

This man was closer to my age, tall with broad shoulders and arms that reached for mine to steady me. For a moment, I was stunned—both from nearly being knocked to the ground and by the grip of his hands. When I looked up at his face, though, my stomach twisted into a knot.

I knew those dark brown eyes, that sharp jaw, that intense gaze. Standing with his hand firmly on my biceps was the one guy I'd never expected to see again as long as I lived.

James Fielding.

He stared at me for a what felt like a full minute, and I thought that maybe he didn't recognize me. Maybe we could avoid any and all awkwardness. But then he gave me his trademark smirk, and that hope went right out the window.

Chapter Two

JAMES FIELDING LOOKED JUST AS ANNOYINGLY attractive as he had in college—though his frame was more muscular, he still had a head full of unruly almost-black hair and dark brown eyes that took on a devilish glint when he grinned. Dressed in a fitted black tee shirt and snug jeans with a leather motorcycle jacket, he looked like a slightly more polished version of his college self. Now, his rough edges looked intentional.

His piercing gaze though—that hadn't changed one bit. James had always had this way of staring at whatever object or person had captured his interest and focusing on it like there was nothing else in the room. Now his gaze was fixed on me— and I felt that familiar tingling on the back of my neck, like what happens when lightning strikes close.

Being the focus of James Fielding's attention was a lot like being struck by lightning.

"What on earth are you doing here?" I said. There was no use in pretending I didn't recognize him, because who could ever forget James Fielding? My heart was doing this weird somersaulting thing, and I could feel all the blood rushing to my head. I knew I should be civil—because should I really hold a grudge after eight years?

Yes, actually. Yes, I should.

His lips lifted into a tiny smile as he released me. "Hi to you, too, Harper."

My jaw tightened. I'd hated when he used to call me that. Which was always.

The way my name sounded on his lips, though, still sent shivers straight down my back. He had one of those deep drawls from coastal Georgia that was all soft edges and sweet promises —as soothing as a lullaby.

I could have easily fallen for him back at Cambrick College… if he hadn't been so determined to outdo me every chance he got. One night I'd come dangerously close, because for all his faults (and there were many) James Fielding knew how to make you feel like the most fascinating person on Earth.

That had always sounded cliché to me, until he'd managed to break through all of my insecurities one night, under a blanket of stars, and made me feel like I had some kind of rare alluring quality, too.

Somehow, he'd only gotten hotter since then.

Stop it, I thought. *Stop staring at his perfectly tousled hair, his gorgeous eyes, his mischievous grin. Stop.*

"You run this place?" he said, sliding his fingers along the antique bookcase by the door. "It's quite lovely." The way he said *lovely* sounded like an insult, even though his tone was as sweet as caramel.

Just as I was appreciating the way those jeans seemed to be tailor-made for his muscular thighs and perfectly curved backside, he turned and caught me staring.

"You didn't answer my question," I said, trying to ignore the way his eyes raked over the decor—and then over me. "Are you lost?" It wasn't hard to guess what he thought of this house: quaint, small-town, a little shabby chic. Probably exactly what he'd thought of me back when we were trying to constantly one-up each other in college. This was no doubt exactly where he'd pictured me ending up, despite my greatest efforts not to, and I wanted to knock that satisfied smirk right off his face.

How the universe would bestow such striking looks to such a jerk was criminal. And why the universe had decided to send him here, to my precise location, was inexcusable.

His eyes landed on mine, and his teasing smile was back. "I'm checking in," he said, his voice gravelly.

I snorted with laughter. "Yeah, okay. Why are you really here?" I could think of exactly zero reasons why James Fielding would be in Jasmine Falls. We had a cute tourist thing going on here, but James hadn't been the kind of person to either (1) hike in what was until recently called a national swamp, or (2) recreate in places that were considered quaint. The James Fielding I knew was the opposite of quaint. He was methodical, calculating, and laser-focused on what he wanted.

He arched a brow. "The room's probably booked under another name. Try Ashley Bennett."

I blinked at him, feeling utterly nauseated because the last thing I wanted to think about was all the things James would do here with a woman—and seriously, would the universe really be that cruel?

Suddenly I was very grateful for the carriage house. These walls were paper-thin.

A million thoughts went racing through my brain: how had he found me? Had he tracked me down and come here just to antagonize me? Make me feel like a complete failure because I was still stuck in my tiny hometown while he'd become a jet-setting writer? (Yes, I'd semi-stalked him on social media enough to know that he'd become a travel writer, and not a horrible one. The man could craft sentences, I'd give him that.)

But how would he even know I was here at the inn? Yes, I posted about my park job on social media, and Congaree was easy enough to find with Google, but Jasmine Falls was basically the middle of nowhere. I hadn't heard from James since my college graduation, and now here he was, standing in the foyer acting like it wasn't unusual at all to run into me in a town so small it only had two stoplights.

There were three things I knew for sure about James Fielding: he aimed to be the best, he made friendly rivalries into all-out war, and he never did anything accidentally.

With a rakish smile, he said, "She's our P.A. Among other things."

And that's when two things clicked together in my brain: the last article I'd seen of James's was a travel piece in a national magazine. The crew checking in today was filming a travel show.

James must be the writer.

"Oh no," I breathed. How could this be happening?

"Is there a problem?" he said, his voice light. He shoved his hands into his pockets and raised a brow. He'd always had these perfectly expressive eyebrows that punctuated every emotion that flashed across his face.

Problem? That was one way to put it.

In college, James and I had been on the same track for a degree in hospitality for three years, until I'd finally switched concentrations in my next-to-last semester. We'd been rivals the entire time, always neck and neck for awards, internships, and the highest grades in our class. What started as simple competition that kept me on my toes had soon grown into an epic rivalry, and it didn't end until we tossed our mortarboards up into the air and went our separate ways.

At least we had different goals for our degrees. Because James was bent on adventure tourism and I was enamored with parks and conservation, there was virtually zero chance we'd ever cross paths again.

Or so I'd thought.

Since college, James had become a travel writer—and much to my dismay, a really good one. I'd seen his pieces in a few national magazines, and some big-time online publications, too. And yes, I'd even hate-read them all because some rivalries just never die. (It had started with following links to his articles, curious if he'd accomplished all of those *#goals* that he went on and on about on social media—but his posts made me want to gag because he seemed to always be posing smugly in some exotic, beautiful locale, grinning as if he had a glamorous, flawless life.) James had made a name for himself, and had everyone fooled into thinking he was this charming, humble storyteller who was smitten with hidden-gem towns and luxurious escapes, and wanted nothing more than to show everyone on Earth the exciting parts of life that they'd been missing.

YOLO, and all that.

But every time I saw his smug face attached to an article, I just thought of the guy who made my college life miserable and rubbed my failures in my face. Whenever he'd be selected for an internship we'd both applied to, he'd say, *Don't worry, I'm sure you'll find one, too* in that condescending tone that meant he thought hell would freeze over first. When he'd beat me out for awards, he'd say, *Maybe you'll get the next one.* When his GPA bumped above mine, he'd say, *Most employers don't even care about grades anymore.* And when I'd win something over him? He'd smile and say, *See, the dark horse pulls ahead sometimes.*

He said these words in a friendly tone, but I knew the subtext. He thought he was better at everything and thought my park service dreams were silly. He had Big Dreams and Serious Plans, and even though he had an ego the size of a small planet, people in our class still liked him. Everybody did.

And based on his writing career and his social media account, that had not changed. He was a wolf in sheep's clothing, and the internet loved him. Usually as I was scrolling, I could tamp all those feelings down because I'd finally found a job I liked—it might not be glamorous like his, but it meant something to me. It made me feel like I had a purpose, and that I was a force of good in the world.

Having that taken away was devastating. It made me feel like I'd been wrong all along: like I wasn't good enough, I was easily replaceable, I wasn't so special after all. To fail at the thing I thought I was best at was utterly humiliating. It made me feel like I wasn't good at anything—and nothing I'd worked for had mattered.

And now James was here bearing witness to my darkest moment, when I'd lost the only job that had ever really meant something to me.

So, was there a problem here? Yes. One hundred percent, yes.

I took a deep breath to calm myself—the kind that three years of working in a government agency had helped me perfect—and pulled up the day's reservations. At the top was one for Ashley Bennett.

Four rooms.

"No problem," I said, gritting my teeth. "Here you are."

"She's getting in later this evening," he said, his big brown eyes locking on mine again. "With the rest of the crew." He said that last word as if to reiterate that she was his colleague, and that he would be sleeping alone in his bed.

Super. Now I was picturing James in his bed, and this room felt ten degrees hotter.

"Cool," I said, taking a deep breath. *Great, Sadie. Now you're reduced to one-word sentences.*

He smiled that warm smile again—deceptively sly, like an alligator at the water's edge. "We'll be here shooting all week. Ashley didn't mention that when she made the reservation?"

I swallowed hard. The last thing I wanted was to have James Fielding explain anything to me in that condescending tone he'd always taken with me in our classes. The way he'd spoken so slowly, placing emphasis on certain words had always made me want to slap him silly, and with no witnesses here, I wasn't sure I could hold myself back if he started that nonsense again.

"Of course," I said, keeping my tone even. "I just wasn't expecting you to be here, too. What a delightful surprise." *You won't get the best of me today, James Fielding! The best thing about rock bottom is that you can't go any lower!*

He gave me a teasing smirk and I forced myself to smile. Just as he opened his mouth to respond, the front door swung open and he turned his head toward the sound.

Paula Sue Hinson blew in like a hurricane, her bright pink floral dress billowing behind her like a sail. She pushed her big black sunglasses up into her platinum hair and made a beeline for us, her wedge heels clopping on the hardwood like pony hooves. "Oh my goodness," she cooed, her eyes going straight to James. "James, you've already arrived. We were just coming by to drop off a surprise welcome basket for you in your room. You're just entirely too punctual."

He smiled so his dimples showed and shook Paula Sue's

hand. "Mrs. Hinson, I presume. Lovely to meet you at last." This time, *lovely* did not sound like a jab.

Paula Sue blushed all the way down to the deep V-neck of her dress.

Barf.

"It's so wonderful to meet you in person," she said. "We're just so honored that you're here."

I rolled my eyes so hard they hurt. Paula Sue loved to hobnob with famous people (we had actors and politicians come through occasionally, plus the regular visit from America's most popular weatherman during hurricane season), but James was hardly a celebrity. Sure, he'd published in magazines, but he was a far cry from a household name. This kind of attention was the last thing that his monstrous ego needed.

"And I see you've met Sadie," Paula Sue said. Her bracelets jangled together as she motioned toward me. "We're going to have such an exciting week!"

"Oh, yes," he said, giving me a charming smile. "Sadie and I go way back."

"Do you?" she said, arching a brow.

Double barf. I stared at him hard, willing him to stop right there. But to my absolute horror, he did not.

"We went to Cambrick together," he said with a glint in his eye. "Spent practically every day together there for a while, in the same major." He turned to me and raised a brow. "Feels like yesterday."

"Well isn't that wonderful!" Paula Sue beamed. "Won't that make an interesting angle for the episode!"

"Episode?" I said, back to multi-syllables.

"Didn't your mother tell you?" Paula Sue said. "James is here to shoot a brand new travel show he's hosting—and it's all about Jasmine Falls!"

Oh. My. God.

My heart dropped into my shoes. James was a writer. Why was he hosting a show? Did this man never run out of luck?

"Can we talk about it yet?" she asked James, placing her hand on his forearm. "Or is it still a secret?"

He smiled so his stupid perfect teeth showed and said, "Cat's out of the bag. They made the official promo last week." He turned to me and gave me a sly wink that simultaneously made my traitorous heart flip and made me want to smack him. Of course he'd show up here when he was wildly successful, at the top of his game. And when I was at the bottom of mine.

Could an asteroid please strike the earth already? Like right now, please?

Paula Sue squealed with delight. "Sadie, James's show got picked up by a big-deal streaming service—we're going to be famous!"

"Famous might be a stretch," I said, unable to help myself.

James arched a brow at me and his lip quirked into a tiny smile—the same tiny smile that used to say *Game on*.

She pursed her lips, ignoring my comment completely, and said, "Think of what this will do for our tourism. James, we're all just so excited that you're here. We have dinner reservations for six o'clock at my favorite restaurant, and we'll show you around tonight if you like. Let you get a feel for the place."

"Sounds great," he said. "I might just rest my eyes a bit before the others get here. I started my day with a three-hour traffic jam in Atlanta and saw an actual high-speed chase. I could stand to unwind a little." He glanced back toward me and smiled, and it felt like a solid minute until my brain started firing all synapses again.

Paula Sue gasped. "You poor thing!"

"That's certainly a lot of excitement for one day," I said.

"Yeah. Not the kind I like." His brow lifted and for a split second I wondered about the kind of excitement he *did* like.

Key, Sadie. Room. Hospitality.

Ugh.

"We put you in the Magnolia Room," I said, aiming for my best fake-polite tone. "It has the nicest view of the garden. It's upstairs, the first room on the right. The key's on the dresser."

Paula Sue's eyes widened, like she was horrified I wasn't leading him up the stairs. If it were anyone else, I would have. But James Fielding could go find his own room, and wander down the halls and fall out a window for all I cared. The last thing I was going to do was wait on him hand and foot.

"Thanks," he said, his eyes twinkling. "I'll see you later, Harper."

Paula Sue smiled and kept her eyes glued to him as he headed up the stairs. "He's even more handsome in person," she cooed.

I rolled my eyes so hard they hurt.

As soon as he was out of earshot, she grabbed my arm and said, "I can't believe he's here already. We need to get you up to speed on things because this is a once in a lifetime opportunity for us."

Before I could ask what that meant, she hauled me back into the library and onto the couch. When she plopped down next to me, there were only a few inches of space between us and I felt like a mouse trapped under a cat's paw. She smelled like gardenias and looked about ten years younger than her actual age of sixty-six, and she had a surprisingly tight grip for a woman so petite. Paula Sue was friends with my mom, and also head of the Jasmine Falls Beautification Council. Most of their work was seasonal (like the annual Christmas decorations that stretched from one end of the town limits to the other), but sometimes there were special projects like redesigning the green space in the town square or commissioning a new official welcome sign. The council's job was to make the town look more adorable than a Hallmark movie set, and she took her job very seriously.

"Did your mother really not tell you about this?" she said, leveling her big green eyes on mine. "It's a huge deal to have him stay here and we need to make sure his time with us is absolutely perfect."

"She kind of left in a hurry," I said. "Maybe you can fill me in?" Heat rose to my cheeks as I thought about my old rivalry with James, how I'd complained about him nonstop when I came home back then, and how my mom had laughed it off and told me he was just a boy with a crush. She'd never known the extent of our feud, but she knew he'd gotten under my skin and stayed firmly planted there until graduation day. Had she known James would be part of this and intentionally not told me?

The realization hit me like a hammer. Of course she'd left this part out. She knew there was no way I'd agree to watch over the inn if it meant being *hospitable* to James Fielding for a whole dang week and treat him like some kind of royalty. My mother had upped her game.

I was going to murder her and bury her in the garden. Or just bring Elvis the king snake back for a surprise visit.

Paula Sue gave me a stern look and arched a finely penciled brow. "There are a few things we need to go over, dear. First, I want to reiterate that this is a very important moment for the whole town. We've all got to pull together to make sure every part of the next six days is picture perfect." She gave me a pointed look. "I picked up a bit of a vibe back there—you say you know each other?"

"We were in the same program at Cambrick," I said.

Her eyes widened. "So you're old friends, then?" She clasped her hands together. "That's wonderful, Sadie. That gives us a huge leg up."

"I wouldn't say friends, exactly." But I could already see the wheels turning in her brain.

"I can't wait to tell the others," she said. "This is fantastic!" She dug through her purse, which was big enough to hold a Labrador, and handed me a folder with the town seal on the front. "I have an extra itinerary for you. Everything we have planned for James is inside."

I swallowed hard, opening the folder. There were several loose pages stuck in the pocket, plus a notepad and fancy blue pen that had a little white palmetto tree on the side, along with the words *Jasmine Falls - Stay awhile!*

"The top page is the daily schedule," she said. "We're taking turns doing interviews, and you can see all the participants listed there in the packet. Yours is on Friday afternoon. It's a packed week, but we want to make sure that everyone puts their best foot forward the whole time James is here. Pretend you're being recorded at all times." She dropped her hand to my knee and said, "I can't emphasize that last part enough. You never know what will make it to the editing room, and you know how reality shows thrive on conflict. We want to avoid that at all costs."

Paula Sue never wanted the wrong kind of attention.

"Interview?" Nausea washed over me like a rogue wave. Mom *had* mentioned the crew might ask me a few questions. That I *might* be on camera. I'd brushed all of that off at the time, but Paula Sue was serious. This was not just a few casual questions that "might make it into the episode." It was one thing to put on my fake smile and be a good hostess, but an interview with James? Like in the same room with him? Letting him pick my brain like a carrion bird? No, thank you.

The more she talked, the more my head spun. Paula Sue went over all the details excitedly, gesturing with her hands like she was showing off the prizes on a game show, but my head felt like it was full of bees and I thought surely I was going to faint. Was it possible to die from annoyance?

James Fielding was the absolute last person I wanted to see here. Or ever again. The last time I'd seen him, we'd been in our caps and gowns and I'd tried my best to ignore him—hard though, since he'd graduated summa cum laude and had given our student speech. It was a rousing one, of course, which had made the crowd erupt into cheers and made me wish I could rewrite that last paper for Professor Erickson that had earned me a B—enough to drop my GPA just a fraction of a point below James's, thus putting him up on that stage. He'd always been an overachieving perfectionist, but he was also conceited and arrogant. Problem was, he hid it well. James was a showman and knew exactly how to work a crowd.

Of course he'd ended up on TV.

We'd had one brief encounter that wasn't entirely awful—and it crept back into my mind despite my greatest efforts to keep it out. He'd probably considered that moment just one more way he'd bested me.

It had begun, innocently enough, with my birthday party. I'd made a fatal error in hanging out with him that night, in a way that would have felt like a date between normal people. It ended in a scorching kiss that could have upended my entire world and I'd completely panicked. Afterward, I'd chalked that whole night up to loneliness and margaritas—and pretended in the days that followed that it had never happened. James dated a lot of girls back then, and never for longer than a few weeks. It was like none of them could hold his interest. Our rivalry was no secret, and for him, that night was likely just a different kind of competition—one he figured he'd won. I'd been the ice queen, and he'd finally won me over with tacos and a slow dance that would be burned into my brain forever. But I'd come to my senses and for the last year of school, I'd avoided him as much as possible and hoped that a cruise ship would take him to the other side of the world so we'd never have to cross paths again.

The thought of being stuck in a room with him, even after all this time, was enough to make me sick.

And even worse, now he was a celebrity? He'd had a bad enough ego back in school—by now, he'd need to pack another suitcase for it. Or ten.

"So," Paula Sue said. "He'll of course be staying here for filming, and your job is to make sure everything is perfect and that he has a splendid time." She clapped her hands together in a way that meant a plan was coming together. "And of course, we'll need you to be stealthy and get as much intel as you can about what they plan to feature in the show and what he thinks about everyone he interviews here. We don't want any surprises, and if there are any rough patches, we need to address those before he leaves. This week must be absolute perfection."

I took a deep breath and pinched myself on the arm, thinking for sure that I'd just fallen asleep on the loveseat while reading a book. There was no way that James Fielding would be staying here, no way I'd be tasked with entertaining him, because that would be a nightmare of epic proportions. Nothing was a bigger waste of my time than trying to make James Fielding happy.

But the pinch just made my arm hurt, and Paula Sue Hinson was still sitting next to me, her big eyes narrowed like a cat's.

"This is vitally important," she said. "It's imperative that you do everything humanly possible to make sure that James has a wonderful time and leaves here singing our praises. Understand?" She leaned over and squeezed my knee for emphasis, her nails pinching my skin.

"Yes ma'am," I said. "Copy that."

She gave me a firm nod, releasing me from the grip of her bright pink nails. "I know you'll do great," she said. "You've dealt with the public enough to know how to put on a good face and address any and all problems with grace and ease." She patted my knee then and said, "Just don't let us down. The whole town is depending on you."

With that, she gathered her purse and strode out the door, leaving me alone in the library with a growing lump in my throat.

This was going to be a disaster.

Chapter Three

JAMES

SADIE HARPER LOOKED EVEN MORE gorgeous than I remembered. She was all luscious curves with long muscular legs, and still had those piercing blue-gray eyes that could stop me in my tracks. Those eyes were one of the many wondrous things about her: they went from bright blue when she was excited to a stormy gray when she was annoyed, and sometimes it was entirely too tempting to see if I could make her eyes shift from one color to the other.

Today, she wore a blue wrap-style top that fit like a second skin and slim-cut jeans that seemed designed to draw my eyes straight from her feet to her delightfully rounded hips. Her dark hair fell just past her shoulders in loose waves, and I was dying to know how it would feel slipping through my fingers. She had one of those soft accents that made everything sound sweeter, even when she was madder than a rattlesnake.

I'd done plenty to rile her up back in college. Partly because she was cute when she was sassy, but also because she was super smart and driven. She wasn't easily distracted—you had to be extraordinary to hold Sadie Harper's attention.

I liked that challenge.

She'd kept her tone breezy, but I could tell from her steely gaze that I was the last person she'd expected to bump into today.

So she still didn't like surprises. That hadn't changed, either.

This was going to be fun.

I'd learned a lot in college, but some things had remained a mystery to me. And the biggest one of all was why Sadie Harper loathed me so. There had always been a weird tension between us, and most of the time I couldn't tell if she wanted to kiss me or shove me into a fountain. I'd finally gotten an answer to that question one night when I'd miraculously mustered up the courage to make a move that she couldn't misinterpret. But in the end, it just muddied things between us even more.

Finally, just so I could concentrate and get out of there with my diploma and my pride intact, I'd convinced myself that she hated me. It was easier if I thought I didn't have a chance with her.

With a sigh, I collapsed on the big king-sized bed and stared up at the ceiling. This room was gorgeous—decorated in a neutral palette, it had just enough color added in with throw pillows and a quilt that was definitely made by a sweet little grandma somewhere. A couple of muted abstract paintings that looked like originals hung over the bed and the dresser. The walls were painted a dove gray that made me think of winter mornings, and there was a faint scent of lavender hanging in the air. Windows on one side looked out over the side of the property, and a window on the back wall looked out over a flower garden and a cozy carriage house.

As I started to unpack my clothes, I saw movement outside and stepped to the window. Sadie was walking down the stone path toward the carriage house. Even from here, I could see the hard set of her shoulders. She'd looked tense earlier, and had only grown more so when Paula Sue had arrived. When Sadie came back outside a few moments later wearing a different shirt and carrying a tote bag, I realized that she must be staying in the little house behind the inn.

From my poking around on the inn's website, I'd learned that Sadie's parents still owned and operated the inn. I'd been surprised to see Sadie here today, and not at all prepared. When I'd bumped into her downstairs, it had nearly knocked the breath out of me.

It was a reaction I hadn't expected. But then, few things with Sadie ever went as expected.

Three months ago, when my producer Tetia had first pitched this show idea to me, I'd been shocked. For starters, I hadn't been the network's first choice for the host (not surprising at all). The show had been written with Jack Hartwell in mind—he was a comic-turned-TV-personality and having him as host was like a guaranteed Emmy. He'd passed on the show for some reason I couldn't fathom, and then my name had come up as a replacement. And by that, I mean Tetia had dropped my name to her producer friends and lobbied hard.

I'd jumped at the chance to host, of course, because my career was in a tailspin.

Before the ink on the contract was dry, Tetia had sat me down and told me exactly what the stakes were. The last time I'd seen her, she'd had long, neat braids that she sometimes threaded a bright color into. Today though, her hair was cut short, sculpted on the top and shaved on the sides. It made her look more like a rock star than a producer. Based on her years of experience in TV, she had to be in her forties—even though she didn't look a day over thirty. But when she fixed her big brown eyes on you, it was like being stared down by the high school principal.

I knew I'd better pay attention because she had her serious face on.

"I had to twist some arms for them to consider you," she said. "But I know you're a good fit. This could be the boost you've been looking for."

"I appreciate that," I told her. We'd worked together on several projects, but never on a ten-episode series, and never something that could really make this kind of difference in our careers. A successful show like this one could be a boon for both of us. And the last thing I wanted was to let Tetia down after she'd stood up for me. I knew the kinds of rumors that were swirling around about me. After my breakup with Melanie, I'd been blackballed in publishing. Tetia had worked a miracle to get anyone in TV to even consider me.

"That last web series was a good move," she said, referring to a pet project I'd done with another friend of mine. Together, we'd done some small-budget web shows that had blown up online, and my six hundred thousand Instagram followers hadn't hurt, either. People seemed to like watching me travel— probably because there was a lot of fumbling toward adventure involved. (Not on purpose. That was one hundred percent natural Fielding, always a fish out of water.) At the time, I'd just wanted to do something enjoyable that took my mind off the way my life was falling apart. Turns out, people found it fun to watch.

"See, not all my ideas are bad," I said, teasing.

"It's also good that you kept writing," she said. "I had plenty of material to show the execs, so they were willing to give you a shot. The catch is that they'll only spring for one episode to be filmed and edited. They want to see that before they make a decision to keep going."

I sighed. That's the way it was now, too often. You got one

shot to make a killer impression. If the first episode flopped with a test audience, you were done. And I'd already been down that road once before.

I'd already struck out enough times in the last few years. This needed to be a home run, and we both knew it.

Tetia had gone over a whole list of places with me that day—the show was meant to highlight small quirky towns across the US, mostly in the southeast, with the idea that we'd expand further with subsequent seasons—bless her, Tetia was already optimistic about expanding. Jasmine Falls was one of Tetia's top choices for the first episode—she loved that it had an eclectic mix of business, artists, and festivals and was also next to a national park. When I dug into the research (I tend to geek out over research), I found plenty of people that we could profile for the show—and then I took a drive down here to scout it out myself with Ravi, our cameraman.

When I took all my notes and photos back to Tetia, she was thrilled.

"This is perfect," she'd said. "There's plenty for us to feature, and I like the arts angle."

It was on that trip with Ravi that I realized this was Sadie's hometown. Sabrina Harper was listed as the owner on the Jasmine Inn's website and as I read her bio, everything came into focus: I remembered from our days at Cambrick that Sadie's mom had owned an inn; that she'd wanted Sadie to help her run it, but Sadie had other dreams; that Sadie was from a small town, just like me. And then everything else had come rushing back and Sadie was all I could think about. There was plenty I'd forgotten about my college days, but it was impossible to forget Sadie Harper.

And that ridiculous rivalry we'd had.

It had started as just the typical competition between two

caffeine-fueled perfectionists. As part of a small program, we were always competing for the same internships, the same summer jobs, the same awards. At Cambrick, I'd been hyper-focused on being at the top of my class and making all the connections I could that might get me fast-tracked into my dream job. I wanted to travel the world and work in adventure tourism. It was a competitive field even ten years ago, so I put most of my effort into making myself irresistible to employers who were looking to expand into a wider market. My head was full of ideas about how to make adventure tours appeal to younger travelers, and I was ready to do whatever it took to fill my passport. Going to college had been my ticket out of my tiny hometown outside of Savannah, and a job in travel meant that I'd never have to go back. Not ever.

I'd sensed a similar need in Sadie—we never talked about things like family (she hardly talked to me at all if she wasn't forced to by a group assignment), but I could tell she had big dreams, too. She worked harder than anyone else I'd ever met, and that meant she was moving toward something. I was dying to know what that something was, and wanted to learn everything about the mysterious Sadie Harper—but every time I'd tried to talk to her, she seemed hurt or annoyed and just put more space between us. She never let me get close enough to understand what I'd done wrong.

She'd been whip-smart and studious, and completely irresistible in a nerdy kind of way. She brought a challenge to my mostly boring coursework and made me actually think harder about what I wanted from my life—when I wasn't devising ways to spend more time with her. Sadie never backed down from a challenge and didn't give a flip about the status quo. You were more likely to find her in a library than a frat party, but you were just as likely to find her taking an elective like *Astronomy for Non-Physics*

Majors simply because she wanted to get outside the bubble that was our department. Plus, she had exactly zero patience with me and called me out on my antics one hundred percent of the time.

I loved it.

And then there was that party at her dorm, where she finally let those walls come down just for a moment and she'd kissed me until I thought my heart might stop. No one had ever made me feel like she did—not then, and not anyone since.

So when I found out that her parents owned the Jasmine Inn, this project became a no-brainer. I hadn't met with Sadie's mom in person when I took my little research trip with Ravi, because I didn't want word to get back to Sadie that I was part of this project. I wasn't ready for that yet—I'd done enough snooping to know that she lived and worked in Jasmine Falls, but I needed to orchestrate a casual way to bump into her again.

Colliding with her in the downstairs foyer wasn't what I'd had in mind—but feeling her hands against my chest, even for that brief moment, had made my pulse skyrocket.

My mouth had gone dry and my heart had hammered against my ribs so hard that I thought surely she could hear it. And judging by the look on her face, I was the last person she expected to see today, too.

More than that though, her expression was not unlike that of someone who bites into a delicious-looking homemade chocolate chip cookie, only to realize that it's full of god-awful raisins. She looked completely annoyed to discover that I still inhabited the earth. It was kind of adorable in a weird way, seeing that she still had this aversion to me for reasons unknown.

Pity, because seeing her was like finding a warm ray of sunshine on a winter day. And for a second, I thought I'd seen a spark in her gaze, too. It took everything in me not to kiss her right there against the bookcase and run my fingers though her hair until she purred.

Sadie had been the one puzzle I could never solve. After college, I'd shoved my memories of her way down deep, until she became as intangible as a goddess from a myth. But then this assignment came across my desk, and it felt like fate. What were the odds that Tetia would send me to this little town that was a speck on the map, the same town that happened to be home of Sadie Harper, the girl I never thought I'd be lucky enough to find again?

My phone buzzed in my pocket, reminding me that other things existed in the world, aside from Sadie Harper.

A text from Ashley read, **Hey, we're on our way. ETA is 5 or so.**

Great, I replied. **Our host has dinner reservations for 6. Please don't make me go alone.**

The thought of being alone with Paula Sue and a few friends like her made me shiver. That woman was aggressively friendly, and obviously part barracuda. She probably had lots of ideas she wanted to share about how we should do the show—a meeting with her needed backup.

Hope it's fancy, she said. **I've had nothing but coffee and gas station snacks. Situation is dire.**

How's the drive? I typed. Ashley was driving up from Atlanta with Tetia and Ravi. They'd all been working together for years—a small but mighty crew.

Tetia's driving like a demon and Ravi's making us listen to a murder podcast nonstop. So, you know, the usual.

Drive safe, I wrote. The idea of them all in a van together made me laugh—it'd be less awkward than me trying to make small-talk with Sadie, though.

Ashley sent a thumbs-up emoji, followed by a string of coffee cups.

I flopped back down on my big fluffy bed and stared at the painting that I'd decided was an abstract mountain landscape. This really was a beautiful old house—not at all the kind of place I'd pictured Sadie in. She'd been interested in ecotourism before she switched onto the Parks and Recreation track—she was into the adventure element, but conservation was her angle. I figured she'd either be in a remote part of the Alaskan wilderness or running kids' camps on a secluded island that promised total communing with nature. She liked challenging people, making them curious. Doing that sparked a fire in her, and that passion was contagious.

It was also wildly sexy. She'd always seemed so laser-focused on what she wanted. It made me imagine how it would feel to have that laser-focus pointed at me.

Still, I wondered: a little B & B in her hometown seemed like it was way too easy for her. So, what was she doing here?

I closed my eyes, wishing I could sleep for an hour before the crew rolled in and I had to put on my extrovert suit. This was a great gig, and I knew it could be a stepping stone to something life-changing—but no matter how much I traveled, and how many people I met, I never got used to doing the whole friendly chitchat thing. Being around people could be exhausting—even when I liked it. When people already had big expectations for you when they met you, well, trying to live up to that expectation was even more exhausting.

And this gig was a big deal. I couldn't afford any missteps.

I pulled my phone back out of my pocket and called my sister Phoebe, who lived in Savannah. She'd tried to ease my mind about this whole trip right before I left, when I'd had one of my classic last-minute panic attacks.

When she answered, I said, "Tell me again this isn't a huge mistake."

"I just did the electric slide at a wedding reception and I'm pretty sure it's going to go viral. That's what you call a mistake." She sounded out of breath.

"Where are you?"

"Fleeing to my car and making a break for the state line. Where are you?"

"I'm in a cute B & B that has suddenly started to feel like a cell," I said. "What if this is a huge flop?"

"Just be your same irresistible self," she said. "You're like, network gold. Like if Mike Rowe and Jack Whitehall had a sweet, sexy baby."

"Umm, thank you?"

"Seriously," she said. "You have nothing to worry about."

"I have literally everything to worry about. If this show isn't picked up, where does that leave me?"

My dream of travel writing hadn't panned out like I'd imagined. But then, that was the case with most parts of my life.

She sighed, and I heard her car pick up the call. Phoebe was always at a wedding somewhere—I couldn't imagine how she had any single friends left. "Just breathe," she said. "Have fun with it. You're doing the thing you love, remember?"

Because of one bad breakup and an angry ex who could pull serious strings in the publishing world, I'd gone from a travel writer with a book deal to a guy whose agent was begging to find him guest spots on travel shows. After proving I could co-host on TV and then doing a quirky YouTube series with a friend, I'd finally gotten this break.

But if I'd learned anything over the last few years, it was that big opportunities could vanish just as quickly as they appeared. There was no room for error this time.

"This might be my last chance to prove I belong in this business," I told her.

Raking my hand through my hair, I thought of how Tetia had told me she'd convinced the streaming folks to give me one more shot at a show of my own.

"If this doesn't work out, there's always something else for you," she said. "But I think you'll be just fine."

I didn't believe her at all. But it was nice to hear her say the words.

"Thanks, Phoebe."

"Keep me posted," she said, and ended the call.

Even with the pillow pulled over my face to block out the sunlight, I couldn't push those swirling thoughts far enough away to take a nap. I'd ruined so much in the last couple of years, and this was the best opportunity that had come around since the breakup that had blown my whole world apart. Tetia had helped me pick up the pieces, though, and now she was counting on me, too.

My stomach rumbled, reminding me that I hadn't had anything to eat since the bagel and coffee I'd had on the drive down, and I finally gave in and peeled myself off of the bed.

"You got this," I said aloud. "You are not your failures. You are not your fears." If I said the words enough, I might start to believe them.

Chapter Four

SADIE

PAULA SUE HINSON had left me one exceptionally detailed itinerary.

Reading over the daily schedule, I didn't see how James would hardly have time to breathe. Each day was broken up into morning and afternoon slots for filming, and listed each person that James was set to interview. Breaks for meals were built in, and reservations were listed at different restaurants in town—any of which were fair game for the episode. Judging by the list of interviewees, the show was geared toward highlighting the town's small businesses and artisans. Like Gus and Natalie Richardson, our local flower artists who made the most amazing arrangements in town; Max Eckhart, a master chef who owned the Spare Time Grill; and of course, Gwen at the Sentient Bean.

James was also scheduled to do a special day of filming with Maxine Bell at the Arts Council, and interview her grandson Eli and his friend Alex, both of whom were remarkable metal artists. Reading through the schedule, it was easy to envision each of these people talking excitedly about how they'd built their businesses from nothing but a dream. All of them would benefit from having a few moments in the spotlight, and Paula Sue was right: this really was one of the most important weeks for the town as a whole. Being featured in a TV series could bring a lot more visitors here.

As much as I hated that James Fielding was the person who might usher in this boon for them, I needed to be on my best behavior. These folks meant a lot to me, and if this could bring them new customers and fans, then I could tamp down all my feelings about James Fielding long enough to make that happen.

The bells on the door clanged again and I startled, thinking that Paula Sue had come back with more suggestions for how I might be hospitable. I straightened up the loose pages that were scattered on the sofa and coffee table, not wanting to leave her any reason to start criticizing my housekeeping skills.

A voice called, "Hey, you," and I turned to see Leah, who'd been my supervisor in the park for the last two years. She poked her head into the library and said, "You forgot something." Dressed in her typical slim jeans and tank top, she was wearing my ranger's hat and carrying my sad-looking money plant that had obviously not lived up to its name.

"You didn't have to bring these over," I said. "I could have come by the office."

She shrugged, setting the plant down on the coffee table. So much for all the good fortune it was supposed to bring me. Its little coin-shaped leaves were shriveled and drooping.

Leah pulled off the hat and put it on my head. "Didn't want anyone to steal this," she said. "You know seasonal rangers are a bunch of scavengers when it comes to wardrobe."

"I miss you already," I said. "I even miss the rowdy kids and the alligators."

She smiled, her light brown skin showing off her glorious

cheekbones, and pushed a lock of curly hair behind her ear. "We miss you, too, babe."

To say I was sad about leaving the park was an understatement. I was gutted. Congaree National Park had a small staff, and three years ago they hired me as an interpretive ranger. Some people might think it was a nightmare to spend every day in a swamp filled with mud, mosquitoes, snakes, and tourists, but for me it felt too good to be true.

Turns out, it was. Even though the job was categorized as "temporary seasonal," it had been renewed every year. I'd had stellar performance reviews, and even had visitors tell Leah how much they enjoyed my programs. (Okay, two of those people were my friend Fiona and her aunt, but still. People loved my programs.) Without interpretive rangers, the park wouldn't have the growing number of visitors that it had—people wanted to learn about the ecology of the swamp and go on birding tours and nature hikes. And that's what people like me gave them.

I'd loved doing programs that made people see the park as more than just snake-infested wetlands. I loved seeing kids' faces light up when we went on nighttime walks to find owls. It made my heart swell to hear people talk about all the cool things they'd learned about pitcher plants while they were there. I was a total nature geek and I'd happily poured my heart into my job. Being kicked out felt like a personal blow.

"I had to work eight seasons before I got a permanent position," Leah said. "If you want to stay in, just go do a winter season down in Florida or something. Stay in the game."

I shrugged. "I don't know."

"They're going to realize this was a big mistake, and they'll hire again—but in the meantime, go get more experience and get more time in. Then when they want you back, you'll make the short list easily."

Leah was one hundred percent dynamo: she loved the outdoors, did programs that kids and parents raved about, and didn't take guff from anyone. She was tall and wiry, built like a swimmer, and had lush curly hair that seemed to defy the South Carolina humidity.

Even the weather bent for Leah.

She shook her head and said, "You're one of the best, Sadie. I'm sorry this happened to you—but Congaree isn't the only park out there, and you're too good at what you do to give up because these bureaucrats made a bad call."

I smiled, feeling like a big piece of my heart cleaved away like a glacier. I got called a lot of things, but not *the best*. "Thanks, Leah."

"Sometimes I'd like to march into that district ranger's office and thump him right on the forehead," she said frowning. "I can't believe he claimed it was more important to hire another wildlife biologist. I mean, how many dudes does it take to count baby gators? Those guys don't even interact with the public. We're the ones getting people excited about nature and conservation. You won an outreach award, for heaven's sake."

"He was mad about Joe," I said.

Leah rolled her eyes. "Don't even get me started."

Joe was also a seasonal ranger. I made the bad decision to date him for a short while, despite the fact that his father Mike was the district ranger. Suffice it to say that when we had our epic breakup (like the kind Taylor Swift writes songs about), it came as no surprise that his father took it out on me—even though Joe had been the one cheating. When the move to cut jobs came, Mike's decision to send me packing was likely the easiest decision he'd made all year.

Probably the wildlife department hadn't needed another biologist. But District Ranger Mike frowned on fraternizing within the department—especially when it involved his son. (Spoiler alert: I wasn't the first ranger Joe had *fraternized* with, and I most certainly would not be the last. Sorry, Mike.)

Before Joe, I'd had a strict no-dating-colleagues policy that Leah had told me was the first rule of Ranger Club—if you wanted to go farther than a seasonal hire. People talked in small parks, and there were no secrets between rangers who worked in small confined spaces every day. (Spend an eight-hour shift in a ticket booth sometime, and see if you don't spill all of your secrets.) Plus, you never knew who you'd be partnered with on a kayaking tour or a visitor program, and let's just say it's better if you're not stuck in the swamp with someone who'd like to see you fall face-first into a lagoon full of feisty baby gators.

But Joe was fun, and goofy, and looked at life like it was an endless adventure. And I'd fallen hard because the romantic in me loved a good adventure. Plus, something casual with no high stakes didn't have to lead to heartache, right?

Wrong.

When I found out Joe was seeing someone else, I broke things off. He begged me to take him back, and when I didn't, he went whining to his dad about how I'd broken his heart and he couldn't bear to see me every day. And then he had the nerve to say I'd been the one cheating.

Then the cutbacks came, and I'd been completely blindsided. District Ranger Mike got to decide which seasonal jobs were renewed and which ones were not. And deep down, I thought that if I'd just been a little better at my job, had a few more exemplary reports and one more award, then maybe I could have stayed on. If I'd been good enough, the thing with Joe wouldn't have been bad enough to end it all.

"The good news is that now you can date Ranger Chris," Leah said with a wink.

"Oh, please."

"He's totally digging on you," Leah said. "Has been all season."

Chris looked more like a surfer than a law enforcement ranger. He had wild reddish-blond hair that got light in the summer and made his tan look even deeper. He'd flirted with me plenty over the last few months, but then Chris flirted shamelessly with everyone.

"I'm not interested in being scooped up in a wide net," I said. "I'd like to be properly courted like the rare creature that I am." I fluttered my lashes for emphasis.

Leah snorted with laughter. "Well all right then, Lady Bridgerton. No wild flings for you. Not unless they put some serious effort behind their intentions and make it worth your while."

"I mean, a woman has to have standards."

She looked over my shoulder and her brow arched.

"Sorry to interrupt," James said from behind me, his voice all gravelly.

I felt my insides turn to goo. When I turned, he was standing in the doorway to the library, his hair somehow even messier than it was before and his eyes laser-focused on mine. How much of that had he overheard?

Enough, judging by his teasing smile.

Be friendly, I thought. *You're doing this for the town.*

"Hi," I said. "Can I help you with something?"

"I was hoping you might know a good coffee shop," he said. He shoved his hands into his pockets and that sent my gaze straight to a place that it definitely should not rest.

"Sure," I said, ignoring the butterflies that were swarming in my chest. "Take a right on Oak out there, and go three blocks. It's called the Sentient Bean."

"Need a coffee?" he asked. "Maybe a snack?"

Ignoring the offer, I said, "Ask for Gwen and tell her I sent you. If you're extra nice, she might let you be a taste-tester and give you the special top-shelf coffee."

"Thanks," he said. "Can I bring you anything?"

"No, thank you," I said, wondering what he was up to.

He smiled so his dimple showed and moved toward the door. "Nice hat, by the way."

I pulled the ranger hat from my head and placed it on the coffee table. When the door shut behind him, Leah said, "Who's the cutie pants?"

"Not you, too," I grumbled.

"Does he need someone to show him around?" She peered out the window, watching as he walked down the porch steps.

"Trust me, you don't want to be stuck with him for that long. It'd make our safety training feel like a vacation day."

She arched a brow. "Someone you know?"

"Ugh. Wish I didn't."

Leah laughed. "You're such a little grump. He's cute. And he totally wanted you to go with him. He was just a little shy."

I snorted. "No, he didn't. And James Fielding is anything but shy. I'd sooner drink coffee with the devil himself."

"Wouldn't be nearly as fun," Leah said. "We gotta work on your game. That man's stare was like molten lava."

"He's only here for the week anyway," I told her. "Filming for a streaming show. He'll be gone by Sunday, and it'll be like we never existed to him." Soon we'd be just another item checked off James's to-do list.

"Ooooooh, he's famous?" she crowed. "Tell me more."

"There is no more." But there was so much more. Just seeing him again was making me feel itchy all over, like I was wearing a scratchy sweater that was too tight. Heat rose in my cheeks as I thought of the first day we'd done presentations in junior year seminar. When I'd finished mine, he'd said, *It's like science meets cute escapism,* and made me want to crawl under my desk. From that day onward, he'd always acted like my plans weren't serious enough, weren't big enough to make a difference to anyone.

Leah was already scrolling on her cell phone. "Okay, handsome, let's see what's made you famous."

Admittedly, I'd done the same, hoping against hope for some scandal that would make this town's collective jaw drop so they wouldn't be one hundred percent smitten with him. But the little bit of snooping (okay fine, a lot) that I'd done in the last few hours revealed nothing worse than a goofy snort-laugh during a radio interview.

Somehow, big bad James Fielding had endeared himself to everyone who'd ever met him. This week was clearly going to be no different.

Before she could get too far into her sleuthing, Leah's phone chimed with a reminder.

"Shoot," she said. "I've got to run. But think about what I said, okay? Go do a winter season in your dream park. You're smart and talented and unattached. You could go anywhere you want."

As the door closed behind her, I thought: *Could I?*

Chapter Five

JAMES

By the time the crew arrived, it was nearly five-thirty. Paula Sue had texted me twice already to remind me of the location of the restaurant, using far more emojis than necessary. I was in the sitting room when Ravi, Tetia, and Ashley rolled in and gave me a quick wave as Sadie walked over to greet them. Tetia looked poised, as always, in a black blouse and slim-cut jeans, still sporting her rocker haircut with perfectly tousled top and the shaved sides. Ravi looked like he'd rolled down a hillside—his dark hair was standing up in every direction and his tee shirt had permanent wrinkles. Ashley looked like she was wired from about a hundred cups of coffee, her blue eyes wide and already searching the rooms for a good light source and establishing shot. They were an exceptional crew, and I was lucky to have them working with me. The three of them could work on a shoestring budget and make it look like we'd spent a million.

In short, they made me look good. Like, *really* good. And right now, I needed all the help I could get.

Sadie was all smiles when she spoke with Tetia. "We're so happy to have you staying with us," she said. "I understand you have dinner reservations, but I'm happy to tell you all about the inn when you have more time. It's on the historic register and may or may not have a friendly ghost that hangs out in the downstairs."

Tetia smiled. "I'd love to hear some ghost stories. Wouldn't you, Ravi?"

Ravi shook his head. "Nope."

I grinned. Ravi was terrified of ghosts. We'd taken him on a cemetery tour in Savannah one Halloween and he hadn't spoken to us for three days. And then as payback he'd snuck into my house and filled it with the creepiest dolls that he could only have found in the darkest corners of the internet. I hadn't been able to sleep for a week.

Life lesson: don't mess with the quiet ones like Ravi. He looked unassuming with his lean frame, big brown eyes, and thick-framed glasses, but he was a deviant little mastermind.

"This is quite the place," Tetia said. "It'll look great on film."

"Thank you," Sadie said.

"One question," Tetia went on. "The person we were supposed to interview tomorrow afternoon asked to reschedule. Could we do your segment after lunch tomorrow instead? Do you think your mom could talk to us then? I'm sorry for the short notice."

Sadie's eyes widened. "Actually, my mom had to go out of town for the week. I'm here in her place."

Interesting. So that's why Sadie was here.

"Oh," Tetia said. "So, you'll be doing the interview instead?" I knew where this was going and there was no way Sadie would ever agree. Tetia quickly looked her up and down in that way that no one ever seemed to realize was a quick calculation of how that person would translate to the screen. "That's even better. How's tomorrow at one-thirty?"

I bit my lip to hide my smile. Sadie looked like she'd been touched by a live wire, but Tetia never took no for an answer.

Sadie blinked at her for a moment, then glanced over at me. I gave her a big smile and a thumbs up, and I swear it took everything in her not to roll her eyes at me. "I'd love to," she said. "Sounds like fun." Her voice was chipper, but she bit her lip in that way she did back in college before she had to give a big presentation. She was nervous.

And watching Sadie suck her full, perfect lip between her teeth still made me forget about everything else going on in the room.

"Wonderful," Tetia said. "And if you're interested, we're shooting downtown in the morning, just for some establishing shots and background. I'd love to have you help with that, too. Maybe give us some back story about the town?"

Sadie's eyes widened. "Really? Me?" She looked terrified.

"If you're game," Tetia said.

Sadie smiled her polite smile again. "I'd love to." It was a total lie, and I couldn't for the life of me figure why she'd agree to something she so obviously didn't want to do. That wasn't her style.

She glanced at me again and tugged on the hem of her shirt. When I stood and walked toward them, Sadie quickly looked back to Tetia and the others and smiled. "Looking forward to it."

"The restaurant's not far," I told them. "Can I help take any bags upstairs?"

"I just need a few minutes," Tetia said. "Is it walkable?"

"A couple of blocks," I said. "I scoped it out earlier."

"Great," Tetia said, looking at the team. "Can we meet back down here in twenty?"

Ashley and Ravi nodded.

Tetia hoisted her bag over her shoulder and said, "See you in a few." She turned to Sadie and said, "Lovely to meet you, Sadie. I have a great feeling about this. Tomorrow's going to be a strong start."

Sadie nodded and said, "If you need anything at all, just let me know."

As my three colleagues headed upstairs, I went back to the library, where Sadie sat on the sofa with her laptop.

"Is there something you needed?" she asked, her voice almost friendly.

"You up for a day of shooting with me?" I asked, sitting in the chair across from her.

She snorted. "Of course."

"You sure about that?"

"You think I can't handle one interview, Fielding?" Her eyes sparkled, and there was a flash of that fire she'd had in college—that fire that meant she'd decided what she wanted and wouldn't think of letting go. "You think you're going to put the whammy on me and render me unable to form coherent sentences?"

Actually, it was more likely she'd have that effect on me. Ever since I'd seen her here, my brain felt like it had been short-circuited. I was both delighted and terrified.

"How about we grab a drink after dinner tonight," I said. "I could tell you a little about what to expect tomorrow and how Tetia operates."

She rolled her eyes, but I could see the mention of Tetia had made her recalculate. Sadie still wouldn't back down from a challenge, and still didn't want to need anyone else.

"That's not necessary," she said. "I think I can manage to use my words just fine."

"Suit yourself." I pulled a book from the bookshelf and

opened it in my lap. If I had to wait a few minutes before dinner, there was no place I'd rather be than right here by her.

"What are you doing?" she said. She was still adorable when she was irritated. Her eyes narrowed and her nose scrunched up like a rabbit's. She looked like she wanted to bludgeon me with a couch cushion.

"Um, reading?"

She gestured toward the book. "You suddenly have an interest in canning seasonal vegetables from the Lowcountry?"

"I'm interested in a lot of things." I held the book up and pointed. "Look at the color on these heirloom tomatoes. Just gorgeous."

She leaned closer then and said, "I don't know what you're playing at here, Fielding, but if you think you're going to embarrass me and get it on film, you've got another think coming."

"What if I told you I thought you'd be great on TV?" I said.

"I'd say you were full of it. And I don't have the bandwidth for your games."

"I think you like the idea of being on TV with me."

She stared at me, her eyes a frosty blue. A blush crept into her cheeks and I bit back a grin.

With a snort, she stood and said, "I'll be in the back office if the others need anything."

"And if I should need something?" I asked, teasing.

"You won't," she said over her shoulder.

I couldn't help but watch her as she stalked down the hall to the back of the house, her heels clacking on the hardwood floor, her hips swaying with every step. She was still gorgeous and full of fire, and I couldn't take my eyes off her.

I was in deep trouble.

Chapter Six

SADIE

"So that's why you're all hot and bothered," Gwen said. "Your college crush is back in your life."

"He's not my crush! Stop saying that." Heat rose in my cheeks and even I could tell my voice was too insistent. "He was my biggest rival. A constant thorn in my side."

"Fine, I'll let it go," she said with a grin that told me she wouldn't be letting it go at all. "Your biggest rival is in town."

"And enjoying every minute of it," I said, sipping my beer. "The bastard."

She snorted, picking at our plate of nachos. Piled with chili and jalapeños and about a pound of cheese, they were like a soothing balm for today.

"This is going to be a disaster," I groaned. Already James Fielding was stuck in my head, and I didn't like it one bit. Stupid James Fielding with his stupid big career, and his stupid sexy grin, and his stupid charm that made everyone love him.

Ugh.

We sat in a tiny booth in the corner of the Wonky Donkey, our favorite hole-in-the-wall bar in town. It was on Main Street, just a few blocks from the inn—but not the kind of place that would be featured in the streaming show, and not the kind of place that would catch Fielding's eye. Tourists stumbled into it every now and then, but usually left because it wasn't fancy enough for their vacation experience. It was tiny, dark, and had a mix of '50s-style diner tables and chairs—the kind with brightly colored vinyl seats that stick to the backs of your legs in summer. There was a pool table in the back, plenty of vintage neon signs on the walls (my favorite was the winking alligator with a martini), and a functioning jukebox that played actual records and nothing produced later than 1989.

In short, it was a treasure. Our sanctuary.

"Was he a good kisser?" Gwen said. She gave me a catlike smile.

Yes. Definitely.

"Omigod. Stop." I did not need to be thinking of kissing James Fielding. No matter how good it had been.

"He's a cocky, arrogant, entitled jerk." I took a long drink from my beer, trying to tamp down my hammering heart. "He's completely insufferable." And obnoxiously good-looking, but that didn't need to be said aloud.

Gwen shrugged. "He seemed nice."

"Nice?!" I shouted, a little too loudly. A couple of heads turned our way as the jukebox switched to the next record—an old Dolly Parton song that was like an arrow in the heart. This place would always get bonus points for having Dolly on the jukebox.

Gwen smiled. "He came by the shop earlier—thanks for the heads-up, by the way." She sipped her beer and leaned back in the booth. "He told me a little about what they'd like to see in my interview, which is great to know in advance. I was kind of nervous, but talking with him actually made me feel better."

Gwen was a lot like me: she liked to have plans, to manage her expectations. She wanted to know the when and where of everything, and needed to have contingencies in place—because things didn't always the way we hoped, especially when other people were involved.

"You've got nothing to worry about," I told her. "People love you."

She sighed, pushing her hair behind her ears. It had just been cut into a cute wavy bob, so all the brightest blonde from summer was gone. "I'm really flattered that they asked me, but the idea of being on TV is legit terrifying. I've already had that dream where I realize I'm naked and no one else is. Like ten times."

"You'll be great. I'm sure they'll edit out any rough spots."

"Still, though. This stuff lives forever on the internet." She grimaced. "One false move and you're a meme for eternity."

"You won't be a meme. You've got the ideal energy for TV. All bubbly and sweet. People eat that up."

"That's what James said." She shrugged. "I think he has good energy, too. He seems genuinely curious. And laid-back. It's nice."

I rolled my eyes. "What is it about him that's so dang charming? I mean, you should see his Instagram. It's ridiculous." I pulled my phone from my pocket, determined to pull my best friend far away from Team Fielding before he sucked her into his orbit completely.

Lord knows, once people got yanked into his orbit, they never escaped. They were Team Fielding forever.

Gwen smirked and I handed the phone out toward her. "Look," I said. "Start scrolling and tell me he's not a big fat egomaniac."

Gwen scrolled through the feed and said, "He's got a bazillion followers."

"Barf."

"Wow, you really hate this guy."

I sighed. "I don't hate him. I just find him extremely annoying."

"Yes, being sweet and charming is very annoying."

"It's a trap," I said. "Don't fall in."

"What did this guy do to you, anyway?"

I sighed. What hadn't he done? "He was just always pushing my buttons, trying to get a rise out of me. Everything was a game. Everything was a competition, and I felt like I had to constantly bring my A game. He made me miserable." Sometimes, back then, competing with my own standards was enough—it was exhausting to feel like I had to outdo James and his perfectionism, too. "He always knew exactly how to goad me. There was just no way to ignore him."

He'd found my weakness—I hated to lose to someone who didn't take the game as seriously as I did. (Whether the game was beer pong or a grade point average was irrelevant—it was the condition that mattered.) My parents had made me believe that you had to work hard to get your rewards in life—if you weren't working hard, then you weren't doing it right. The flip side of that was when I worked as hard as I could and still failed at something, I thought there must be something wrong with me —because according to them, excellence was supposed to shield you from failure. So when great things came to someone who wasn't working hard, it seemed completely unfair—like they were getting a prize they didn't earn. And James was the embodiment of that thought: he had an easygoing attitude that always made his wins seem effortless—whereas I had to work my butt off to beat him. I hated that the wins came so easy to him, and if I had to be the one person who made him work hard for a win, then so be it.

I'd have happily died on that hill. And some days, it felt like I did.

"Sounds like he liked you," Gwen said with a smile.

"Ugh. No. He liked getting under my skin." But even as I said the words, I thought of all those times he'd put me on edge. Teasing me around my friends, making everything a competition: from who could raise more money in our department fundraiser to who would get the internship we'd both applied for. Only James could make a bake sale feel like a death match and still make his triumph seem effortless.

And then there was that night of the party. That kiss that came out of nowhere. But then he'd blown me off and as quickly as the spark appeared, it had been extinguished.

Still scrolling, she said, "Aww, look at the puppies. Swoon."

"Seriously, Gwen?"

She slid over to my side of the booth and held the phone out so I could see. "Look at all these cool travel photos. And these profiles of people. It actually looks like he's giving attention to organizations that could use a boost." As she scrolled, she paused long enough to read his captions—and stopped way too long on one that was about animal adoption at Atlanta's biggest no-kill shelter.

I bit my lip as I read the next one, a friendly commentary about a profile he'd done of a guy who lived out of his van and spent every day catching feral cats just to get them vaccinated, spayed, or neutered, and then released so they could continue to hunt mice and go about their other cat business in their neighborhoods. The collection of photos was vibrant and poignant, like a photo essay. Robert was his name, and he had a few cats of his own that he posed with in the photos. That post had half a million likes and tens of thousands of comments. I could see why, though—it was a solid profile of a person who was doing something kind for the community and getting lots of love in return. When I clicked over to Robert's page, I saw that he also had a couple hundred thousand followers, and had a thank-you post about his most recent fundraising effort and the profile by James.

It was like I'd stepped into the upside-down. Since when did James Fielding care about feral cats and senior dog adoption? Did he run out of yachts to take selfies on?

Just a fluke, I thought. Or a PR stunt. I scooted in closer and swiped my finger on the screen, looking for those posts like I'd seen months before: James in the ritzy hotels, with the women who looked like supermodels, indulgent selfies of him grinning on a gorgeous beach, talking about his *#goals* and *#YOLO*. I scrolled through several weeks of posts but saw nothing like that. These posts were different—they weren't bragging, and they weren't self-indulgent. There were beautiful landscape photos of a wide variety of places—not just the kind you'd imagine as vacation destinations for the wealthy. His photos of other people looked like real slices of life, from a painter in Savannah to a couple running community rooftop gardens in Richmond.

Before I knew it, I had scrolled all the way back to last April, stopping to read captions that gave links to his articles, profiles of people doing things that were interesting, inspiring, groundbreaking.

"Maybe he's not the same guy you knew in college," Gwen said. "People change, you know."

"Fielding was always good at figuring out what people want," I said. "That's how he worms his way in." He was a chameleon. A master of disguise. He could insert himself into any situation and immediately go from outsider to darling just by swapping a few stories and buying a round of drinks. He'd certainly entered into my friend group that way, effortlessly charming them so they invited him into the inner circle.

Which meant I saw him everywhere.

Cambrick was a small campus nestled in a tiny town in Western North Carolina, so there was no escaping him. Not in the library, not in the cafe in the basement of our building, and not in the on-campus apartments where my friends had their parties.

And certainly not in the classroom, where he was always ready with a barb. Like that time he'd given me a knowing smirk and said, "You're like the Mr. Rogers of tourism. All about the team-building adventures." As if using travel to build community was such a repulsive idea. It was clear to me that James didn't know the first thing about building community with people—he could worm his way into any place, but he didn't know how to stay.

No matter how I tried to ignore him, his smug face was wherever I was: in every class I took, at every awards ceremony, at every departmental potluck. To my horror, he even showed up at my evening ballroom dance classes—I couldn't even escape him long enough to learn to tango in peace. Soon he was flirting with my girlfriends until they blushed and playfully smacked him on the arm, working his way into every crevice of my life, as if on purpose. Just to prove he could do everything better than I could—including being with my friends. He made everyone love him, but I saw right through him. Fielding just wanted to be the best at everything, and wanted to be adored.

Somehow, he'd learned how to do both.

Me though, I learned early that there was no way I'd ever have both. When I was a kid, the better I did in school, the more people hated me for it. I wasn't exactly a wallflower, but not part of the popular crowd, either. When I didn't have my nose in a book, I was building model dinosaurs and going horseback riding. Instead of arranging furniture in dollhouses, I built complicated dioramas that depicted heroes and goddesses of folklore. I got in big trouble when I turned Mom's vintage Barbie into Medusa, but I still say that was one of the best makeovers ever.

Anyway, it was about that time that I first learned just how much I'd never fit in, and how important it was to choose between doing well and having friends. Fascinated by all things science, I went all-out for the fourth grade science fair and created a robotics project that took me weeks to complete. I was so proud of that thing, and so excited when I won first prize. It felt like all of my dedication and hard work had paid off, and someone besides my parents thought I was good at something. And then Lilly Mae Murphy, furious that she'd come in second place, had made a big show of uninviting me to her birthday party that weekend, telling everybody at school that my parents had adopted me after someone had found me abandoned in a barn with a bunch of baby pigs.

After that, my brother Sean teased me endlessly because he'd said all along that there was no way I could be such a weirdo and still related to him. *But we both know you weren't adopted,* he'd said, *You were dropped off from a different planet.* But fourth-graders are fickle creatures, and it was easy for Lilly Mae Murphy to turn everyone in my class against me. I didn't go to another birthday party for three years.

I'd gone home after school that day and smashed my project to pieces in my bedroom, wailing like a banshee until my mother came to see what all the noise was about. I'd sat on the floor, bits of wire and circuit board scattered all around me, feeling like the whole world had imploded. Dad had planted his hands on his hips and said, "Doing your best is more important that having friends. People come and go, but you just keep working hard for what you want. The only person you can count on in this world is yourself."

Mom had sat next to me and hugged me close, and finally told me, "There will always be people who are jealous of your success, but don't let that stop you from sharing your light. You shine bright, kiddo."

But even then, I'd known the truth. It was like what all those science books I read said: nature seeks balance. When something good happens, there will always be something bad that happens to balance it out. I worked hard to get what I wanted, but I had to remember the balance: if I shined too brightly, the universe would be there to knock me down again. I needed to do well, but not *too* well.

I'd seen that pattern through my whole life. Won a scratch-off ticket? My car got towed a week later. Won an award for best graduate paper? The next day my cat died. Recognized as ranger of the year? A month later my job was eliminated. Each reward was matched with a blow—the universe's way of keeping me humble, I figured. If I brought too much attention to myself, I was bound to pay a price. This week would be no exception—assuming anything good came out of this whole fiasco at all.

"I never should have agreed to do the interview," I said. It had been tempting fate, pure and simple. But Paula Sue's voice had rung in my head like a bell—*This is important for everyone in town.* And then the words were out of my mouth before I knew it.

"I think it could be good for you," Gwen said with a shrug.

"Or this is just one more way for him to prove he's bested me."

"What does that mean?" she said.

"This is the worst possible time for Fielding to be here. I think he wanted to see where I'd ended up after all these years, after all of that competing. And now he gets to draw attention to my big fat failure. And see me humiliated."

"Sadie," she said. "Why would you think that?"

"He made a sport of outdoing me in college. He was always trying to one-up me. And look at the timing—if he'd been here two weeks ago, it would have been fine. We might never have crossed paths. And even if we had, he'd have seen me when I was having fun in a job I loved." I took a long sip of my beer. "But no. He's here now, when I'm at my absolute lowest point, and he's going to enjoy every minute of that. And with my luck, it'll go viral."

Gwen's brow furrowed. "What do you mean your lowest point?"

I hadn't told her all the details about the park job. Biting back tears, I thought of that day a few weeks before, the way District Ranger Mike had so coldly told me there wasn't a place for me anymore. He'd sat at his big oak desk, his badge gleaming under the fluorescent light. I'd focused on the crisp lines pressed into his gray wool shirt, the way he'd shoved his reading glasses into his hair. He'd clasped his big hands on his desk and said, "Your position wasn't funded for next year. Sorry, Sadie." He wasn't sorry, though. Not even a little bit. He was annoyed that I'd dumped his son Joe, and then showed Joe up by doing things like arriving to work on time and giving ranger programs that didn't make people fall asleep. I'd so badly wanted to tell him I knew exactly why he was cutting me loose, but if I did, that would be the nail in the coffin of my park service career. If I kept my mouth shut, I might get into another park someday. His jaw stayed tight and his eyes shifted back to his computer screen.

While I sat there weighing those odds and biting my tongue, he said, "You'll need to be out of housing the day after your pay period is over."

And just like that, I was out. Like I'd never been there at all. All of my hard work had been for nothing.

"I'd finally found what I was good at," I told Gwen. "I thought I was making a difference, after all those crappy jobs that felt like a huge waste of time. But it's just another failure. And the last person I need around here to see that is James Fielding."

She looked sad. "You know failures are nothing to be ashamed of, right?"

"Then why do they hurt so bad?" Even though I knew it was silly, I did feel ashamed. Ashamed for being caught breaking the rules, ashamed for being so easily let go, and ashamed of letting it hurt me so deeply.

Shame was a useless emotion. But that didn't mean I stopped feeling it.

She sighed, reaching for my hand. "It does hurt sometimes," she said. "Believe me, I've failed more times than I can count. But I wouldn't be where I am if I hadn't."

And look where I was. James was probably just dying to paint a picture of how I'd come back to work at the quaint little inn in the quaint little town after all of my big dreams had gone up in flames.

She leaned back and said, "I won't say it gets easier, but it's a part of moving forward. You just have to believe you can get to where you need to be. Fall down five times, stand up six. Failure is just evidence that you're being brave."

Heat rose in my cheeks. My chest tightened. "I can't let him do this," I said. "I won't let him make me feel ashamed."

"Correct," Gwen said. "You will not."

"I'll beat him at his own game."

"Wait. What?"

"Out-charm the charmer. Be the B-actress that steals the show from the Oscar winner. Be better at his show than he is." I tapped my fingers on the table, trying to sort out exactly how that might work.

"Sadie," she said. "Is it possible you're making this into something it isn't?"

"Fielding has an angle. He didn't just find me here by accident." I could see it in that stupid devilish twinkle in his eye, that same knowing smirk he'd always given me in class—he knew he'd find me here, and he was happy about it. "If he wants to outdo me, he's going to have to work a lot harder this time."

Gwen arched a brow.

"But I don't know anything about being a beloved show host. I'm not sure I can be that charming."

"Oh, I can teach you that part," she said with a smile. "If all my years in community theater taught me anything, it was how to be a delight onstage." She clasped her hands under the chin and fluttered her lashes.

I smiled. "Secret weapon. I like it. Think you can teach me the basics?"

"Did you get a list of questions they were planning to ask you in the interview?"

"Yeah, I think so." They were probably still stuffed in the folder that Paula Sue had given me.

"Good. Hurry up and finish that beer. We've got work to do."

Chapter Seven

SEPTEMBER IN JASMINE FALLS was my favorite time of year—it was when the tourists thinned out, the summer heat died down, and the sky turned this crisp shade of blue that felt like the whole world was about to reset. After a fast-paced tourist season, autumn was when you felt like you could breathe again.

Usually, that is. If you're not walking around with a production crew and worried that any misstep you make will be recorded and then uploaded so it can go viral and take you down like a slow poison.

It was just after nine-thirty and the town square seemed oddly populated for a Monday. I'd led Tetia, James, Ashley, and Ravi here after breakfast so they could shoot some footage of the town, but as soon as we got to the square, it felt like something was awry. Our town was cute, but what I saw around us was next-level Hallmark-channel cute. The big gazebo in the center of the square had been decorated with strings of outdoor lights with bulbs as big as softballs. Heaps of flowering plants were set up around it, as vibrant as a feature in a magazine spread. Off to the side, a group of little kids sat in a circle, totally mesmerized by two teachers I recognized from the primary school who looked to be acting out a story from a book, dressed up like a dragon and a warrior queen.

Since when did we have story time on the town square?

And since when did we have a candy apple booth? On the opposite side of the park, there were tables set up with red gingham tablecloths and a couple dressed in matching overalls and tee shirts. They seemed to be selling apple cakes, pies, and other delights while a gray-haired man next to them strummed a banjo. There was a couple playing frisbee with a golden retriever that looked like the happiest dog on earth, and a group of older ladies sat painting on easels by the duck pond. It looked like our fall festival had been smashed together with one of those peppy pharmaceutical ads that promises you a shiny, perfect life.

The effect was surreal. It felt like a committee got together and made a list of all things wholesome and small-town America. Overnight, someone had turned the town's quaint dial up to eleven.

And then I realized: this likely *was* a committee. The spiffying up had probably been going on for days—I just hadn't noticed because I'd been so preoccupied with losing my job and moving into the carriage house. This was Paula Sue's doing—she always dialed everything up to eleven. If there was anything she could do to try to make Jasmine Falls more TV-ready, she'd do it. Even if it meant hiring child actors and planting begonias in the middle of the night. As if on cue, a family of ducks waddled past the gazebo, headed toward the nearby lily pond.

Mercy. She'd even hired ducks.

"Are those caramel apples over there?" Ravi said. "I haven't had one of those in years."

"Seriously?" Ashley said. "You just ate your weight in scones.

Where do you put it all?" Her blond hair was pulled up in a high bun today, so you could see the pink streaks underneath.

Ravi shrugged. "There's always room for caramel apples. Second breakfast."

James simply said, "Wow," and gave me a look I couldn't quite decipher. Had he already seen through this charade? The weight of his gaze sent a current of electricity down my spine and straight to my toes. If he figured out that Paula Sue was doing all of this as an act, I'd never hear the end of it.

The internet wouldn't, either.

Tearing my gaze away from Fielding's, I sipped my coffee, keeping Gwen's lessons from the night before firmly in my mind. She'd coached me through the questions and helped me keep my snark to a minimum. She'd made it seem so simple to stay upbeat, but I knew it was going to take everything in me to be extra friendly and charming with James Fielding today. Even though he'd made himself appear warm and approachable, I knew how his brain worked: he'd come here with an agenda, and we were just a tiny piece of his big picture plans. James had always kept his motives close to the vest, but I knew that something big was at stake for him to be out here in the middle of nowhere.

If I'd learned anything about James Fielding, it was to always remain skeptical of his motives. In the end, he was just trying to win.

But I wasn't going to let him win this time. He wasn't going to spend a week with surly Down-On-Her-Luck Sadie and leave here with the satisfaction of seeing me at my worst. No, he was going to spend a week with Super Amazeballs Sadie and regret that he ever came here with that hope.

But for the sake of everyone involved in this project (and for the sake of my pride), I could do what Paula Sue and my mother had demanded for the good of the town. I could be friendly and open, welcoming and warm, the embodiment of all the southern charm of Jasmine Falls. I could still do all of that and beat him at this game.

Or, I was roughly seventy-two percent sure that I could.

"So," Tetia said. "We've got the morning to shoot some B-roll, and I'd like to get as many exterior shots as we can while we have this gorgeous light." Today she wore tailored gray trousers and a navy blouse, and I immediately felt underdressed in my jeans and checkered shirt. My hair had been extra rebellious today, so I'd spritzed it and pulled it back into a ponytail.

Ravi nodded, glancing toward the main street. "Can never have enough B-roll," he said to me.

"Why's that?" I asked him.

"No matter how good the talent is, you always need filler. Pretty scenery, extras walking around looking happy, cute dogs in costumes." He ran a hand through his raven-black hair and scanned the square. His round face made him seem younger than me, but he spoke like someone who'd been doing this for decades.

Ashley smirked, following his gaze.

I supposed *talent* referred to Fielding.

Ugh. He must love that.

"Let's get a pan of the square," Tetia said to Ravi. "Then an intro from James, walking along the sidewalk here."

James nodded. "You got it."

After more discussion and direction, I stood a few yards away with Ashley while Ravi shot some footage of James strolling along the sidewalk as he spoke. "Today we're in Jasmine Falls, South Carolina," he started, his voice more perky than usual, and Tetia nodded along as she watched him.

"How far's the bakery from here?" Ashley said, keeping her voice low.

"A couple blocks that way," I said, pointing down the street.

"Cool. We can head there next, and then the florist? Aren't they close together?"

"Everything's close around here."

She smiled. "Fair enough."

"Have you shot many streaming shows?" I asked her.

She shrugged. "A few. This one's the first big deal."

I nodded, sipping my coffee.

"I mean, it's more of a big deal for James," she said. "The last show they pitched totally bombed after the pilot."

I nearly spit out my coffee. James Fielding? Bombed? I was dying to hear more of that story and part of me felt a little bit bad for that.

But only a small part.

"Shoot." She bit her lip, looking worried. "I didn't tell you that."

"Nope. My lips are sealed."

She shook her head. "It just slipped out. It's at the forefront of everyone's mind right now, even though every one of them will tell you it's not."

"Understandable."

"I mean, our crew does all kinds of production work, but this is kind of a Hail Mary for James," she said. "That last show was supposed to be his big break, but then... well, none of us expected it to fall apart the way it did." Her brow furrowed as she said, "It was just extra hard because it was right around the time of his awful breakup. We were all rooting for him, but the network wouldn't budge."

James pointed at something behind him, flashing his brilliant smile as he talked about our town's proximity to the national park and our popular annual festivals. I felt my jaw tighten, thinking of Ashley's words, willing myself not to feel one bit sorry for the guy who had made it his mission to outdo me at every turn. Had the unsinkable James Fielding finally felt the sting of failure?

Okay, maybe I did feel a little sorry for him. Thinking that a big break was coming just to have it fall through? That would definitely sting.

"He'll be fine," I said. "You could shoot Fielding out of a cannon and he'd still land on his feet."

Ashley gave me a sideways look as I sipped my coffee.

"He looks nervous," she said, watching him saunter toward the camera with his typical cool swagger. "He's got to shake it off. That's like blood in the water in the screening room."

James didn't look nervous to me at all. He looked like a man who was accustomed to drawing all the attention in the room. But maybe Gwen was right: maybe this happy-go-lucky look was just a facade. No matter how perfect things looked on the outside, we all had secrets to hide.

"I felt bad for him after last time," Ashley said. "It was a great plan for a show, but he just fizzled onscreen. It was like the fire had gone out. That ex of his really did a number on him. After Glossy Gate, we thought it was all over."

I snorted. "Glossy Gate?"

She raised a brow. "It's no joke. His ex-girlfriend nearly ended his career. He was getting articles in all the glossies—you know, the big print magazines—and even had a book deal. Then that horrible woman cheated on him, and when he broke things off, she was so spiteful that she told everyone who'd listen that he'd fabricated his sources."

I bit my lip. That was one of the biggest taboos in journalism. Even I knew that.

"It was a total lie, of course, but she was big enough to pull everyone's strings. She wanted to set fire to his whole life because he left her—and she's the one who cheated!" She took a deep breath and pressed two fingers to her temple. "Sorry," she said. "That woman was just awful to him and I really wish karma would hurry up and find her. Anyway, after that, all the glossies dropped him. The book deal fell through, and then it was all his agent could do to get him guest spots on other travel shows. He finally got lucky when Tetia pitched that pilot, but then it all fell apart." She sighed, giving me another hard look. "It was horrible. I wouldn't wish that on anyone."

"I had no idea," I said, feeling about three inches tall. I wouldn't have wished that on him, either.

She lifted a brow. "You must be the last person on earth who didn't."

James smiled his megawatt smile as he spoke toward the camera, gesturing at the town square behind him. He seemed so confident, so relaxed. It was easy to picture him on a TV screen. Even though he was super annoying, he had this way of speaking that seemed friendly and warm. Even when he was standing on a sidewalk just a few yards from someone who, until just a moment ago, had crossed her fingers hoping he might trip on a crack and fall flat on his perfectly shaped butt.

"Does it seem like the fire's back?" I asked her.

"Not even close." She frowned. "This one might not make it past the dailies, either. Execs aren't willing to give a show a few episodes to get their legs anymore. It's not like it used to be. You've got to wow them early."

Not like it used to be? This woman looked twenty-five, if that.

She shrugged. "We'll just hope for a miracle, I guess. Crazier things have happened."

I turned back to James, still reeling from everything Ashley had told me. It must have killed him to have everything he'd worked for stripped away like that.

When they paused filming, Tetia walked over and started talking to James, pointing toward Main Street. He nodded as she leaned over to straighten the collar of his shirt. For the first time, his smile faded and there was something else there that looked like—worry?

"Yoo-hoo!" A voice called from behind us. I turned to see Paula Sue Hinson headed toward us, wearing pink yoga pants and a matching pink hoodie, walking her standard poodle, Thelma.

"Hi, Paula Sue," I said, noting that she had on much more makeup than usual and that her pink outfit looked like it had never been worn. Her hair was extra fluffy, like she'd just had a blowout at the salon, and her nails had fresh French tips. It was probably her idea of camera-ready. Thelma even looked freshly groomed, her gray fur shining and her bright pink harness sparkling in the sun. When the dog leaned down to sniff James's expensive-looking shoes, he knelt down to pet her and she licked his hand.

Traitor.

"Good morning!" Paula Sue chirped. "I just wanted to pop by and see how the first day was going. I hear you had to reschedule Max."

There really were no secrets in this town. If you sneezed, someone a mile away would call to say *bless you.*

"We did," Tetia said, "but we're all good."

"Well, if you need any extra interviews, I'm happy to fill in," Paula Sue said, beaming as she glanced over at James. She'd been Miss South Carolina back in the day, and apparently once you get that crown, you never lose the ability to summon that megawatt smile. "There are just so many interesting things to see in our little town. We're a place like no other."

James gave her a friendly smile. "No doubt."

While Paula Sue went on and on about the town's main attractions, Ashley and Ravi stepped a few yards away to shoot more footage of Main Street. Tetia and James nodded along as Paula Sue spoke, looking like two people trapped in a corner at a cocktail party with the chattiest guest there. Paula Sue was like a jukebox—once you put the dollar in, you've got to listen for the whole song. She kept putting her hand on James's forearm when she said something she thought was especially interesting. Clearly, she was itching to get on camera and thought James was the person to get her there. He gave her a friendly smile, but I didn't miss the way he kept edging away from her—until Thelma blocked him on the other side, her leash straining against his legs.

James looked over at me and his eyebrows rose in that way that means a universal plea for rescue, but I just raised my hand and wiggled my fingers at him in an extra friendly wave. Paula Sue snorted with laughter at something she'd said as she grabbed his arm, and my heart swelled with glee.

Watching James squirm felt like seeing long overdue karma in action. He'd made me squirm plenty of times back in college, and made me wish I could sink into the floorboards more times than I could count.

"Thank you so much, Paula Sue," Tetia finally said. "I appreciate that." Her tone was pleasant, but all business, and it was a clear signal that the time allotted for chitchat was over. She turned then and called to Ravi. "We should get to the next spot while we have the light, don't you think?"

"Of course," he said, headed back toward us.

Tetia turned to walk away and gave Paula Sue a friendly wave.

"We'll see you around!" Paula Sue called. As I walked past, she grabbed my elbow and said, "How's it going? Do they have everything they need? Did they have a good first night at the inn?"

"All good," I said. "Happy campers."

She raised a brow and that smile went from pageant-ready to sharklike. "You just make sure it stays that way." She gave me a wink and sauntered off, but not before Thelma the poodle narrowed her eyes at me as if to hammer the point home.

As we walked the two blocks to the bakery, James fell back so he was in step next to me. "I was hoping you might rescue me back there," he said.

"Not used to so many adoring fans?" I said, teasing.

He smirked, running a hand through his hair. "Something like that."

I shrugged. "Guess that's the price you pay for fame and perfection."

He glanced at me, his eyes sparkling. "Is that right?"

"Thought you'd be used to the star treatment by now."

"Star's a bit of a stretch." His brow furrowed again in that way that almost looked like worry.

My phone buzzed in my pocket, and when I pulled it out, the screen flashed with a text from Leah. Inside was a link to a job posting at a park in the Everglades.

Time to work on your tan lines, she wrote. **Dust off your resume, babe.**

I smiled and texted back: **I'll check it out.**

My phone dinged with another link to a job in Arizona. **How do you feel about cowboys?** She wrote.

"Everything okay?" James said.

"Yep." I quickly texted Leah a thank-you and shoved the phone in my pocket. It wasn't a terrible idea to look at other park jobs, but a little voice deep in my head kept piping up to say, *What if you're not as good at this as you thought you were?* Ordinarily, I'd tamp that little voice down, but this time, I had to wonder: if I was as good at my job as I'd thought, wouldn't Chief Ranger Mike have kept me around? Yeah, I dumped his son, but I wasn't the first and I most definitely wouldn't be the last. It was easier to tell myself I'd been let go because I'd done something reckless—it was harder to realize that maybe I wasn't as valuable as I'd once believed. If I'd been good enough at my job, Joe wouldn't have mattered.

I should have been better.

"Hey," James said, touching my arm. "Are you upset that I'm here?"

I stopped walking and stared at him, surprised by the frankness of his question. "Why *are* you here? I mean, of all the small towns you could have picked for a travel show, why'd you pick this one?" I stepped closer and said, "Wait, let me guess. You were looking for some place that was cute and quaint—not too much going on below the surface."

Just like he'd said in college, so smugly: *Is it more cute escapism?*

"You seem angry," he said, sounding hurt. "What did I do?"

"I just want you to be honest with me. Why are you here, Fielding?"

He shoved his hands into his jeans pockets and shrugged. "I wanted to see you."

My heart dropped straight to my feet. So, it was true: he did want to check up on me, to see if I'd accomplished what I'd set out to do. And now he'd caught me at my worst, when I felt completely unmoored. "Well, you must be delighted," I grumbled.

"I am," he said, his eyes resting on mine.

The nerve of him, to just tell me that out loud. Heat filled my cheeks. "Well, soak it up while you can, Fielding. Take a good look. This is me when I've managed to fail at everything. It figures you'd show up at the precise moment that my life imploded. But I guess that's exactly what you were hoping for."

He cocked his head to the side. "What do you mean?"

My eyes stung as I bit back tears. I would not cry in front of James Fielding. Would not. He might get to see me fail, but he did not get to see me fall apart. To think I'd felt so bad for him just a few minutes ago—this man who had come here for such a petty reason.

"Hey!" Ashley shouted. "You guys coming, or what?"

"Be right there!" James yelled.

Before he could say anything else to me, I turned on my heel and walked down the block to where Ashley and the others stood outside the bakery. I could finish this one day with them, and hold it together long enough to do the stupid interview this afternoon. And then I could lie low the rest of the time they were here, and then they'd leave, and I'd never have to let James Fielding remind me of my old dreams and my new failures ever again.

I could do this. I could survive one full day with Fielding. No problem.

Chapter Eight

JAMES

Today wasn't going the way I'd hoped.

When we broke for lunch, Sadie avoided me completely. Perched between Tetia and Ashley, she answered all of their questions about Jasmine Falls and gave us plenty of fodder for voice-over that I could add in later in editing—all without speaking one word to me.

After lunch, we went back to the inn for the interview and tour. Sadie was a natural storyteller, and would no doubt look great on camera. Ravi filmed us both as she led me through the main floor of the inn, pointing out some of the more charming features of each room. She'd changed into a powder blue button-down shirt and pencil skirt that hugged her curves, and it was all I could do to drag my eyes away from her muscular legs when really, I just wanted to know what they'd feel like tangled up in mine.

Evidently though, she did not spend her time thinking about this same scenario. I still didn't understand why my being here upset her so, and the hurt that flashed in her eyes earlier today had taken me by surprise. Sure, we'd been competitive in college, and certainly I'd gotten under her skin just as she'd gotten under mine. Not in precisely the same way, because I'd been over the moon for her and she'd pushed me away with one callous comment that cut to the bone. I hadn't expected her to throw her arms around me in a bear hug when she first saw me again, but I hadn't expected her to be angry, either. She'd been the one to put distance between us just when it seemed like she might feel a fraction of what I'd felt for her. After all this time, I should have gotten over her.

But there was no getting over Sadie Harper, and this time I wasn't going to let her push me away without telling me what was in her heart.

I was just going to have to try harder.

"The house was built in 1899," Sadie said, leading us through the foyer. "The woman who built it also built the first library in Jasmine Falls. She was a sucker for hand-carved woodwork, and she loved rabbits. So you'll see there are lots of rabbits carved into the wood accents, sometimes partially hidden by leaves." Sadie slid her hand along the doorframe and pointed to the carved vine in the corner and all I could think of was how her slender fingers would feel sliding along my skin.

Lord help me. I was doomed.

"We have a standing tradition," she said. "If you can count all the carved rabbits in the house, you get a prize."

"Oh?" I said. "What do I win?" *Please let it be a whole night counting bunnies together.*

She snorted playfully and then her voice dropped to an octave that made my heart do a barrel-roll. "Like I'd spoil the surprise. You're just going to have to count them all and find out, Mr. Fielding."

My breath hitched at the coy way she said *Mr. Fielding* and I tried hard to shove aside thoughts of all the different situations where she might say that again. For example, not in a room full of my colleagues. "There's a rumor you may have a ghost here," I said, following her down the hallway and trying not to stare at her lovely legs.

"A few," she said, "but they're all friendly." Her voice was light and teasing, but I knew that was for the sake of our filming. The way she glared at me between takes could burn this house to the ground.

"Got any stories you can tell us?" I tugged the collar of my shirt as Ravi panned back to her. This room felt like the floor was lava, but she was cool as ice.

"Martha lives in the turret upstairs," she said, pausing by the dining room. She pointed to an old black and white photo on the wall. It was faded, but you still could see a group of surly looking women posing on the front porch. They wore long, dark dresses with high-necked collars, and looked fierce enough to slay dragons with their bare hands. "Martha used to own this place in the 1930s, when it was a boarding house. Sometimes guests see her at night, but we figure she's just checking to make sure everyone's inside and safe. Occasionally a book or a set of keys goes missing, but that's about as mischievous as she gets."

"A ghost who likes to read?" I said. "Does she haunt a particular part of the house?"

Sadie scrunched her nose. "We don't say *haunt*, Mr. Fielding. She visits us. Like a friend."

I grinned. "Does she visit any particular part?"

Sadie smiled. "Actually, your room is her old bedroom. Better keep an eye on your books."

I couldn't tell if she was joking, but Ravi shook his head, muttering, "Nope." The thought of a ghost moving my books around was oddly endearing, but Ravi's scrunched brow told me he wouldn't agree.

"She's partial to romances," Sadie said. "Fair warning."

When we moved onto the big wraparound porch, Ashley did a quick check of Sadie's make-up and Tetia said, "You're doing great. Keep going, y'all."

When Ravi was rolling again, I tried hard to think of anything except Sadie's piercing blue eyes and said, "What do you like about Jasmine Falls?"

She blinked at me and smiled. "It's a great place to grow up. A friendly town with a strong sense of community. People look out for each other here."

It was a canned answer. Nothing personal about it. "What makes it different from every other cute, friendly town?" I said. "What made you want to live here?" I was going off-script, but I genuinely wanted to know the answer. Sadie had had such big dreams, and this town seemed too small for them. I wanted to know what made her want to be here.

There was a lot more I needed to know about her, but I'd settle for an easy question now.

She arched a brow. "Obviously the friendly ghosts and the hidden gem restaurants. And this gorgeous national park that's just down the road." She leaned against the doorframe and smiled. "On the outside, this town might look quaint and simple, but a town's just as layered as people are. It has histories, and dreams, and aspirations, and sometimes you have to look hard and take your time to see the complexities. It's like peeling back the petals on a peony."

I smiled. "Peonies. I like that."

She shrugged. "Layers of onion are gross and make you cry."

"What's your biggest dream, Sadie Harper?"

Her eyes widened just a bit, enough to let me know I'd knocked her a little off-guard. Sometimes I went off-script when it felt like people's answers were too rehearsed. I liked the spontaneity, and sometimes I only got one shot to surprise people when the camera was on them. If we went to multiple takes, then the surprise was gone—and I'd get another planned, dull answer. I had to pick my surprise questions carefully and slip them in when I felt like the wall between me and the subject was coming down. Sadie had relaxed a bit since we'd moved out onto the porch, and I took a chance. Deep down, I did want to know her dream. I wanted to know everything about her.

She bit her lip and her eyes darkened to a stormy gray. Without meaning to, I'd hit a nerve.

"To do work that has meaning and inspires people," she said, her tone still light. "What's your dream, James Fielding? What mark do you want to leave on the world?"

Ravi turned the camera to me, and for the first time in a long time, I was stunned speechless. It was a simple question, and one that I should have seen coming, and yet in that moment, it felt like all the air had been sucked out of the room. In all the years I'd asked people this question, no one I interviewed had ever turned it around on me.

A lump formed in my throat.

I could have replied with a dozen canned answers. I could have deflected. But something about the way Sadie looked at me with that fierce, curious gaze made all of those thoughts fall away.

"I want to peel back the petals on peonies," I said.

Her eyes snapped away from me when Tetia yelled, "Cut!"

But not before I saw the blush in her cheeks.

AT DINNER, Tetia was quiet, which meant she was turning a problem over in her mind. We'd stopped at a food truck parked on the town square, along with Ashley and Ravi. While they joked about the latest reality show they couldn't get enough of, Tetia sipped her iced tea and stared out over the square like she was searching for the answer somewhere far off in the evening sky.

"What did you think about today?" I asked her. "Are you worried?" After the last show had been cancelled, I knew the possibility had to be on her mind. I'd been off my game that time around because my love life and my career had just imploded. Even now, I wasn't sure I was back to the version of James Fielding that got good ratings and high engagement.

She turned toward me and grabbed her to-go cup. "Let's take a walk. I have something to run by you."

Those words usually meant trouble. Swallowing hard, I followed her as she walked across the grass and toward the gazebo. Those big strings of lights were shining bright tonight, and it looked like it was set up for a party. As we got closer, she said, "How do you think it went today?"

"Good," I said. "It feels nice to be on camera again. Like coming home." I wanted her to think I was eager and excited, even though I felt like there was a tornado forming in my chest.

"What do you think of Sadie?"

She's gorgeous. Talented. Amazing. Wishes the earth would open up and swallow me down right into its fiery core.

"She's great," I said with a shrug. "Good on camera."

"I think so, too." Tetia arched her brow. "I think you two play off each other nicely, and I think she should do the whole episode with you."

For the second time today, I felt like the wind had been knocked out of me. All I could manage was, "Oh."

"You two have good chemistry. This whole series is about a fish out of water, right? And she's a kind of anchor—she's the small-town to your big-city. She's a natural way to bring out your sense of curiosity about this place—she's a spark." Tetia smiled, sliding her fingers along her chin. "Plus, she's not afraid of you, and she's not star-struck."

"True on both counts," I said. "But I don't think she'll go for it."

Tetia cocked her head. "What makes you say that?"

I shrugged. "Lots of reasons." *She hates that I'm here. She wants to spend as little time with me as possible. She'd like me to fall face-first in the duck pond on a livestream that breaks the internet.*

Tetia scoffed. "Don't be all vague with me, James. What's the deal with you two?"

"We barely know each other," I said, which was not a complete lie because when had I ever truly known her? "We went to college together and were in the same department. I just think she doesn't like me much." There was no need to share the details. Tetia didn't need to know about how I'd worked my way into Sadie's friend group to hang out with her, or how I'd applied for the same internships in the hopes of working with her outside of classes. She didn't need to know that I'd timed my walk to class so I'd have the best chance of bumping into her and walking the rest of the way together, or that Sadie had been the only girl that I'd been terrified to ask out on a real date. Or that the night I came closest to her was the moment everything backfired.

And she definitely didn't need to know about the kiss that nearly cleaved my heart in two.

Tetia stared at me, sipping her tea. Her eyes had that steely glint that meant she'd already made up her mind. "People will put up with a lot to be on TV."

"True. I'll give you that. But Sadie's not one of those people looking for fifteen minutes of fame."

Tetia smiled so the tiny wrinkles at the corners of her eyes showed. "In my experience, no one turns down their fifteen minutes."

"You might have just met the one exception." The Sadie I knew liked working with people and rooting out adventure, but she didn't like being the center of attention.

"Look," she said. "You know I love you, and I want this new show to be a big success for you. I just think that it has a better shot if we give her a bigger role to play. She brings out something in you that frankly isn't there when you're going solo."

I knew she didn't intend to be mean, but her words stung just the same. It hurt to think that I couldn't do this on my own, that I needed someone else to make me palatable. The execs had already said so when they killed the pilot, but it was harder hearing the same thought from Tetia. "What kind of something?" I asked.

She shrugged. "Something like actual joy, James. Something I haven't seen in you for a long time."

She wasn't wrong about that. Before coming here, pitching the show had felt like a lifeline, a necessary move for my career. But being with Sadie made it feel less like work and more like I'd found my way back to my purpose.

AFTER THE OTHERS went back to the inn, I sat there in the gazebo until the sky turned violet. Tetia was right. My career hadn't exactly gone the way I'd planned, and the last few years had been rough. In the two years that we'd worked together, though, she'd never done anything that wasn't supportive. Magazine articles were impossible to get now, since my ex had me blackballed—and the last TV pilot had bombed so badly that I'd been shocked when this offer came my way. If I hadn't done that YouTube show with another travel buddy of mine, Tetia probably wouldn't have gotten five words into her pitch with the execs for this show. This was a chance to turn my career around, and deep down I knew I should do whatever Tetia suggested. Even if it meant being in close quarters with the woman who would clearly feed me to the alligators if given half a chance.

Could I convince Sadie to fake some friendliness for the sake of a TV show? And for the sake of my failing career? And, if I was being really honest, have a chance to get to know her better, like I wished I'd had the guts to do all those years ago?

Being here might be the best second chance I'd ever have—both for my career and for my heart.

IT WAS dark by the time I walked back to the inn, and once I turned off of Main Street, there were no more streetlamps to light the way. The moon was high and bright though, and it wasn't far to the inn. By the time I got there, I was feeling too fidgety and anxious to go to bed. It was barely eight-thirty and there was zero chance of falling asleep. Thinking a walk in the garden might clear my head, I followed the rock path around the side of the house and into the backyard. The small garden in the back was lined with big camellia bushes that still had blossoms as big as my hand. Most of the other flowers had stopped blooming, but there were fragrant herbs and a moonflower curling along a trellis. It was calming to hear the crickets chirping, to feel the touch of chill in the air that comes at the end of summer. I followed the path through the garden to where it ended abruptly near the carriage house. About the size of a two-car garage, the house had a cute front door and tiny deck off to the side. When I heard music, I couldn't help but follow the sound to the side of the house, where the windows were filled with golden light.

Sadie was in the kitchen, dancing as she dried dishes by the sink.

With the blinds open and the lights on, it was easy to see her. I knew I shouldn't be there, but I couldn't help watching her move through the room, waving her arms and shaking her hips like she was in her own personal music video.

It was pretty freaking adorable.

She moved just out of my line of sight, so I stepped a little further to my right, closer to the deck and the railing. Now she had a big spoon that she appeared to be using as a microphone, and something swelled in my heart to the point it felt like it would burst.

I chuckled to myself and stepped closer the deck railing, and then tripped on something in the dark that sent me sprawling. In a blink, three things happened simultaneously:

A clatter split the night as I stumbled into a metal trash can.

The can toppled, sending trash spilling onto the deck.

Sadie froze at the window, turning her head toward the sound.

Who has metal trash cans anymore?

"Dang it," I said, staggering to my feet. Somewhere beyond the trees, a dog barked like it thought the whole world was on fire.

The door banged open and Sadie came into the yard, barreling toward the deck with a giant pot and a big metal spoon. "Get lost!" she yelled. "Git!"

I froze, having never before been told to "Git," and by a gorgeous woman, no less.

"James?" she said, her voice dropping back to a normal octave. "Is that you?"

She was wearing plaid pajama pants and a tight tee shirt and was holding the kitchenware like a sword and shield.

"Sorry," I said. "I was just in the garden and—"

"I thought you were a raccoon," she said, stepping closer.

"No, just clumsy." I looked at the pot and spoon. "Were you planning to make raccoon stew?"

She banged the pot with the spoon and I flinched at the racket.

"Good plan," I said. "That would make anyone leave."

"And yet you're still here." She sighed, staring at the trash.

"Let me get that," I said, hurrying to right the trash can and pick up the mess.

Her face softened as she seemed to remember that she was an innkeeper, at least for the moment. "Is everything okay?" she said. "Did you need something?"

I shoved the lid back on the trash can and pushed it into the corner of the railing so it wouldn't topple so easily. "I was just out for a walk," I said. "But now that you're here, can I ask you something?"

She hesitated for a minute. "Um, okay."

It seemed weird to talk like this, standing in the dark, Sadie in her pajamas and me mistaken for a hungry raccoon. And if I was being truthful, I didn't want her to give me a quick answer and then go back inside and shut the door in my face. I wanted her to drop her polite act and talk to me like a real person. I wanted to tell her about all these feelings I'd had since she'd checked me in the day before. And even more, I wanted to tell her all the things I'd been afraid to all those years ago in school. That was all too much though, to discuss in the yard as a cloud passed over the moon.

"Is there somewhere we could go to talk?" I said. "Maybe get a drink?" I felt like my whole world had been knocked off-kilter after everything Tetia had told me, but somehow I thought Sadie might make it better. She certainly couldn't make it worse—worse was me being alone in my room, working myself up into a frenzy as I let myself overanalyze all of the catastrophic scenarios that might play out if this week didn't go the way we needed it to.

She raised a brow, and good lord, she was hopelessly beautiful in the moonlight. Her skin seemed to glow and her eyes were as deep blue as the ocean. She pursed those full lips and planted one hand on her waist, drawing my eyes straight to her curvy hips and, mercy, she was entirely too far away.

I was drowning, and I wasn't sure if she was the anchor or the life raft.

"Are you all right?" she asked, her voice softening.

"I'm not sure."

She nodded, then went inside the house. I stood for a moment, not sure of what would happen next. But then the music switched off inside, and I heard her heavy walk on the hardwood floor, the slam of a door, and then the outside light by the deck came on.

Sadie came back outside dressed in slim jeans and a tee shirt, a lightweight jacket and purse draped over her arm. She locked the door behind her and said, "Come on, Fielding. I know a nice hole in the wall that's in walking distance."

Chapter Nine

SADIE

UNDER THE DIM lights of the bar, James Fielding looked weary. Standing in the yard, he'd had this weird expression come over his face, and it was like his famous-person facade dropped long enough for me to see a flash of real uncertainty—and worse, pain. I recognized that brand of hurt—the kind that eats you from the inside out. The kind that shows itself to other people only when you're worn down enough that you can't help becoming vulnerable because it's just too exhausting to keep the walls up.

I couldn't leave him in the yard like that, though I really wished he'd just been a raccoon in the trash can. Raccoons were much easier to handle. And they certainly didn't come with baggage like we had.

Now, sitting in a booth in the back corner of the Wonky Donkey, James looked more anxious than anything else. He'd leaned back in the booth and was picking at the label on his beer bottle. His brow was furrowed and his jaw was tense, and I couldn't stop looking at him and trying to figure out exactly what was rolling around in that head of his—and how, precisely, it pertained to me. Was he also stuck in his memories of our time at Cambrick? I wondered if maybe Gwen was right after all. Perhaps he did want to make amends. There were certainly some regrets I had from my early years, and definitely a few people I'd apologize to if I ever crossed paths with them again. (Such as Carly Dennis, for example, for that time I scattered raw shrimp in the trunk of her car after she told everybody some lie about how I'd gone all the way with the captain of the soccer team in the back of his car during the winter formal.) Sometimes, it's hard to know where to begin.

A beer in a dive bar seemed like a decent way to start.

He leaned his head against the back of the booth, staring up at the ceiling. "This is an interesting light fixture we have above us."

"Local artist," I said. "This is my favorite booth." The fixture above was a big star, almost three feet across, made from handmade paper and maps. Since the paper was translucent, you could see all the lines and shapes in the map when it was illuminated. Lucinda, the artist, had a gallery in town full of paper sculptures like these that could be lit and hung from the ceiling.

"So, you want to tell me about it?" I asked him.

He peeled off his leather motorcycle jacket and I got a glimpse of tan skin just above his belt. He wore a navy plaid shirt with the top two buttons undone, the sleeves rolled to his elbows, looking more casual than he had since he'd arrived. I'd forgotten how big and solid his hands were, how muscular his forearms were.

Stop, I thought. *You are not allowed to think about his big arms and solid hands, and all the things they could do.* Nope.

"It's this show," he said. "It's completely psyched me out."

"What?" For a moment, I'd thought that he wanted to talk

about the College Party Incident that I'd sworn to never speak of again. Or that he wanted to apologize for being a jerk all those years ago, making me feel simplistic and naive. But no. Of course, James only wanted to talk about his career. It shouldn't have surprised me, but here I was, letting Fielding get my hopes up again—if only for a few moments.

And yet, I still didn't want to leave him there in the booth alone. I knew how awful it felt to think you were on the edge of losing something that mattered.

He took a long drink from the beer. "I really screwed up the last time," he said. "And sometimes I feel like everyone's just waiting for me to screw up again." He sighed, raking his hands through his hair. "I'm not going to get a third chance at this."

"You have a lot of fans," I said, keeping my tone friendly. "I think you'll be fine. And the internet loves a good comeback story."

"Fans don't always equal revenue. Or job security." His soft brown eyes rested on mine and he said, "Don't get me wrong, I love my fans, and I'm flattered that people even read my work or watch what I do. But the network took a loss on the last show, and if this one tanks, well, I'll be looking for a career change."

"Would that be so bad?" It felt weird to say, since I could have asked myself the same question. James seemed to be skilled at the art of pivoting, though, and that wasn't something I'd say about myself.

He looked at me like I'd just suggested we knock over a Piggly-Wiggly. "I've already been run out of publishing," he said. "If this goes away, I'm sunk."

"How were you run out of publishing?" His articles were actually quite good, but I wasn't going to add that, because Fielding's ego didn't need to be any bigger.

"It's a long story."

Glossy Gate. Ashley had mentioned this. There was no way I'd betray her confidence, but I was curious: would James share this part of his life with me? Or would I get some sanitized version that wouldn't reveal any wounds?

His eyebrows had that sad arc to them again, and now I was intrigued. "Did you have other plans tonight?" I waved in the space around us—empty because it was Monday. "The only reason you come to this place is for cheap drinks and a long story."

"Fair." He smirked and shook his head. For the first time, I felt like I was seeing the real James Fielding again—not the polished Instagram famous version, but the college kid—the rumpled, flannel-wearing version that had cute messy hair and a crooked smile that threatened to melt my heart. "Once upon a time," he drawled, "I had a sweet writing gig at *Great Travel*. But that was partly because I was very close with the editor-in-chief."

"How close?"

"Close." He grimaced. "But when that fell apart, she wasn't so keen on keeping me around. In fact, she wasn't keen on me being in print ever again—anywhere. And she has a lot of strings she can pull to make that happen."

His lip lifted in a tiny smile. "I'm a great example of why workplace romances are a bad idea."

Same here, I thought. But what I said was, "I'm sorry that happened. It sounds awful."

"Burned that bridge pretty thoroughly, I'd say." He raised a brow and sipped his drink. "The opposite of success."

"And yet, you're still standing."

"Some days."

I rolled my eyes. Humble wasn't something I was accustomed to seeing on him. But it seemed genuine. "James, you can do anything—it's really irritating, actually. But I don't think you need me to tell you that."

"That I'm irritating?" He gave me a hint of a smile, the devilish glint back in his eyes, and I felt the back of my neck tingle again.

"You really are insufferable," I said.

"Apparently the last test audience thought so, too."

I felt a pang of guilt. "Sorry." The beer seemed to have loosened my tongue a little too much.

He gave me a cocky wink. "It's okay. I know you mean insufferable as an endearment."

"In your dreams."

He smirked and my heart did that weird flip-flop again. "Win some, lose some," he said. "Audiences are fickle. The problem is, this is officially a losing streak and I'm running out of time to break it. My agent, a total miracle-worker, managed to get me some guest spots on other travel shows, and I did this goofy YouTube show with a friend of mine. That kept me out of total obscurity, but this is my first real break after transitioning away from writing." He sipped his beer and was quiet for a moment, deep in thought. When his eyes locked on mine again, there was no hint of teasing. "Sometimes I'm afraid I'll never get back on top again. Like my best days are just behind me, you know? I don't like that feeling."

"You're only twenty-nine. I think that's highly unlikely."

"Thirty," he said. "And I thought it was highly unlikely I'd get you alone, but here we are."

I studied his eyes, trying to ignore the heat blooming in my chest. "Why did you want that?"

"Your turn," he said, his gaze pinning me. "What's this about your life imploding?"

I felt my cheeks turn hot, thinking of how I'd stalked away

from him on the street earlier today, so angry about those words he'd said years before. "Nothing."

He leaned back in the booth, draping his arm across the back. "Come on," he said. "I told you mine."

"I didn't bring you here so we could talk about me." Laying myself bare in front of Fielding seemed like a very bad idea.

"It can't be worse than being blackballed by the entire print industry, laughed out of a studio exec's office, and being turned into fodder for gossip blogs that usually focus on who got a rose on the big reality show this week."

"Does everything have to be a competition with you?" I said.

He gave me a rakish smile that raised goosebumps on my arms. "Isn't life more exciting with a little competition? Come on, humor me."

I groaned, leaning back in the booth. He'd never let this go. "I got fired from my park job. Or, more precisely, my position was terminated. It might as well be the same thing."

"I'm sorry," he said. "That sucks."

"It does suck!" I cried, taking a long drink from my beer. It felt good to say that out loud. "It was a great job. But I wrecked it. I sort of dated the chief ranger's son, and when that went sideways, he retaliated. But I keep telling myself that if I'd been good enough, it wouldn't have mattered what happened with Joe. I'd still have my job."

He arched a brow. "I imagine you were more than good enough."

I blinked at him for a moment. Those were not the words I'd expected to hear.

"I finally felt like I was on the right track, doing something meaningful. And then blammo—gone in a blink."

He nodded and I knew he understood. These things that felt so right could disappear so quickly.

"Working at the inn is just temporary, while Mom and Dad are out of town. But being back here feels like rubbing salt in the wound, you know? It's bad enough to lose a job I loved, but it's worse to have my parents think I need their charity, like I can't survive on my own."

He raised a brow. "I get that. But Harper, it's pretty obvious you can survive just fine by your own devices. You're smart, resourceful, independent. Any idiot can see that."

I stared at him, feeling like a deer in headlights. Once again, not the words I expected to hear. "That sounded like a compliment, Fielding."

"Honestly, I was shocked to see you at the inn," he said. "But now I get it—you're helping your folks while you're in between things. I'd expect nothing else from you." Before I could open my mouth to argue, he said, "Relax, Harper. What I mean is, it's admirable and sweet, and you'd do anything to help your family."

I stared at him hard. He was making it awfully difficult to stay irritated with him.

"I know your family means a lot to you," he said. "I'm not a complete dolt."

"You're right," I said. "On both counts." James was many things, but he was never oblivious.

"Maybe you need a big change," he said. "Something to set you on a new course and shake you out of the boring, familiar place so you can grow properly." He pushed his sleeves up further and I caught sight of a curious tattoo curling by his elbow. My traitorous brain was trying to determine how much of his muscular biceps and shoulder it might cover as he said, "My grandfather used to shake his pear trees for that same reason. He swore that shaking the tree caused it to make better fruit."

"That's ridiculous."

He shrugged. "We had the tastiest pears in town. Sometimes growth is uncomfortable. Usually it's worth it."

"I've been looking at job postings for other parks, but I likely won't get a good reference. The park service is a small world, and our chief ranger seems to know everybody."

"That's why I went into television," he said. "My ex shut every door. I had to make a big change."

I sipped my drink, admiring that adaptability. "Makes sense."

"What if your change was big, too?" he said.

"Such as?"

"There might be a way we can save this show before it sinks." He leaned forward, resting his elbows on the table. His intense gaze was back. "How would you like to be in the whole episode? Like a co-host?"

I nearly choked on my beer. "Is that some kind of joke?"

He shook his head. "Tetia's idea. I thought I'd give you a heads-up, because I know you hate surprises."

"I don't hate surprises."

He snorted. "Yeah, okay. I thought you'd actually murder your roommate when she threw that surprise birthday party for you."

The memory of that night hit me like a gust of cold wind. A tingle ran along my skin again as I thought back to that night with James on the lawn outside our dorm. What else did he remember about that party? Did he remember going with me outside to get away from the crowd? Did he remember how he'd kissed me, so tentatively at first, before making me so dizzy I saw stars? And then how after, he'd acted like that night had never happened?

"Fine," I said. "Surprises are not my favorite thing in the world. But surely you misunderstood."

"Tetia thinks I'm better with a co-host," he said. "I agree."

I felt like the room had just turned upside down. "I don't have any TV experience. Why on earth would your producer want me as a co-host?"

"Tetia thinks you're a natural. I mean, a little rough around the edges, but she loved what you did today. She wants a whole show like that."

"No way." The idea of being filmed, my mistakes living forever on a streaming service, made me want to gag. Being in the spotlight was never good for me. This was supposed to be a one-and-done thing. One segment to show him up, to prove I wasn't some bumpkin who couldn't hold her own with the pros. I could fulfill the rest of my promise to Paula Sue from the sidelines.

"Her exact words were 'Sadie is your perfect complement.'" He raised a brow and sipped his beer. "She said she liked our chemistry."

My neck tingled again when he said *chemistry*. There had definitely been a spark between us during that surprise party, but thankfully we'd been interrupted before we could make a bad decision. My roommate Kara had run out onto the lawn looking for me so we could team up and play a round of charades and James and I had split apart as if a bolt of lightning had struck the ground between us.

"No," I said, thinking of the way his lips had moved against my neck that night, achingly slow and deliberate. "But I appreciate the offer."

Shaking his head, he leaned back in the booth. There was that annoying smirk again—the one that said he was already thinking three moves ahead of me.

"What?" I said. "What's that face?"

He shrugged. "I knew you'd say no."

"What's that supposed to mean?"

His eyes gleamed. "You're not really one for adventure."

I felt my jaw tighten. Just who did he think he was, waltzing into this town after not seeing me for eight years and telling me what I was and wasn't capable of? What I did and did not enjoy? What I was and was not terrified of?

"I like adventure just fine," I said. "Maybe I just don't want to spend a whole week in close quarters with you."

He gave me a tiny smile. "People like green beans *just fine*," he said. "They like tap water *just fine*. You either love trying new things, or you don't." His eyes sparkled, daring me to prove him wrong.

"Don't pretend like you know me just because we had some classes together, Fielding. You don't know me at all." Even as I said the words, I knew they weren't completely true.

He leaned forward again and stared at me so hard I felt an ache in my chest. He was so close that I could smell his woodsy scent, which only made me want to be closer. "You're a perfectionist," he said, his voice gravelly. "You always worry that you're not good enough, even when you clearly are. You're bored out of your mind at the inn, but you're still working there —probably because you want to make your parents happy, even though you shouldn't have to. And you love a good challenge and a chance to outdo me—even more than you like peanut butter chocolate cake."

I stared at him, feeling like all the air had whooshed right out of my lungs.

"And you've got some pretty killer dance moves," he said, his tone lightening.

At first I thought he was talking about college and that ill-fated party, but then I remembered the clatter of the trash can outside my window. I felt heat rising in my cheeks. "You were watching me?"

"I couldn't help it," he said. "I wasn't trying to be weird and stalker-y. You just looked so..."

"So *what*?" The words sounded harsher than I intended, but the thought of James standing in my yard, watching me through the window when I thought I was safe from anyone's scrutiny and all by myself in the world made me want to chuck my beer bottle at him.

"Happy," he said.

I frowned. "Not exactly. And for the record, it is very stalker-y to stare into someone's window when you don't have their permission to do so."

"So you dance around like that when you're unhappy?"

I sighed, knowing I should pull myself from this booth and run away into the night and put James Fielding and his annoying smile and magnetic stare behind me forever. That would have been the smart move. But the beer had loosened me up just enough to be honest and not care too much about what James Fielding thought of my reasoning. Plus, I hadn't felt this zip of electricity from someone in a really, really long time.

Like, since he kissed me on the lawn outside our college apartment.

I took a long drink from the beer and said, "Manifesting."

He cocked his head to the side.

"It sounds all goofy and woo-woo, but I was reading about the law of attraction, and manifesting your dreams and whatnot. And one of the lessons was to get yourself into a place where you're really feeling what you want. For things to really manifest, you have to think about the things you want as if you already have them, and really feel it in your bones." I shrugged. "Some people say the best way to do that is hype themselves up so they're feeling really good. For me, that's dancing it out."

He stared at me for a minute, his eyes nearly black in the dim light. "What is it you want to attract, Harper?"

Mercy, he could melt steel with those eyes. A little zing of electricity rippled over my skin again, all the way down to my toes.

No, I thought. This is James Fielding. You cannot feel this way about Fielding. He only sees you as a means to an end, a way to get what he wants. Stop looking at his eyes, and his lips, and his big perfect hands. *Stop.*

"Why are you talking to me like we're friends?" I said.

There was a hint of a smile. "Can't we be friends?"

"No."

"Then let's be co-hosts."

"No." I didn't need to be stuck with James Fielding every day, pretending to be happy and amicable so it looked good on film. The last thing I needed was to be stuck in another charade.

He smiled his rakish smile. "Come on, Harper. It's just for one week. Take it as a challenge. Prove to me you don't hate adventure."

"A train wreck is not adventure."

"Depends on who's on the train."

"You have a ridiculous answer for everything, Fielding."

"What better things do you have to do this week? Search boring job postings? Chase raccoons in the yard?"

"I do have an inn to run, you know." I didn't like the way those words tasted in my mouth—they were just a reminder of how badly I wanted my old job back, or to get a new, better one that hadn't been offered out of sympathy and necessity. On the Venn diagram of jobs and need, this was the deadly area of overlap that made me sick right down to my core. As badly as I wanted James Fielding to be wrong about me, I did need something new.

"I don't think your guests will need you at all waking hours. But we can work around your schedule. No problem."

I frowned, hating that he had an easy answer for everything. But it seemed all things came easy to James. "What's in it for me?"

"Tetia will talk to you about talent fees. It won't knock your socks off, but it'll make it worth your time."

"This all sounds terribly cute," I said. "Two hosts with banter, one fish out of water. I thought cute escapism wasn't your brand."

"Cute escapism is a money-maker. Networks lose their minds over cute escapism." He said this matter-of-factly, his tone light.

I snorted, thinking back to the way he'd used those words against me years before, making me feel like my ideas were simplistic, not even in the same universe as his. *Cute* wasn't compelling. It wasn't serious and important. It was amusing, fluffy. Easy.

"You don't remember, do you?" I asked him.

He stared at me, his eyes wide and steady on mine. Of course he didn't. It was silly of me to think that he'd spent a single second thinking about those words he'd thrown at me so carelessly. Words that had stung me to my core at the time, and made me feel like my dreams weren't big enough, not the stuff that built real careers.

"It wasn't so long ago that you thought cute escapism was the worst fate imaginable," I said. "A waste of time and effort."

He leaned forward again, so we were only inches apart. I wanted to move away from him, but there was no way I was backing down again. Never again would he make me feel small.

"I never said that, Sadie."

"But that's what you meant. Insignificant. Unimportant. Silly." He knew what I was referring to now—I could see the shift in his expression, the way his jaw tensed.

"That was never what I meant." His gaze dropped to my lips and I felt my heart do that weird flip-flop again. "There's a reason people love cute escapism. It makes them feel light, and hopeful, like it's easy to find things to love about the world. Sometimes I think we need that now more than ever." He tapped his finger on the table between us and it felt like he was chipping away at the wall I'd so carefully built around my heart. "Some of us can do that naturally, though. And some of us have to work so hard at it that it comes across as insincere. And an audience can tell the difference. Just like a good producer can."

I swallowed hard. He was very good at saying what people needed to hear.

"You've always been able to cut to the heart of things and make people care," he said. "You make it look easy. It's actually kind of annoying." He gave me a playful smile. "Don't bother arguing with me, either. I saw one of your ranger programs."

"You what? How?" My one beer had suddenly made the whole world fuzzy and none of what James was saying made sense.

"We came to scout things out a month or so ago," he said. "I went to Congaree one day to get a little dose of nature and I saw your name listed on one of the ranger programs, so I stuck around."

"You did what?" My heart hammered in my chest. James had seen me do a program? And then slipped away and not even spoken to me? "You said you didn't expect me at the inn!"

He shrugged. "Not at the inn, no. I expected you at the park, because I saw you there that day. You were amazing."

"Not amazing enough," I muttered, still reeling from the idea of James being in one of those crowds, and me having no idea.

"I think you should give this a try, Harper. What do you have to lose?"

I finished my beer and leaned back in the booth. James Fielding did look sincere.

"Just think about it," he said. "Tetia's going to ask you about it tomorrow. She'll want an answer quick so she can keep shooting and put out this dumpster fire."

"It's hardly a dumpster fire."

He frowned. "You haven't seen the dailies."

"Fine. I'll think about it. But no promises."

"Great," he said, slamming his hand on the table. "Next round's on me." That devilish twinkle was back in his eye, and his lip lifted in a satisfied smile that made the nape of my neck tingle. I swallowed hard, pushing away the thought.

As he walked toward the bar to get another two beers, I found myself staring a bit too long, admiring his broad shoulders and muscular frame. I couldn't help but think that I might have been wrong about James Fielding—he might have changed more than I was giving him credit for. But he still had that spark in his eyes that lured me closer, daring me to back down from the challenge.

He wasn't here to humiliate me—that much was clear. And now I felt petty for thinking that was reason enough for him to come here in the first place. He'd made co-hosting sound like a win-win, but if what he said was true, this would obviously affect his career more than mine. Unless of course, it led me somewhere entirely new.

As much as Past Me would have hated to agree with him on anything, Present Me could see that he was right about one thing.

At this point, I had nothing to lose.

Chapter Ten

SADIE

TETIA WAS VERY CONVINCING.

I'd been up half the night replaying the whole conversation that James and I'd had in the bar, and sometime around sunrise had decided that I was going to say no. I needed to focus on the next step for my career, and dabbling in TV was not part of that plan.

But then Tetia came down early for breakfast and pitched her idea to me while I finished arranging a plate full of mini-quiches, and my plan went right out the window.

"You're the spark this show needs," she said, and another little chunk of that wall I'd built to protect myself fell away. The recovering people-pleaser deep inside loved to hear that she was good at something, and that part of me needed to hear those words now more than ever.

Tetia gave me a script to read over before we met Gwen for my first real interview. With a solid list of questions from both myself and James, it still left plenty of room for banter.

"The more teasing, the better," Tetia said with a wink. "We can always edit down, and everybody loves the goofy fish-out-of-water trope. Adding in this old rivalry y'all have is the secret sauce, and we want to lean into that as much as we can. Just think *Dirty Jobs* vibes, and keep it casual."

As she popped a tiny quiche into her mouth, I couldn't help but wonder: What exactly had James told her about our history?

Once Ashley and Ravi set up the extra lights in Gwen's kitchen, this became real. When Ravi started filming, I felt a knot forming in my gut. We were all squeezed into the kitchen, which was behind the main part of the cafe. Gwen had kept the cafe open, which meant we heard the din of the usual crowd out front, plus the occasional burst of steam from the espresso machine. The plan was for me and James to pepper Gwen with questions while she taught us to bake one of her crowd-pleasing cupcakes. The kitchen that had once seemed huge and airy now felt like it was the size of a coat closet.

Keep it together, I thought. *You can do this.* Friends talking. Friends baking. No problem.

Gwen stood between James and me, telling him about how she first opened the cafe while handing him ingredients to add into the mixing bowl. Today she looked like a real-life kitchen goddess, with her blond curls just this side of messy. She wore a bright pink shirt that almost matched her lipstick and I was suddenly grateful that Ashley had insisted on taming my hair into a cute ponytail and doing my makeup camera-thick. If I was going to be in the spotlight, they were going to make sure I looked good in it.

James tossed in eggs and sugar while Gwen answered his questions, flinching when the big standing mixer sent up a cloud of flour that covered his apron.

"Easy there, Iron Chef," Gwen said, teasing.

"I've made cupcakes exactly once in my life," James said.

"Was anyone harmed?" I asked, mostly on cue.

Ashley gave me an encouraging thumbs-up as James smirked. "Can't really discuss details," he said, "But I'm feeling hopeful today. I like to think I'm a fast learner."

"I'm sure you are," Gwen said. "Thorough, too." She shot me enough devilish side-eye to tell me she was thinking about her whole he's-your-college-crush theory and considering some other things he might learn thoroughly.

I took a deep breath and pushed that thought as far away as possible.

Ashley held up a little dry-erase board every few minutes, reminding me of the next question I was supposed to ask. There were only twelve in my script, but ever since that red record light had started blinking, my brain had stopped working entirely. I couldn't remember which questions to ask in what order, and I was already sweating through my blouse. The room felt hotter than a tin roof in July, and we'd only just pulled the first batch from the oven.

James gave me a reassuring smile and said, "Gwen, did you ever think you'd be baking cow-face cupcakes when you were in high school here?"

"I did not," she said. "But life is full of surprises."

"What was it like growing up here?" he said. "What's the wildest thing you ever did in Jasmine Falls?"

"Oh James, I can't tell you about most of the things I did in high school," Gwen said, giving me a playful nudge. "We'll have to take those secrets to the grave."

"We wouldn't want to break the internet," I said.

"These cupcakes will break the internet," James said. "Now how do these get made into cows?"

The plan was to have Gwen show us how to make adorable cupcakes that looked like three-dimensional cow faces. It was a design she'd perfected for last year's summer festival, and was one of her most-requested items for kids' parties. If this show went the way we all wanted, she'd likely be making a lot more cow-cakes in her future.

When I felt myself getting nervous again, I heard Paula Sue's voice in my head, telling me that the whole town was depending on me. Then I told myself *This is why you're doing the show. This could help a lot of people in this town.*

"Do you have any secret ingredients?" I asked her, sticking my finger into the batter for a taste.

"Love," she said. "I know it sounds totally cheesy, but you can taste the difference when you think about something you love while you bake."

I licked the batter from my finger and glanced at James. He was staring at me with a look that was one hundred percent smoldering, and my heart did that weird flip-flop again.

"Plus vanilla bean," Gwen said. "And just a hint of moolasses." After a beat, she said, "Man, that one kills with the kiddos."

His eyes fixed on me, James broke into a sexy half-smile that would absolutely break his Instagram and I thought I might actually combust. When was the last time a man had looked at me that way?

At my twenty-first birthday party, in our big college dorm apartment. That was when. It was the night that had been the end of everything and the beginning of something else.

THE APARTMENT HAD BEEN PACKED the night of the party, mostly with people from our department. James had shown up, to my surprise, but we'd somehow managed to dodge each other for most of the night. Eventually we'd been shuffled in with the dancing crowd, each of us trying and failing to squeeze out of the fray, because the one thing we had in common was being introverts. We were both feeling a little braver from a few drinks, and when we ended up next to each other James had pulled me into a dance with a shrug that said, *If you can't beat 'em, join 'em.* He was all heated stares and fiery touches, and in that moment I knew I could no longer deny the attraction between us. Despite the sniping and competition, it had been there all along.

With one hand on my hip, he drew me closer as I tangled my hand in his hair. We'd both laughed at the surprise of it, the two of us finally coming together in a moment where we weren't clashing, and then when the song ended, we'd snapped apart just as quickly as we'd come together, as if waking from a trance.

Later, I'd snagged a piece of birthday cake and slipped outside to the courtyard to get away from the crowd. There was a warmth in the air, the kind that comes in late March in Western North Carolina, teasing you into thinking it's spring. When I hopped up onto the brick wall outside, James stepped out from under the shadow of a tree and leaned next to me on the wall. We'd ended up talking for a while, the cake forgotten. My skin was still on fire from the way his hands had held me so firmly against him, and each time his eyes rested on mine, I felt my breath catch. The music from the party was booming through the open windows, and when an '80s playlist fired up, James said, "Fun fact, this song is a tango."

"*Wake Me Up Before You Go-Go* is not a tango," I scoffed.

"You willing to bet a piece of birthday cake on it?" He cocked his head to the side and said, "Quick-quick-slow, quick-quick-slow."

"No way." Before I could argue further, he lifted me off the wall and pulled me into the same hold we'd practiced a few weeks before in our ballroom class. In a flash, his feet were moving in the familiar rhythm, sweeping me through the courtyard. I tripped over his feet as he sang along with the song, laughing until I was sore.

"Told you," he said, his lips close to my ear.

When the song ended, I dropped my hand from his shoulder, and he let me go. "You owe me cake," he said, his tone teasing.

I swiped the plate from the brick wall and said, "I'll split it with you, because the tempo was too fast to be an actual tango."

He smirked as I held the plate between us. "Agree to disagree."

When I broke off a piece for myself, he quickly grabbed my wrist and pulled it toward his lips. I laughed as he stole the bite, and then stopped when his teeth pinched my finger. His eyes burned into mine as he slowly licked the bit of frosting from my thumb like it was the last trace of chocolate on earth. Just like that, I was like a bunny caught in a snare.

His focus was entirely on me. I was surprised, delighted, terrified, and when he set the plate on the wall and leaned in to kiss me, I thought surely my heart would explode. This was James Fielding, after all—I shouldn't be swooning over him like he was Mr. Darcy. He he was basically my nemesis.

But not tonight.

He was a surprisingly good kisser, and even though my brain told me to pull away from the clutches of my arch-rival, my traitorous body had other ideas. Before I could work out how I felt about all of that, my roommate Kara had burst into the yard looking for me and stopped us from careening toward a terrible decision.

Later, Kara had cornered me in the kitchen and said, "I knew it! You two are like gasoline and a lit match. It was only a matter of time."

"Ugh, no," I said, burning with embarrassment. "Not in a million years." I'd blamed it on having one too many shots, insisting that what she'd seen was nothing but a moment of weakness and that we would be terrible together. When I'd scooted past her back into the hallway, I'd bumped into James. My blush burned all the way to the tips of my ears. He didn't say a word, but he had to have heard me.

His brow was furrowed, his eyes sad, and I felt like I'd been kicked in the chest.

We were like two magnets: most days, we went through our lives with the wrong sides touching so the closer we got, the more we repelled each other. When we weren't misaligned, we'd clicked with an intensity that took my breath away—but then I'd said that stupid thing in the kitchen, and James had never mentioned it again.

On Monday, James and I were right back to being misaligned magnets again. It was like that night in the courtyard had never happened. He quit coming to the ballroom classes, and I didn't see him quite as often in the cafe or when I was out with my friends. After that, he seemed to always have a different girl with him, but never the same one for very long. He didn't avoid me entirely, and he was never rude—but the teasing wasn't the same as it was before. It was less intense, less personal.

And I missed it.

ALL THESE YEARS I never stopped wondering what might have happened if Kara hadn't interrupted us. Or if I hadn't said those awful things.

And thinking of all that now, one truth was crystal clear: James Fielding never had it out for me. Not in the way I thought.

I had it wrong all along.

Focus, I thought. *You have a job to do.*

Gwen snorted at her joke and nudged James. "These are

ready to pour up, cowboy. Remember, be gentle and don't knock all the air out."

And here I was, struggling to breathe. His gaze flicked back to Gwen and he said, "Yes, ma'am," and spooned the batter into our baking cups in a slow, deliberate way that made me think of a kid trying hard not to mess up. He carefully placed the baking tin in the oven and we took a quick break as Ashley grabbed the tray of cupcakes that had been baked ahead of time and cooled.

"Y'all are doing great," Tetia said. "Keep it up."

James stepped out the back door while the rest of us prepped the kitchen for the frosting demo. Ravi helped himself to a cupcake that had rolled off the cooling rack while Ashley touched up my makeup.

"You look a little wooden," Ashley said. "You okay?" She put her hands on my shoulders and moved them back and forth like she might shake a little tension loose. "Don't be nervous. Just you and your old friends having fun."

I nodded, rolling my neck and shoulders to loosen up. "Right. Old friends. Fun."

I was not a good enough actor to pretend my whole world hadn't just tilted on its axis. Why had I never let myself believe that James had real feelings for me? Why had I just assumed he was trying to hurt me?

Ashley smiled. "Don't worry about millions of viewers. Just focus on Gwen and James."

My chest tightened. "Millions?" Why had I not given more thought to what I was wearing today? What hadn't I gotten a haircut? Why had I ever thought this would be okay? I was so far out of my depth here. Who was I kidding, thinking I could fake my way through being a co-host? *With a man who could knock me off-kilter with one lingering gaze?*

"Relax," she said. "You got this."

"I'm just going to get some air," I said. "Take a quick walk down the block." Part of me wanted to run straight for the inn and never look back, but I knew that wasn't an option.

"Let's take ten," Tetia said, breezing past us. "Ravi, let's you and I grab a coffee and look at lighting for a minute."

I slipped out the galley doors that separated the kitchen from the cafe and nearly collided with Maggie, the head barista.

"Hey, Sadie," she said, out of breath. "How's it going?"

"Trying not to have a heart attack," I said. "You?"

"Slammed." She hustled back over to the espresso bar, where four customers were waiting to order. The cafe was more crowded than I'd seen it since the peak summer season, and there wasn't an empty chair in sight. It seemed like half the town was squeezed in here.

I'd almost made it around to the front of the counter when Paula Sue Hinson swooped up next to me and grabbed my forearm. She was the last person I needed to collide with right now. Paula Sue did not need to see me panicked and frazzled.

"Sadie," she said. "I trust everything's going well today."

"How'd you know I was here?" I squeaked.

Her big green eyes widened. "I heard you've got a bigger role in the episode now."

There truly were zero secrets in this town.

"Maybe you could get them to come out and shoot a little footage out here," she said, glancing around. "It looks good to have a crowd, don't you think?"

"Paula Sue, did you tell all these people to come here this morning?"

She sniffed. "I might have sent a group text that encouraged folks to stop by while the segment was filming. Everyone wants to show their support."

Lord have mercy.

"I'll see what I can do," I told her, gently prying my arm from her grip. "If you'll excuse me, I have to run outside for a minute." I slipped away before she could latch onto my arm again, and heard her calling out more instructions as I headed for the front door.

Once outside, I made a beeline for the end of the block and didn't stop until I was around the corner and out of Paula Sue's line of sight. I took a deep breath and closed my eyes, and tried to will myself to forget about James Fielding's big hands, and smoldering looks, and stupid mischievous grins. And how what I'd said so long ago must have hurt him so much worse than I'd imagined.

"Hi," he said.

My eyes popped open and there was James, sitting on a bench just a few feet away. How was it that this man could be everywhere all at once?

He'd stripped off his apron and was sipping a bottled water, looking as relaxed as if he were out for a stroll in the park. "You doing okay?" His button-down shirt was straining against his shoulders and biceps and I definitely needed to look at something else.

I let out a deep breath and tried to will my heart to go back to its normal rhythm because the last thing I needed was to faint on the sidewalk. "Sure. It's just stuffy in that kitchen." I sat down next to him on the bench and he passed me the water bottle.

"I'm glad you said yes to all this, for what it's worth," he said. "I wasn't sure that you would."

"It could be great publicity for the town," I said, taking a long drink. I was hot and flustered, and feeling the warmth from his knee touching mine was not helping. Not at all.

"Is that the only reason?" he drawled.

"Yes."

Nope.

He'd caught me in a weak moment last night—or created one —and today I felt like I'd made a huge mistake. I could handle working with Fielding, but feeling like I had to perform perfectly and not embarrass myself, or my parents, or this *whole town*— that was too much.

What had I been thinking?

"I think we're good together." He raked a hand through his hair and I saw little flecks of flour there. "Don't you?"

I shrugged, trying to act cool while my started heart racing again. "Sure."

He laughed. "Careful, Harper. All that enthusiasm's going to make me think you like me."

"I didn't think this through," I muttered.

"What's there to think about? Do the segment, have fun, make a better cupcake than mine. I thought you'd enjoy making me look like a doofus in the kitchen." He rolled his sleeves up over his elbows and I forced myself not to study the corded muscle of his forearms and the edge of that mysterious tattoo.

I took another sip and handed the bottle back to him. "This is hard for me, okay? I really don't like being in the spotlight."

He arched a brow, curious. "Why not?"

My whole body tensed up. "It never goes well."

"What does that mean?"

"It means it's always a disaster!" I said, and two ladies who were window-shopping nearby turned to stare at us. I waved to them and smiled—*nothing to see here! No meltdown on this block!*— and turned back to James. I took a deep breath, trying to tamp down all my fears. "The idea of being filmed and plastered all over the internet is even worse," I explained. "I can't handle any more humiliation, okay?"

"'All over the internet' might be a stretch," he said. "I mean, you'd have to be a subscriber to see our episodes, so it's not like—"

I turned to face him. "If I'm in another horrible viral video, I will die. I will spontaneously combust and disappear into smoke, and moonwalk right off this mortal coil."

"You were in a viral video?" he said, his voice lightening.

I squeezed my eyes shut and said, "Are you telling me you didn't see it? The park ranger who got chased by the elk and climbed up a tree? It was on the nightly news, for heaven's sake."

He started to chuckle and I swatted him on the arm. "It's not funny. It was awful. I had to stay in the tree until another ranger drove his vehicle over to scare the elk away and rescue me. And then I fell out of the tree."

"I'm sorry," he said, choking back a laugh. "Now I'm going to have to google it later."

"If you do, I'll never speak to you again." My cheeks were on fire, and I felt the heat all the way in the tips of my ears. I'd never wanted to think about that day again, either, and now I'd just blurted out all the details right here on the sidewalk.

"It can't be that bad," he said. "And how did you get chased by an elk? Aren't they in the Rockies?"

"They're also in the Smokies," I said, dropping my face into my hands. "We had to go there for a training session and a couple of the wildlife biologists there took us out to see the elk. Unfortunately it was during the rut, and I made the mistake of accidentally getting between the bull elk and all his ladies."

"Oh, darlin'," he said, biting back a grin. "Did David Attenborough teach you nothing?"

I gave him what I hoped was my most fearsome, iciest stare.

"It couldn't have been that bad, Harper."

"I became a cautionary tale. Not only did the rangers use it as material for their safety training, but it was posted literally everywhere on social media. I was a total laughingstock." It made me want to die just thinking about it. Tourists did those goofy things all the time, but park employees were supposed to know better. It had been a rookie mistake, and one I'd never live down. Even though you couldn't clearly see my face in the video, and even though I was pretty sure the average person who saw it couldn't pick me out of a line-up, it still felt like the whole world had seen me screw up and laughed about it.

And they were still laughing. Because the internet is forever.

"I'm sorry," he said, and when I looked up, he was still biting back a smile.

"I hate you," I said.

"There are worse ways to get yourself plastered all over the internet, Sadie." The way he said that made me think I might need to google him later, too.

"I'm telling you," I said, "whenever I'm the center of attention, something terrible happens." The elk incident had been humiliating, but at least it wasn't as bad as some of the other times I'd been in the spotlight. Like the time I won the science fair in fourth grade and then lost all my friends overnight. Or the time I won the award for Best Graduate Paper and then got food poisoning and ended up in the emergency department. Or back on my twenty-third birthday, when I'd stayed out all night with my friends and finally given myself permission to cut loose and have fun in a karaoke bar—only to learn the next day that my grandmother had died that night while I was making a fool of myself with my friends.

People always told me those were coincidences, no doubt trying to make me feel better. But they were wrong. For me, this fact was as certain as gravity: if I tried to step into the spotlight, the universe would knock me right out of it with surprising force and cruelty.

"The other shoe always drops."

"Did you ever think that maybe that's just a story you're telling yourself?" he said. "Maybe something else could be more true?"

"That sounds like something a therapist would say."

"Actually, it is," he said. "It's something my therapist said. Turns out, she was right. I'd been telling myself a story that really wasn't true for a long, long time."

"And what was that story?" I said.

"Come to dinner with me, and I'll tell you."

Was he asking me on a date? My heart squeezed as I considered this. Was I attracted to him? Sure. Was I reading too much into this? Maybe.

"What's the matter?" I said. "Not getting enough quality time with me in our marathon shooting schedule?"

"Come on, it'll be fun." He smiled and nudged my arm.

"That's exactly what they said about the elk."

"I promise not to run you up a tree."

"I think I need to finish that walk," I said, and left him there on the bench. Even though I was mildly curious about the story he told himself, the last thing I needed was to have James Fielding trying to solve my problems.

That was something I needed to do on my own.

GWEN'S DEMO cow cupcakes were ridiculously cute, with their little black fondant spots and pink marshmallow noses. They had sweet little eyes and tiny horns and ears, because Gwen was serious about details, and that woman did not skimp when it came to baked goods. Once Ravi started filming us again, she expertly frosted the first one while James and I struggled to keep up, all while she told James about why she'd decided that Jasmine Falls was the place to start her business.

"I didn't think to do this until after my grandma passed," she said. "She had a bakery back in the day, and taught me how to do everything I know. When she died, she left me her house, and I decided to move back to Jasmine Falls. And then this storefront came up for sale, and the rest is history. This wasn't the path I started on, but now it seems inevitable that I'd be here."

"Funny how that happens," James said, glancing at me.

I swallowed hard, looking at Ashley's cue card and struggling to get my words out.

After the demo, Gwen said, "The rules are simple. You two have ten minutes to frost as many cupcakes as you can. Winner gets a prize." Gwen set her baking timer and we were off, tackling the remaining cupcakes.

James grumbled while he struggled to make little cow ears out of fondant. I worked quickly to cover my first cupcake and do the piping for the nose. James hip-checked me playfully as I reached for my next cupcake and I tossed a handful of marshmallows at his face to retaliate. He laughed and whipped a handful of powdered sugar at me as he cried, "Mooove out of the way, Harper. Eyes on the prize!"

"Keep your hands to yourself, Fielding!" I said. "No cheating."

He bent back to his little cow faces, grinning as he added in their cute button eyes, and something in my chest was knocked loose. Watching him clumsily attack the cupcakes, giving me a teasing nudge when I finished another, it was actually hard to imagine how on earth he wouldn't go over well with test audiences. James, in front of the camera, was funny and self-deprecating, and full of wonder. He asked questions that cut to the heart of things, and made Gwen's eyes sparkle with joy. He knocked down defenses and put people at ease.

He was a total sweetheart.

Cupcakes, I thought. *Focus on cupcakes.*

"That's time!" Gwen called, as her timer beeped.

James braced himself against the counter dramatically, wiping his brow with the back of his hand. He left a streak of frosting on his cheek that I desperately wanted to wipe away.

"Don't look so moo-rose, Harper. Yours look pretty good."

I snort-laughed and threw another marshmallow at him.

Gwen stepped between us, examining our work. "Sadie has four cows and James has three and a half vague animal shapes with ears and eyes."

"Hey," he said, laughing. "They're definitely recognizable as cows. They're not an *udder* disaster."

"Winner, winner," Gwen said, grabbing my hand and holding it up. I couldn't help but laugh, finally feeling the nervous tension slip away. And then James was smiling at me—flashing his genuine lopsided smile, and giving me a sly wink that melted me to my core.

With the frosting demo complete, Gwen had moved on to the segment where she showed off some of her other cake designs. For months now, she'd talked about expanding into creating cakes for special events, but she hadn't gone all in yet. It struck me as unusual for Gwen, who seemed to never let anything hold her back.

"So," James said, admiring a giant carrot cake, "What's the best thing about owning your own business?" He seemed to genuinely be having a good time as Gwen answered his questions with the grace and self-confidence that I'd wished for about a million times.

"You mean aside from getting to eat all the less-than-perfects and using them to bribe my friends?" She shrugged and said, "I get to do what I love every day. I didn't always think that was possible, but it was my grandma who inspired me to go for it." She leaned against the counter and smiled. "She said to make my passion my North Star, and as long as I did that, all the other little annoying things that happened along the way couldn't stop me from going wherever I wanted."

"Sounds like a wise lady," James said.

"Life took her to some unexpected places," Gwen said. "And it did the same for me." She looked over at me and smiled. "Now I try to go with the flow and see where it takes me—even though it drives my little inner perfectionist totally bonkers."

James gave me a friendly smile and I felt like the room was closing in on me. All the talk of dreams was just reminding me of how quickly mine had slipped away. I could handle the arrogant, competitive James, but I couldn't handle this version of him that was warm and empathetic, so eager to put everyone at ease.

Somehow, that made my failure seem even more real. And it made this co-hosting gig feel like nothing more than a band-aid. A temporary fix.

You can do this, I thought. *It's only a few more hours.* Then I could go home, sit in my pajamas, and binge-watch my favorite cooking shows while searching for more park jobs that were anywhere but here.

"So," he said. "What's Sadie's prize?"

"A gift certificate for a cake of her choice," Gwen said with a wink. "And James, the runner-up gets to take all the cow cupcakes from today."

"Perfect," he said, pulling her in for a hug. "Thanks so much for letting us do this feature with you, Gwen. It's been a blast."

"My pleasure," she said, giving me a look that said she'd have plenty to say about all of this later.

James had totally won her over. And despite my greatest efforts, something in my heart was feeling warmer toward him, too.

Chapter Eleven

AFTER WE FINISHED FILMING, I took a walk downtown to clear my head. By the time I got back to my room and stepped into the shower, I was right back to thinking about Sadie again.

I'd never been so happy to lose. Yes, the stakes were low for cow cupcakes, but when Sadie had tossed those mini marshmallows at me, it was like another little chunk of that wall around her had fallen down. My fierce competitor had finally relaxed, had laughed her musical laugh as she'd let her goofy side come out on full display while wielding a piping bag like it was a magic wand.

It was so adorable it made my heart ache.

She'd been frazzled earlier in the day, struggling to get through the segment. I could tell she was worried about missing cues and stumbling over lines, so I tried to encourage her between takes and praise those things she was doing so well. (And there was a lot she was doing well.) At Cambrick, she'd set an impossibly high bar for herself, and it was clear today that she hadn't changed in that regard.

She'd looked more anxious as the hours passed, and I could

read her mind like a book. She was in a spiral that I knew all too well: you put pressure on yourself not to make a mistake, and then you do make one, and it makes you even more flustered and you stumble again and you just know that everyone around you is taking notes and tallying those mistakes against you. Pretty soon it feels like every move is the wrong one and you're a sinking ship.

If only I could have snapped my fingers and made that feeling go away for her.

When we'd sat on that bench and she'd explained how she was so afraid to be in the spotlight, it had taken me by surprise. Partly because she was so very good at holding everyone's attention—she really had done an excellent job with the ranger program I'd seen. Sadie was precisely the kind of person who deserved to be in a spotlight: friendly, kind, and inspiring. She was a total dynamo, and I hated that she couldn't seem to see that.

She still seemed to be struggling with my being here, though. In some moments, she acted just prickly enough to keep space between us. Other times, the armor disappeared and her warmth broke through, drawing us closer. There was no denying the sparks that flew between us, but I could feel her holding back. I still wasn't entirely certain how she felt about me, but I wasn't leaving this time without knowing for sure.

If she told me to get lost, I'd let her go. Walk away. But the way she looked at me suggested that was not at all what she wanted. I really hoped that when this week was over, we'd be spending a lot more time together.

I just needed to figure out exactly how to make that happen.

I smiled, thinking of that moment when I'd walked in on her talking to her ranger friend in the library of the inn. *I just want to be courted like the rare creature I am,* she'd said.

She'd been half-joking, but she was absolutely right. She was extraordinary, and deserved nothing less. And I intended to prove it to her.

After my shower, I flopped onto the big bed and thought again (for the thousandth time) of how Sadie had licked that cake batter from her finger and nearly stopped my heart with one flash of her tongue. I'd barely been here two full days and was already aching to spend every minute with her. *Keep it together*, I thought. *You are not some sad sack pining in a Victorian novel. That's not what she wants.*

Before I could think too hard about that, my phone buzzed with a text.

Hey, Tetia wrote. **Can we talk quickly before dinner?**

Sure, I replied.

Is now ok? She typed. **Meet in the garden outside?**

Be there in 5, I answered, happy to have something to take my mind off Sadie and stop me from trying to piece together how she felt about me.

IN THE GARDEN behind the inn, Tetia sat under the shade of a small dogwood tree, at a little table with two chairs. She'd poured herself a glass of cucumber water from the kitchen and brought me one, too.

"Cheers," I said, clinking my glass next to hers.

"I needed my daily dose of sunshine," she said. "And I thought we could catch up for a minute."

"Great," I said. "How did you think it went today?"

She pushed her sunglasses up into her hair. "Very good. I like the idea of having a bit of a contest in every segment."

I sipped my water. "Yeah, that was fun." And it got Sadie to relax, too. By the second half of the segment, she'd loosened up and seemed more like herself.

She stared at me for a moment and said, "I talked to the execs earlier today and wanted to get you up to speed."

Something in the set of her jaw told me it hadn't been an easy phone call.

"What's the news?" I asked.

She leaned back in her chair. "The short of it? They've seen some clips from this week, and they want you to have a co-host for the whole show. It's not a suggestion."

My chest tightened. "Oh." That was not the feedback I'd expected.

"I know what this show means to you, but they're not going to budge. I had a long talk with them, and we went over some options."

I bit back a grimace. This was exactly what had happened before, with the last pilot. One episode, and the execs had said I was terrible on my own. They loved me with a co-host, but in their words, I couldn't carry an entire show by myself. I needed a partner, they said. It was painfully ironic because in the weeks before, Melanie had tried to explain away her cheating by telling me I was a terrible partner. She told me I was distant, that I traveled too much, and I was making it impossible to build a life together.

Apparently I was only partner material when I was in front of a camera.

It had cut me to the bone when the execs last told me that, but I'd convinced myself I could do better. I was bad in the pilot because my whole life had just gone up in flames. To be honest, I wasn't good at anything during that time.

But now I had my life back together. I felt like my old self again—my pre-Melanie self who was quick with his words and sharp in a scene. And they were still telling me I was no good on my own.

The thought made my heart twist in my chest.

Tetia sighed. "They want to bring in Clarissa Davis."

It felt like a full minute before I heard the words come out of my mouth. "Absolutely not," I scoffed. "That woman is a troll. Brash. Rude. You remember when we were both guests on that YouTube show, right? She goaded me about the pilot through the entire segment, and then confused me with that idiot author who was caught plagiarizing his dead mentor's work." I took a deep breath, my pulse already hammering at my temple. "I got hate mail for weeks."

Tetia held her hand up to stop me. "My counter offer was to have rotating co-hosts for each episode. The problem is that it would take longer to schedule multiple people and it could delay production. They didn't go for it."

"Did they float any other names?" I said.

She arched a brow. "A few, but none that I was excited about. They're driven by ratings, and they think you need someone with a social media presence who already has a big fan base. You know how these guys think, though. They want either chemistry or conflict. Anything else is boring."

"This is a terrible idea," I said. They'd get conflict with Clarissa, all right. Enough to send my blood pressure skyrocketing and give me permanent frown lines.

"It might be the only way you get to do the show." She crossed her arms over her chest. "But it could lead to something much better for you. My advice? Don't say no just yet."

It felt like the whole world was closing in on me. My chest was tight and a pounding had started behind my left eye, and none of this was okay.

"What about Sadie?" I blurted.

Tetia raised a brow.

"She's good, right? I mean, she's a little rough, but she's funny, charming, great at getting people to open up to her." The words were out of my mouth before I could fully consider what I was suggesting.

"Keep talking," Tetia said, tapping her finger on her lip.

"She's an unknown, sure, but she's down-to-earth. The cute girl next door with a big sense of wonder. She's got the spark, don't you think?"

Tetia was always on the hunt for *the spark*. It was what turned a show into gold and made a producer's career.

"Agree. She's delightful. But you're right—the unknown is a hard sell. Especially when the known is—"

"Me," I finished.

She frowned. "I'm sorry, James. You know I believe in you one hundred percent. You're one of my favorite people in the whole world and I only want wonderful things for you."

"Ditto." I smiled and gave her a shrug. "It's pretty great to discover new talent, though. Puts you on the map." Plus, it was a huge ego boost for the execs. It gave them something to brag about at all their fancy parties and award shows.

She studied me, her eyes narrowed. "You think she'd go for it?"

"It's worth a shot," I said. "Isn't she a thousand times better than Clarissa?" I shuddered, hating to even have that woman's name in my mouth.

"I love that idea." She nodded, quiet for a moment as she turned that over in her mind. "Let's see how the next two days go. Then I can send more footage to the execs and pitch it."

I let out a deep breath. "Thank you."

"In the meantime," she said, "coach her a little and get her to relax and open up more like she did this afternoon. We don't have much time, and we need to make the execs see what we see in her. Make them swoon."

How could anyone not swoon over Sadie?

"You got it," I said. I knew they'd go for it if they could see Sadie the way I did—if she'd just *let* them see that side of her she tried to hard to protect.

Getting her to agree to do one full episode with me had been one thing, but convincing her to do a whole season was something else entirely. What I needed was to get Sadie to stop putting so much pressure on herself and just have fun with me.

That might be my biggest challenge yet.

Chapter Twelve

SADIE

I FELT like I'd been run through a trash compactor.

Spending a whole day in close proximity to James was exhausting, and inspiring, and terrifying. He was truly skilled at being a good-natured I'm-up-for-anything show host, and it took everything I had in me to keep up with him. He set a high bar, just like he had in college, and I was determined to leap right over it or die trying. Working on his level, making things look fun and interesting and also effortless—was completely exhausting.

But it was fun, too. More fun than I'd expected.

The rush of adrenaline that came from racing the clock to ice those silly cupcakes was no joke. Did I have an unfair advantage from helping Gwen do that before? Probably. Would I ever admit that to him? No way. I'd take my wins wherever I could get them.

The real treat was seeing Gwen shine. I'd never heard her talk so eloquently about what she wanted for the cafe before, and James was able to pull those thoughts out of her with just a few simple questions. It was important to him to keep the show unscripted, because he wanted it to be a realistic portrait of each person in their element. Aside from a dozen or so big-picture questions he and Tetia wrote down, the rest of the shooting day was completely organic. The interviewee could plan what they wanted James (and now me) to do in our time together, but the conversation went wherever it went based on those first few questions. James was really good at mining stories for those parts that would resonate with people, and today's shoot with Gwen had struck a chord with me, too.

It was scary, the way he could see right into the heart of things. It made me wonder what he saw when he looked at me.

Now, sinking into the hot bath, I tried to sort out this tangle of feelings that had been building up all week. Was I attracted to James? Yes. Should I be? No.

Well, maybe.

No, definitely not.

Would it be so bad if I was, though?

Yes. Terrible.

He was only here for a week, and then I'd never see him again. He should be off-limits. End of story.

My phone buzzed from its spot on the window sill, lighting up with a text message.

Hey, Ashley wrote. **We're going to grab tacos for dinner. Want to join?**

It was nearly seven and this was the first moment of quiet I'd had all day. I'd felt like a live wire since breakfast, and now my frayed nerves had finally started to relax.

I should finish up some work stuff here, I replied. **Thanks, though!**

We're going bowling after, she said. **You should come. We'll need a fourth because Tetia won't stay out late.**

How did extroverts never run out of energy?

Maybe, I wrote. **Text me when you're headed over? If I'm still awake, I'll meet you there.** It was sweet that she wanted to include me—they'd done nothing but make me feel like part of the crew—like I belonged. But part of me really wanted to slip into my pajamas and scour the park job postings before turning in early. There were still no new reservations for our empty room, but I did plan to drop off fresh towels for everyone while they were at dinner.

Will do, she wrote.

I leaned back in the hot water, trying to forget about the way James had looked at me earlier when I'd impulsively stuck my finger in the cake batter for a taste. He'd been dialing up the friendly, flirty part of him for the episode, for sure—that was no doubt part of the act. But the heated look he'd given me in that moment wasn't for the benefit of the show.

That smoldering look had been just for me.

And it had made my whole body tingle, right down to my toes.

I shook my head, refusing to think any more about what exactly that meant. Sinking down deeper into the water, I thought instead about Yellowstone, the Everglades, Devil's Tower—all those parks that needed seasonal rangers. This week with James would be a fun detour and a way to make a little extra money to tide me over. That's all it could be. What I needed to focus on was finding my next job. I couldn't stay here at the inn, and I certainly couldn't stay here in the carriage house. One of those park jobs was my best bet, and I needed to find one fast.

AN HOUR LATER, I was scrolling through the job postings while eating my second cow cupcake. (James had insisted on sharing, and I was not about to miss out on Gwen's award-winning treats.) Stress-eating was real for me, and since there were only two even vaguely appealing jobs listed that I was qualified for, I was using lemon cupcakes to manage the anxiety that came with that.

My phone buzzed with another text. When I picked it up, I saw that it was from James.

Get over here, Harper, he wrote. **I need your bowling skills.**

Is that an autocorrect error? I replied.

No. That is an SOS.

Aren't you sick of me yet? I was feeling bold. Probably just the sugar high.

Never, he replied.

That one word awakened the butterflies in my chest. They whipped up into a flurry.

We're at the Spare Time, he wrote. **I'm writing your name on the score card, so you have to come.**

I should stay home. Keep my distance from James and his fiery gazes. Avoid the temptation of this being anything more than working together. But *should* was starting to feel awfully dull.

It's '80s night. You'll love it.

I rolled my eyes. He'd never take no for an answer.

Ravi's already got me on video throwing the worst gutter ball ever. You're missing all the fun.

A pause, and then he wrote: **It's my job this week to help you have fun.**

I sighed. As much as I hated to admit it, today had been fun. But this was tempting fate. We were as different as two people could be, and now we were officially working together. Two good reasons to keep a safe distance.

I need my beauty sleep, I wrote lamely.

There was a pause, and I thought he'd finally given up.

Lies! First, you do not need beauty sleep. Second, I know you're scouring jobs and watching the Vampire Diaries. Get over here or I'll come kidnap you myself.

You wouldn't dare, I wrote. My eyes shifted to the TV screen, where the latest vampire drama was playing out.

I need a partner, Harper. Don't make me come over there and put you over my shoulder.

I'd like to see you try, I wrote, feeling a blush rising in my cheeks as I pictured being hoisted over his very broad shoulder with his very strong forearms. What on earth was wrong with me?

I'm getting my keys, he wrote. **Headed to my car. Last chance to surrender.**

I laughed. **Okay, fine,** I wrote. **You win.**

Atta girl, he wrote.

My butterflies were a hurricane.

At the Spare Time, I found James with Ravi and Ashley, finishing up a practice game. The Spare Time had once been our community center and only bowling alley. A few years ago, a young chef named Max had bought it and done a complete makeover, turning half the building into a farm-to-table restaurant. He'd kept the bowling alley in the back. Partly for nostalgia, he claimed. It gave the restaurant a hip vibe, and the locals loved it. We'd be shooting with Max on Friday and doing a cooking demo, but tonight we had the lanes to ourselves.

James, wearing a slim-cut black tee shirt and snug dark jeans, came right up to me and draped his arm around my shoulders. "Glad you could make it, partner."

"You really didn't leave me much choice." I tried to ignore

the warmth and weight of his arm, but I found myself leaning closer to him instead.

He smirked and said, "You made the right one."

Ashley grinned. Her hair was down tonight, the pink streaks peeking out from the blonde. "Glad you made it, Sadie. We like to blow off a little steam after long shooting days."

Ravi motioned toward the beer pitcher and when I nodded, he poured me one. "Also, we wanted to toast you on your new gig," he said, handing me the cup.

"To Harper," James said, and they all clinked their cups against mine.

"Thanks, guys," I said. "I was super nervous today. Couldn't have done it without all of your help."

"You did great," Ravi said. "We peeked at the footage earlier with Tetia."

Ashley nodded, her big eyes sparkling. "She's like, beside herself happy."

James arched a brow and gave me a self-satisfied smirk.

"Don't look at me like that," I said to him.

He shrugged. "Told you."

AFTER AN HOUR, Ravi and Ashley had pulled ahead by a few points and I had an embarrassing three gutter balls. When it was my turn again, James said, "Nice and easy. If it helps, just picture my face on the one in the middle."

When I picked up a spare, he grinned and said, "Works every time."

Ashley went next and rolled a ferocious strike.

"She does it, too," he whispered.

"Oh please," I said. "They all love you and you know it."

He gave me a tiny smile. "They're a good bunch. I got lucky."

"I'm glad you forced me out here tonight," I said, sipping my beer.

"Forced is a strong word."

"Coerced, then."

"Isn't this better than your vampire show?" he said.

"Depends on which episode."

His gaze dropped to my lips and Ashley yelled, "Come on killer, only two frames left."

James nodded her way and then stood. His movements were fluid, confident. And lord help me, my eyes were glued to his muscular frame as he squared his shoulders and hurled the ball toward the pins. The crash that followed left one pin standing. James gave me a sly wink as he retrieved the ball and took aim again. I tracked the line of his shoulders, down to his hips and then held my breath as the ball thudded on the lane and whizzed straight for that last pin.

The pin fell and he sat back down next to me. Ravi stood up, stretching and bouncing on his toes like a boxer.

"Nicely done," I said to James when he dropped down next to me.

He leaned back in his chair, draping his arm over the back of mine. He was close enough that I could feel the warmth radiating from his skin. "This feels nice," he said. "Being on the same team."

I sipped my beer, feeling heat rise in my cheeks. "Let's see if you still feel that way after my last frame."

He smiled, watching as Ravi lined up his next bowl. "Why'd it take us so long to get on the same team, Harper?"

"I thought you enjoyed trying to bury me. That was kind of your thing."

He raised a brow as if to argue.

I shrugged. "In college, you never let up. Your highest priorities seemed to be to outdo me and graduate, in that order."

"You were the only person in that program who challenged me. You had to have known that." He raked a hand through his hair. "Think what we could have done if we'd collaborated instead of competed."

"Careful, Fielding. That almost sounds like regret." I shifted in my chair, watching Ravi line up his shot and pretending James's confession didn't shake me to my core.

What else did he regret?

The lights shifted as the next song came on—a familiar bluesy song that took me a moment to place. And then it yanked me back to that night at the dorm party, the song that had played as James had pulled me against him, when we were trapped in the crowd and being caged in his arms felt inevitable. The night the walls came down.

His fingers tapped against his thigh and he turned to me, his gaze intense.

"This song," I said.

"I know," he replied, his voice an octave lower. I didn't need to ask him if he remembered that night, how it blared in the background when we'd stumbled into each other's arms. Something in his gaze told me that he did.

"Every time I hear it, I think of that party," he said. "And you."

The butterflies were back, stronger than ever. "What else do you remember about that night?"

He turned to me, his eyes drawing me closer. "Everything." His gaze dropped to my lips. "How could I forget?"

A crackle of electricity rippled along my skin. I hadn't forgotten anything, either. Not the way he'd teased a laugh out of me, not the way my heart had squeezed in my chest when his big hand had slipped around my waist. And certainly not the way he'd made me feel like we were the only two people in the world.

I hadn't known what to do then, and I didn't know what to do now, either. I couldn't tell what was real and what was imagined.

Ashley cheered as Ravi's second bowl brought in a spare, and my gaze snapped to Ravi, doing his celebratory dance. When I turned back to James, he was biting his lip.

"What do we get when we win?" I asked.

"They buy tomorrow's round."

"Huh. Is that all?"

"You were hoping for higher stakes?" He smirked.

"Aren't you?"

His grin turned wicked. "Fair enough. Name your terms."

"I get a strike, I get to ask you anything."

He looked amused. "And if you don't?"

"Whatever you want."

His brow lifted. "Now who's cocky?"

I shrugged. There was one question I was dying to ask him, but more than that, I was curious: with nothing off-limits, what would James ask of me?

"Deal," he said. "Let's see what you've got."

I plucked my ball from the rack and held it up to my chest. Focused on that front pin, I took three big steps and hurled the ball down the lane. It was my most steady shot yet, but after the clatter, there was still one pin standing.

Heat bloomed in my chest as I aimed for the last pin, just to finish the frame.

When I missed, Ravi said, "How about best of three?" We'd beat them by only six points.

"We do have to work tomorrow," Ashley said, reaching for

her jacket. "And they're closing in a few." She and Ravi grabbed our empty glasses and headed for the counter to return their shoes.

I walked back to my chair, where James now leaned against the low wall between the lanes. "Good game, partner," he said.

After swapping out our shoes at the counter, we headed out to the parking lot, where Ashley and Ravi were climbing into the van.

"So, what's the ask?" I said. Ever since missing out on the strike, I'd wondered what James would claim as his prize.

He shoved his hands into his pockets and said, "I'm curious about one thing. How did you feel when I showed up at the inn the other day?"

I blinked at him for a moment. "That's your big question?"

He nodded slowly, his eyes wide in the darkness.

I shrugged. "Surprised."

Annoyed by my one-word answer, he said, "Don't hedge like that. Tell me how you really felt, Harper."

I stared at him, feeling my heart twist in my chest. Telling the truth made me feel too vulnerable.

He took a step closer. "Tell me."

My heart hammered against my ribs, so loud that I was sure he could hear it. "Furious," I said. "Scared."

He arched a brow. "Why?"

"Because I thought you wanted to humiliate me. Make me feel like a failure." My chest tightened as the words came out, but his expression remained calm, like he was just asking about the weather tomorrow.

"Why would you think that?" he asked.

"Because you always made a sport out of trying to best me at everything, James. And now here you are, seeing me at my worst. I know it's not coincidence that you're here." The words came out harsher than I'd intended, and then they rushed out like a tidal wave. "Everything was always a competition between us, and you were everywhere I turned when we were in school, just waiting for the next chance to beat me at something. I could never relax. And then there was that crazy night at the party when we, you know," I blushed furiously, "and I thought maybe I'd been wrong about you after all. And I know I said some stupid things, but they were just stupid, you know? Words I said when I was freaked out! But then suddenly everything changed and then I hardly saw you at all, and when you did show up you gave me the cold shoulder. It was like you just flipped a switch, and it made me think I'd been kidding myself about any connection I thought we had that night."

James just looked at me, his expression calm, waiting for me to finish.

I sighed, feeling like a volcano had just erupted. "For a minute, I'd let myself think that maybe there was something between us—but then you froze me out, with no explanation, nothing! And it just proved I was right all along and I was just another challenge for you and your ego. I mean, why did you do that? Why did you just cut me out that way?"

I was a human firehose, but once all those feelings came up, there was no tamping them back down. Not anymore.

He stared at me for a long moment, that furrow back in his brow. "Because you broke my heart, Harper." His lip lifted in a sad smile, and he stepped past me toward the van. Over his shoulder, he said, "See you at breakfast," as if he hadn't just upended my whole world.

Chapter Thirteen

JAMES

THE AFTERNOON WAS NOT GOING WELL.

Sometimes, you just have an off day of shooting. Things don't go according to plan, and the actors make gaffes, or the weather sucks, or someone just can't get through their lines. It happens.

Usually though, it's not all those things at once.

Today, though, was maybe the worst day of shooting I'd ever experienced—and that included the day that we'd all gotten seasick on a shrimp boat as a tropical depression was slipping by and tossing us around like a toy in a bathtub.

It was my fault, of course. I'd dropped that bomb on Sadie last night, and today she was more flustered than ever. She could barely look me in the eye, and all of us were paying the price— including the Richardsons and their rare succulents.

Gus and Natalie Richardson had a flower shop that was like a tiny botanical wonderland—getting to it felt like walking though some kind of magical portal because from the outside, the building looked like any other quaint, small-town main-street shop. Its brick facade was painted white and a hand-painted sign over the door read simply *Natalie's*. They had a variety of flowers and houseplants, but their specialty was succulents—and they had them in every shape and color. The main window had a display of sun-loving plants that looked like they were living their best life.

Natalie and Gus seemed to be living their best life, too. That is, until we showed up this morning.

Natalie was short with soft, rounded features: dark brown eyes and blue-black hair cut into a sleek bob. She was somewhere in her early fifties, but looked ten years younger— especially when she smiled and her laugh lines showed. Gus, a few years older than her, was tall and lean with short-cropped gray hair and little round glasses that made him look more like a professor than a former advertising exec.

We'd started the interview inside the shop, where Sadie had promptly knocked over an enormous ceramic pot that hit the polished concrete floor and smashed into a million pieces. This terrified the shop cat, Josie, and sent her leaping across the counter and into the safety of a row of snake plants. But not before knocking over a few more potted violets and bud vases in her panic.

Sadie, white as a sheet, had apologized a hundred times and helped Gus sweep up the remainder of the ceramic pot.

The furrow in Tetia's brow deepened. Ashley's mouth formed a tiny O of surprise. Ravi stood back, clutching his camera like it was a baby.

I'd placed my hand on Sadie's shoulder and said, "Hey, it's okay," and she'd jumped like I'd touched her with a cattle brand.

No touching. Point taken.

Then Sadie had gotten all tongue-tied with her lines and limped through the first few interview questions in no less than fifteen takes. She looked like she was standing in front of a parole board instead of a couple of her friends, and every time I looked over at her to say something supportive, she quickly looked away, refusing to meet my eyes. When we all went outside to shoot a segment with Natalie showing off the nursery, the darkest cloud I'd ever seen passed overhead and Sadie and I were soaked to the skin before Tetia could yell, "Cut!"

After we'd all had a wardrobe change and everyone was reasonably camera-ready again, we moved back inside to try again with the rest of the questions as Gus and Natalie showed us how to prune succulents and use the cuttings to make an adorable arrangement. If we were lucky, we'd be able to just use the next portion and shoot a little more outside footage of the nursery later in the week.

Tetia called for a break and went to chat with the Richardsons while Ashley set up the demo table with all of the potting materials we'd need for our little succulent project.

"Hey, are you okay?" I asked Sadie.

She was paler than usual and her eyes were wide, and there were tiny beads of sweat right at her hairline. The last time I'd seen someone look that miserable was when Ravi was curled up on the deck of that shrimp boat off the coast of Charleston, mumbling about a kraken and his last will and testament.

"Super," she said, which was most definitely a lie.

"Maybe I can help," I said. Everyone got jitters in front of the camera. No one was immune. But this was almost certainly more about what I'd blurted out last night and less about stage fright. "Let's just pretend this is Day One. How can I make this better?"

"I'm fine, Fielding. Just drop it, okay?" Annoyed, she brushed past me and went over to help Ashley set up the two workstations for our potting demo. With her spine stiff and her jaw tense, she looked about as malleable as granite.

So, the storm cloud had moved inside.

Side by side, each station had an empty shallow bowl about a foot in diameter, a bag of potting soil, a small bag of tiny stones, and a row of small succulents. A pot full of overgrown plants sat between them, its inhabitants twisting and curling on top of each other. The plan was to have Gus and Natalie teach us how to trim overgrown succulents and tame them into a new arrangement while they told us how they came to land in Jasmine Falls.

The Richardsons had been a little stiff on camera at first, but Tetia had coached them and rehearsed the questions enough that they'd loosened up. Now they seemed right at home and completely focused. Sadie, on the other hand, looked like she was a million miles away, thinking about everything except shooting this segment. Something was bothering her, but she wouldn't say what. She kept tugging on the ends of her hair and chewing her lip, just like she had back in college, when she was irritated over a project. Ever since this morning, she'd been distant. When we'd taken a break for lunch, she'd barely spoken at all.

Now, with her arms crossed over her chest, she looked like she was physically trying to hold herself together while Natalie rattled off the names of plants that sounded like they'd been named by someone who was surely stoned: tiger tooth, blue elf, zebra wort.

Desperate to save us from a twelve-hour shoot, I asked Gus the easiest question of all: how he met Natalie.

"I'd been in advertising and was completely burned out," he said, trimming the dying leaves from an echeveria as big as my hand. "I had the world's best assistant, who kicked me out of the office and booked a vacation for me in the Texas hill country. Wine tastings, a day at the botanical gardens, a drive through the national forest, a tour of a cheese farm. She was determined to make sure I spent zero time inside an office—or any place with too many walls, for that matter—and set me up to spend more time in nature than I had in twenty years."

Natalie handed him a blue-tinted burro's tail and said, "Bless his heart, his feet hadn't touched dirt in about a hundred years."

"Accurate," he said. "I almost cancelled my day at the cheese farm, but I'm sure glad I didn't. While I was there, I met Natalie."

"Love at first sight?" I said.

"Not hardly." Natalie laughed, turning to Gus. "I actually didn't like him at first. I thought he was kind of stuffy and aloof, but it turns out he'd just forgotten how to relax and talk to people outside of a pitch meeting."

Gus nodded. "Fair."

Natalie grinned. "But he remembered soon enough."

"Turns out the farm had a little vineyard, too." Gus said. "And a cabernet that seemed to work a miracle on a poor schmuck like myself."

"It did allow you to talk like a human," she said.

He smiled, wrapping his arm around her waist. "After the tour, we ended up staying for a tasting, and then we had dinner, and then we had plans the next day. Next thing you know, I'm extending my vacation and giving two weeks' notice."

"It took us a while," Natalie said, "but we found out we had more in common than we first thought. But we were opposites in the best ways."

Next to me, Sadie tensed. Her brows pinched together, and something about that tiny movement made my heart squeeze like a fist.

"I thought he'd never leave Texas," Natalie said. "But I guess falling in love does strange things to a man."

"I know when to follow a good thing," Gus said with a warm

smile. "Plus, it was to be closer to Natalie's mom as she started to need more help. Moving for family is a no-brainer."

Sadie grumbled as she tried to work a leggy plant into our pot and then swore when she snapped it in half. Clearly she'd rather murder plants than think about instalove. Resting her hands on the side of the pot, she looked like a surgeon who'd just called time of death. Bits of potting soil clung to her short nails, and she had a little smudge of it on her cheek that I desperately wanted to brush away with my thumb.

She was so beautiful it hurt.

"I think I'm failing at this," Sadie said, trying to make her voice sound light. "Y'all make it look too easy." We'd been trying to follow along with the Richardsons as they pruned and shaped little rosettes into a masterpiece that made ours look like it had been dropped from the rooftop. I kept knocking all the delicate leaves off, and every plant that Sadie put into place promptly fell over.

And then there was the moment when I'd stabbed myself with a cactus and said one of the seven words you're not allowed to say on the air.

Sadie huffed and said, "Sorry," to Ravi as he motioned for her to keep going.

"We'll handle it in editing," Tetia said. "Just keep rolling."

Whatever was happening with Sadie, though, was not about fumbling through lines and maiming succulents. It had everything to do with me, and the only question was how I might fix it.

"They just need a better foothold," Natalie said. She plucked one of the succulents from our pot, trimmed a few leaves low on the stem, and then used a chopstick to move just enough potting soil to put it firmly in place so it stood up straight. She handed me the chopstick and I made a little space in the soil as Sadie trimmed a few fat leaves from a little pink-tinted plant, following Natalie's instructions.

When Sadie stuck the plant into the space I'd carved out, her hand brushed over mine and the warmth rippled along my arm and straight down my body to my toes. She glanced at me and quickly moved her hand, and I wondered if she'd felt the same.

The way her cheeks turned pink, I was guessing she had.

"That's it," Natalie said. "You just have to prop them up a little."

Ashley held up a cue card for Sadie, prompting her next question.

"Do you ever miss the advertising world?" Sadie asked Gus. "Jasmine Falls must have been a big change for you."

He smiled, turning toward Natalie. "Not for a minute," he said. "We've been here ten years now, and I wouldn't trade a single day."

"Well," Natalie said. "Except for maybe that one day when the sewage pipe burst."

Gus grinned. "Nah. Not even that one. I wouldn't trade a single day I spent with the love of my life."

Natalie smiled and Ashley made a little "Aww," sound from behind Ravi. Tetia gave us a thumbs up and Sadie looked like she wanted the floor to open up and swallow her. When I smiled at her, her eyebrows pinched together again in that way that I now recognized as extreme discomfort. I wanted to tell her she was doing fine, just relax—even if it was only half true. But today everything I said seemed to only make her more rattled.

I really wanted to know how to fix that.

"Well, thanks for teaching us a new skill, guys," I said. "What are the chances someone will buy this arrangement out of pity?"

Natalie looked from Sadie to me and said, "Take it home with you. Practice makes perfect."

"I think I'm a bad plant parent," I said. "Can't keep anything alive."

"Echeveria can live through anything," Gus said. "I like their quiet resilience."

When we wrapped for the day, Sadie bolted out the front door in a blur, leaving me to take our newly potted succulents back to the inn.

It was just after seven when I knocked on the door to the carriage house. There was no answer, but I could see a light on inside.

I pulled out my phone and sent Sadie a text: **I brought you a surprise.**

Three dots appeared, blinked for what felt like an eternity, and then vanished.

I think you'll want it, I wrote.

No thank you, she wrote back.

Would you open the door, please? I feel like a doofus. And a target for angsty raccoons.

That's because you are one, she wrote.

A doofus or a target? I wrote.

Yes.

Your snark won't work on me, Harper. I brought takeout that you'd be crazy to refuse.

Not hungry, she wrote.

Open this door or I'll be forced to write a horrendous Yelp review.

Three dots. Then nothing.

I'm so bored, I'll have all night to craft it, I typed. **Once I**

recover from my battle royale with the raccoons and gorge myself on this amazing takeout.

The door opened and Sadie Harper stood nearly nose-to-nose with me, her big gray-blue eyes looking as stormy as ever. She was wearing an old Rolling Stones tee shirt and plaid pajama pants and had her hair pulled back into a ponytail that I desperately wanted to give a little tug.

"I didn't know you liked the Stones," I said. Immediately, I wanted to know if she preferred mainstream rock n' roll Stones or the far superior dirty bluesy Stones. I had my suspicions, and they were a delight to imagine.

She blinked at me, then looked down at the paper bag I had in my hand. "Is that from Marco's?"

"It is." Tetia and Ravi had insisted on trying Marco's Diner tonight, because they'd heard about the famous burgers. Sadie had skipped, but we'd gone over everyone's notes for today anyway, because we just couldn't help ourselves and really, what else were we going to talk about? When the three of them had left to find a good craft beer, I'd headed back here with a peace offering.

Sadie arched a brow. "It smells like an inferno burger."

"He told me it's your favorite."

She pulled the door open—an invitation—and walked back into the kitchen.

I followed her and set the takeout bag on the kitchen counter. While she took a plate from the cabinet, I sat down on a stool at the bar and stole a glance at her open laptop. It was open to a site for job listings in the park service—Montana, Alaska, North Dakota. Even though we'd only had a few days here together, my heart sank at the idea of her being thousands of miles from here.

Thousands of miles from me.

When she turned, I quickly shifted and trained my eyes on her instead. I wanted to ask her about last night, but the look on her face told me that was a very bad idea. As badly as I wanted to apologize, I knew it would only make things worse.

The less said about all those old feelings, the better.

So I deflected, and turned her attention to work. "Don't worry about today," I said. "We all have off days. It's no big deal."

She plopped the burger on the plate and added a handful of fries. "Don't lie to me, Fielding. I'm a big girl. Today was a train wreck."

I rested my elbow on the counter and she sat on the stool next to me, taking a big bite out of the burger. Sadie Harper had never been a dainty girl—she did everything with gusto, whether it was defending her senior thesis project, dancing at a birthday party, or savoring the first bite of a delicious burger. It was one of the many things about her that made it impossible not to watch her.

She built up big strong walls around herself, but she had her weak spots, just like all the rest of us. "I'm just saying, cut yourself some slack," I said, thinking she needed to hear these words, though she'd never admit it. "This is day two on the job for you. No one expects you to be perfect."

She rolled her eyes. "It's not rocket science."

I smiled, holding my arms out to my sides. "It's not exactly easy, either. I know I make it look like a piece of cake, but looks can be deceiving." I was trying to get a smile out of her, but the truth was, it was a hard job—harder than most people thought it was. And glamorous? Not so much. Most people thought being a host of something was easy—just show up and smile and act friendly and curious. But putting myself out there for the world to see was one of the hardest things I'd ever done. Some people created a persona for TV, but not me. The person on camera was the real James Fielding, and when he bombed with audiences, it was pretty hard to not take it personally. I'd had years to do all this, but Sadie had jumped right into the deep end.

Sadie snorted, taking another huge bite. "I think this was a bad idea. I'll talk to Tetia tomorrow and tell her I'm out."

I felt like she'd just throat-punched me. But judging by the look on her face and the way she tore into that burger, she was dead serious.

"Don't do that," I said. "Give yourself a break."

She shook her head. "This is your thing, Fielding. Not mine. I know when I'm out of my league."

I hated the thought of her giving up so easily—especially because I'd knocked her off her game with that remark that I should have kept to myself. I knew what it felt like to screw up in front of everyone, to feel like a failed experiment. But I also knew how it felt to come out the other side and realize you could surprise yourself.

"Give it one more day," I said.

"Why, so I can embarrass myself even more? No, thank you."

"The Harper I know wouldn't give up so easily."

She gave me a hard sideways look. "Maybe I'm not that person anymore. I know when to cut my losses."

"Technically, you signed a contract to finish the episode," I said. I didn't want to play the legal card, but I knew Sadie had an unshakable work ethic. "If you back out now, they have to restructure the episode. It'll look weird to have you in part of it, but not all."

She narrowed her eyes at me. I'd hit the right nerve. "Tetia probably wants to fire me anyway," she said. "I'd be doing everyone a favor."

"Martyrdom doesn't suit you," I said, stealing a fry.

"Why do you even care, Fielding?"

Because I want to spend every minute here with you. Because the last twenty-four hours have been better than the last five years. "Because I want to see you play with fire tomorrow."

She snorted. "You're such a dork."

Tomorrow we were scheduled to do a demo and interview with Eli Bell and Alex Fox, two metalsmiths who had the whole Lowcountry all aflutter with their sculpture and their mentoring.

I sighed, knowing if I pushed harder, she'd just dig her heels in deeper. "Let me take you on a field trip tonight, and get away from all this for a minute. And tomorrow, if you still feel the same way, I won't say another word."

"You can't charm me into changing my mind," she said. "Those moony eyes and movie star smile aren't going to change how I feel about all of this."

This was a woman I desperately wanted to spend more time with. I hated the thought of leaving in a few days and never seeing her again, but the idea that all of this could be over tonight was killing me. Even worse, I hated the idea of her giving up something she could be really good at—just because of one lousy day.

It seemed unlike her to do that. The old Sadie would have fought tooth and nail to prove she could do this job better than I could. So why was she so quick to give up now?

"Noted," I said, stealing another of her fries. "How about if I frown at you the entire time?" I narrowed my eyes, giving her my best broody look.

She stabbed another fry into her ketchup. "I get that all of this comes easy to you, Fielding. But how about you don't keep rubbing that in my face? Just let me mope around in my pajamas."

"How about we settle for not spiraling down into catastrophic thinking? Let's go do something fun instead."

"And where would this fun happen? This town rolls up by eight o'clock, if you haven't noticed."

"It's a surprise."

"You know I hate surprises."

"This one seems to have been a hit," I said, motioning toward the crumbs that were left of her burger.

"That was a known quantity," she said. "But I do appreciate the thought. The last thing I ate today was half a taco at lunch, and I was feeling somewhat murderous."

"So you're saying I *can* be useful sometimes," I teased.

Her brow lifted. "You're pretty good at delivering takeout."

"Change your clothes," I said, giving her arm a nudge. "But don't worry, casual is just fine."

"What, your big night doesn't involve evening wear?" Her tone softened and she almost smiled.

"I took a chance that you'd prefer something more laid back this time."

"How about I throw a jacket on over my jammies, then?"

"You might want to at least put on real pants."

She snorted. "If I agree to this…outing…then you agree to let me strike 'co-host' from my resume and stop giving me grief about it." She didn't phrase it like a question.

The decision was hers, of course, and I wasn't going to twist her arm. But I recognized the fear that was just beneath the surface of her words—I'd been there, too. Sometimes it helped me to stand back for a minute, to get out of the pressurized environment. I thought we might be similar in that way. "If that's what you want," I said. "But humor me and see how the night goes."

She stared at me for a long moment, her eyes narrowed.

"Fine. You've got yourself a deal, Fielding. But if your plan is to hold me hostage in some kind of Hallmark-movie moment, I'll drag you out into the swamp and leave you there."

I smiled as she marched into the bedroom and shut the door behind her. She could take that storm cloud from over her head and wear it like a protective cape, but there was one thing about Sadie Harper that hadn't changed: she never did anything she didn't want to.

I'd take this as a win.

Chapter Fourteen

SADIE

JAMES'S CAR WAS IMMACULATE. It wasn't anything fancy—it was the sort of small SUV that I'd like to upgrade to someday—but it was spotless. Unlike mine, there were no granola bar wrappers stuffed into the cupholders, empty travel mugs rolling around in the foot, or half-filled water bottles stashed in the back seat. There was no fine layer of dust on the dashboard, and no loose change or pens in the console.

It shouldn't have surprised me. James had neatly pressed shirts, perfectly styled hair, and the precise amount of beard stubble that accentuated the angle of his jaw without looking disheveled. Of course his car would be in pristine condition.

"Do I get a hint about this outing?" I said.

He smirked as he drove us to the edge of town and then turned onto one of the two-lane highways that would cut through pastureland and forest for about a hundred miles before eventually ending at the coast. There was nothing out this way, except for the occasional turkey farm and horse pasture. And the state park. The next town over was fifteen miles away, and there wasn't much to do there this time of night, either.

"Are you even using the GPS?" I said. "Do you have any idea where we're headed?"

"Relax," he said, his tone light. "We're almost there."

When he turned off the highway and into the state park, I said, "James, there's nothing to do here at night. What are you doing?"

This small state park, unlike Congaree, was generally closed at sundown. With no camping facilities open, it didn't have a reason to be open at night. It had hiking trails and picnic areas that were day-use only—but when we pulled onto the narrow road to the visitor center, I saw that the gate was open and there were a dozen or more cars in the parking lot.

"It's a stargazing event," he said, turning off the engine. "Or more precisely, comet-gazing tonight. I thought some fresh air would do us good." He gave me a tiny smile. "We've kind of been blowing it in confined spaces, lately."

I couldn't argue with that. Last night had nearly done me in.

Because you broke my heart, Harper.

I'd never considered that he might have had real feelings for me back then. All of his teasing and goading had seemed like a strategy to get under my skin and psych me out. I'd thought it was all a game to him—nothing genuine—and so I'd tamped down all the attraction I felt toward him. And then that night at the party, I'd felt something that was confusing and strange to me, and when Kara called me out on it, I'd responded with a knee-jerk reaction.

But his feelings had been real—if they hadn't, my silly denial to Kara wouldn't have hurt him so.

And now, it felt like the same thing was happening again. Being around him lit me up, but I still couldn't shake the little voice that had been in my head the whole time we'd been at Cambrick: that annoying voice that said no matter how hard I worked, I'd never be quite good enough. And his barbs had made me feel like he believed that, too.

Today's disastrous shoot had made me feel the same way. No matter how much effort I put into it, I wasn't as good as he was. I knew it, and he knew it. Even if he was now too considerate to say that to me, being around him still awoke that voice deep inside my brain. The voice that told me no matter how far I'd come since Cambrick, I still wasn't as good as I should be—at my job, at relationships, at everything.

We climbed out of the car and headed toward the visitor center. This area was densely wooded—not ideal for stargazing, but it was far enough from town that there was little light pollution. Congaree did the occasional night hike, but fortunately James hadn't taken me back into the park that had so callously cut me loose. No, he'd brought me somewhere different, a park I actually hadn't seen in ages.

It felt like a fresh start. A new way to see what had been around me for so long. Ironic, I know, since it was so dark out here I could barely see where I was stepping. Really, though, I liked being in the darkness. It meant that I could relax my eyes and pay more attention to other details, like the calls from whippoorwills in the shrubs, or the scent of fir on the breeze. Every sensation felt heightened in the darkness—including the tingle that spread over my skin when James's arm brushed against mine.

"They meet down by the lake," James said. We followed a lit gravel pathway past the visitor center and into the woods. After thirty yards or so, we came to clearing by a small lake where the sky opened up. Above us was a blanket of stars.

"I forgot how peaceful it is out here," I said. "I think the last time I came to this park, I was in high school."

"Come on," he said, touching my arm. "They've already started."

James led me toward a small grassy area where a dozen or so people had set up telescopes. I could see the blinking of tiny headlamps with red bulbs and hear the chatter of friendly voices, like a bunch of old friends getting together.

"How'd you find out about this?" I said.

"Yoo-hoo!" Someone shouted from the clearing and I turned toward the sound. Paula Sue was headed toward us, carrying a small red-bulbed flashlight. "James," she said. "I'm so glad you made it." She gave me a big smile and said, "Sadie, so good to see you here, too."

"Hi, Paula Sue," James said. "Thanks for the invite."

"Well, of course!" she gushed. "I know there's not a lot to do around here at night, and we wouldn't want you to be bored." She was wearing a gray cardigan and dark jeans with red sneakers—more casual and less sparkly than her usual attire. "Tonight's special because there's a comet passing by. Apparently it's green—have you ever heard of such a thing?"

"No, I haven't," James said. "How interesting."

"Professor Harding is here from the College of Charleston," she said. "She's going to tell us all about it if you'd like to join us." She leaned closer to me and patted my shoulder as she stage-whispered, "I'm so glad you came."

Paula Sue strode back over to the cluster of stargazers and I turned back to James. "So you're into stars, huh?" I asked him.

He shrugged. "Who isn't?"

I motioned toward the group. "Well, since those folks represent approximately point-five percent of the population of Jasmine Falls, I'd say the answer is lots of people."

He smiled that rakish smile again, and I felt warm and fuzzy all over. "There's a difference between being vaguely aware of astronomical phenomena, and being interested enough to find a good location on a clear night," he said. "Some people will see this on the morning news tomorrow, and some people might catch a fuzzy photo in their social media feed. I wanted to see it for myself."

"So you're saying you geek out over stars," I said.

"You say that like it's a bad thing," he said, teasing.

"Not at all, Fielding. It's kind of endearing." If I was totally honest, it was a lot endearing. Like undeniably hot. A guy who liked anything found in nature—and sought it out on a weeknight—ranked pretty high in my book.

"I think you might be a little bit of a space geek, too," he said. His eyes locked on mine, so wide in the darkness, and it was like we were yanked back through time, back to that night on the lawn outside my college dorm. Back to that night of the rowdy party and the birthday celebration I'd later regret. But in that moment at the party, I'd been so content out there in the darkness. The big open sky above us was full of twinkling stars and endless possibilities of how my life might unfold. James had been there next to me, holding out a piece of chocolate cake like it was an offering, a sweet, decadent promise of what might lie undiscovered between us. We had our secret spot there on the lawn, and it was like the whole rest of the world fell away— somewhere far in the distance I heard the thumping of the music and the shouts from our friends, but this place in the dark was just for him and for me.

He'd been different in that space—not my rival, but a challenge just the same. I'd wanted to freeze time and stay in that moment as long as we could, and that was both exhilarating and terrifying. Exhilarating because I couldn't deny there was some kind of spark between us. Terrifying because he was the last person I should have sparks with—I'd never felt so drawn to anyone before, but all my data suggested he was just bored and looking for another challenge. And how better to humiliate me that make me fall for him and give him the chance to reject me in front of everyone? He could have had anyone he wanted back then, and seemed to have an endless parade of girlfriends—so why choose me? It had all been too much, and even though I felt a little electric current zip along my skin as he licked that frosting from my finger, I knew it was a mistake to let him get so close.

So I'd said the dumb thing, and pushed him away. And then he'd gone right back to being flirty with every girl in his orbit except me, and I'd taken that as proof that he didn't have actual feelings for me.

You broke my heart, Harper.

But the truth was that he'd broken mine, too.

Now here he was again, holding my hand under a big glittery sky, pointing at a little green fuzzy dot that might only be visible on this one night in our lifetime. It felt like a different kind of offering, but one that was just as curious and enticing. Before I could say anything else, he gently took my arm and led me across the uneven ground toward the group that had gathered in the clearing. In that moment, I'd have let him lead me anywhere.

Professor Janet Harding was a short, stout lady who looked to be in her sixties. Even in this light, I could tell that her silvery hair had locks that were dyed purple. She had bright pink glasses and wore a NASA sweatshirt and jeans with motorcycle boots. I loved her instantly.

"This woman is my hero," I whispered to James.

"Mine, too," he whispered back.

While the professor told us all about the comet—green because of its special space dust, twenty-seven million miles away—I stared up into the stars and tried not to think about how warm James's hand had felt on my elbow and how he smelled faintly of cloves and spruce. And how his eyes seemed to find mine so easily, even in the darkness.

"Hey, do you want to take a peek?" Professor Harding asked us. Everyone else had brought their own telescope or binoculars, and suddenly I felt like that person who'd come to the potluck without a covered dish.

"Sure," I said. I stepped over to where her telescope was set up and peered into the viewfinder. There, in the center, was a bright green oblong shape. When I finally stepped away to give James a turn, Professor Harding said, "There she is. Last time Earth saw her was in the Stone Age."

"Godspeed, little dot," James said.

Paula Sue came back with a few of her friends, introducing them all to James and telling them as much as she could about shooting this week. While they all cooed over him and asked him a million questions, I slipped away and sat down on a log by the trail, taking a moment to relish the quiet. Somehow, he'd known exactly what I needed tonight.

After a while, James sauntered up to the log and sat next to me. "Hi," he said, his knee brushing mine.

"You might have an official fan club here in Jasmine Falls. Who knew you were such a hit with the septuagenarians?"

"They're my best demographic," he said, teasing.

After a moment, I said, "Why'd you bring me out here, Fielding?"

"Did you not hear?" he said. "There's a once-in-a-lifetime comet passing by."

I swatted his arm playfully and tried to ignore how very solid and well-muscled that arm was.

"I thought you might like to get out of your head for a little while," he said, leaning closer. "How'd I do?"

"Not bad. Bonus points for the comet."

There was a hint of a smile. "Perfectionism is exhausting. It's easy to get pulled into this spiral of picking your actions apart, beating yourself up, wishing you could undo things and do them again, but better. It's always worse when I'm alone. I thought you might feel that way sometimes, too."

He looked at me then, and I knew he wasn't just talking about himself. We were opposites in so many ways, but not this one. The James I'd known had held himself to an impossible standard. Always.

"You didn't want me to be alone tonight," I said.

He shrugged. "I thought a comet would be more fun. Also, I thought of ice cream afterward. Think that gas station on Main Street has any?"

"Thank you. This might be the nicest thing anyone ever did for me."

He shifted on the log and his thigh pressed against mine. Neither of us pulled away.

"You know," he said, his voice gravelly, "I thought you hated me in school."

"Hated? No. I found you annoying. Cocky. Infuriating. But I didn't hate you."

His lip lifted in a hint of a smile. "You drove me absolutely crazy. And you tried so hard to avoid me—that is, when you weren't trying to eviscerate me. Academically speaking, of course."

"You're the one that made everything a competition," I said.

"It was the only way to be around you," he said. "Plus, no one else was as interesting as you. You made me think bigger, work harder. I loved it." He smiled. "But every time I tried to hang out with you and your friends, you high-tailed it away from me as fast as you could. I even tried to time my walk to class just right so I might meet you on the way and we could walk together." He shook his head. "Ridiculous, I know."

I thought back to how James had appeared at the cafe, at the bars my friends went to, how it felt like he'd pop up everywhere I went. He was right—I'd tried my best to ignore him, but he was everywhere.

"I just hoped if we hung out like normal people, outside of class, you might like me," he said. "I mean, I took ballroom classes, for Pete's sake. I almost broke my foot learning to Samba for you." He gave me a sheepish look that almost unraveled me. "But everything I did to get close to you seemed to backfire. Especially at your party."

That stupid party. Where I'd been so afraid of what I was feeling for him, so confused by what it all meant about me.

"I didn't hate you, Fielding. I hated the way you made me feel."

He turned to face me then, his brows knit together in confusion. "What do you mean?"

I sighed, glad that he couldn't see the tears stinging the corners of my eyes. All these years later, it still hurt. "You made me feel small. Like I wasn't as smart or charming or creative as you. Like I just wasn't good enough. And the worst part was that most of the time, it was true."

"Sadie," he said.

"Cute. Twee. Not too serious." He'd said that about my very first presentation, like he'd summed me up in ten seconds. Seven syllables. "Like I was some flaky small-town girl who couldn't measure up to you. So obviously, I had to prove you wrong every chance I got."

He turned to me and took my hand in his. "That's not at all

what I meant. What I was trying, and failing, to say, was that you were fun and unpretentious. I thought you were brilliant, Sadie. And I still do. You were so intimidating back then, it just turned me into a lunkhead whenever I was around you."

I bit back a laugh. "Me? Intimidating?"

"You still are," he said. "You have no idea how amazing you are, do you? It still turns me into a babbling wreck."

There was the crunch of footsteps on gravel behind us, and I instinctively pulled my hand from his, as if we were doing something scandalous there on the log. Then there was a loud thump and shriek that got us both to our feet. In the dim light, I could see a dark shape lying across the gravel path just a few yards away from us.

I scrambled toward the shape, James right on my heels. The person sat up, groaning.

"Paula Sue!" I said, kneeling next to her on the path. "Are you all right?"

James put his hand on her back to help her sit up straighter.

"I tripped," she said. "I think I'm fine except for my arm."

It was hard to see much with the tiny lights along the edges of the path, but I could see small cuts and scrapes on the one palm she held out to me. She gasped when I touched her other arm, so I quickly let it go. "Does anything else hurt?" I said.

"My knee," she said, "But not too bad." She moved to stand and James and I quickly got on either side of her to help her up.

Professor Harding rushed over with her red flashlight, two other women right behind her that I recognized as Ginny and Evelyn, friends of Paula Sue's. "Oh my goodness," Ginny said. "Are you hurt?"

"Her wrist may be sprained or broken," I said, keeping my hand at her back.

"Should we call an ambulance?" Evelyn said, pulling her cell phone from her pocket.

"Heavens, no," Paula Sue said. "That'll cost a fortune. I just need to get home." She took a step toward the parking lot and James slipped his hand under her good shoulder, supporting her as she walked stiffly toward the parking lot.

"Let's at least get you cleaned up," James said. "I've got a first aid kit in my car."

"You do?" I said.

"Of course," he said. That was James, though, prepared for anything. I made a mental note to clean the empty bottles and granola bar wrappers out of mine and make room for a kit, like an adult.

When we got to the parking lot, James and I helped Paula Sue toward the visitor center, where there were two benches out front by the door. The security lights cast us all in a greenish glow. When she sat, James said, "I'll be right back."

"Paula Sue," Ginny said, "We should take you to the hospital and get this checked out."

"I don't think it's that bad," Paula Sue said, wincing.

"We insist," Evelyn said. "You certainly can't drive yourself home."

Paula Sue opened her mouth to argue and Ginny cut her off. "Don't be stubborn, now. We're taking you, and that's that. We'll come back for your car tomorrow."

James reappeared with a small first-aid bag and sat on the bench next to Paula Sue. He handed me some gauze and cotton swabs and then opened a bottle of water he'd brought. Now, in the light, I could see small scrapes on Paula Sue's hands, where the gravel had bitten into the skin. I pulled a leaf from her hair and she winced as James poured the water over her hands and dabbed them dry with cotton balls. Then he pulled an antiseptic spray from the bag and said, "That was some comet, huh?"

"I didn't expect to have a celebrity patch me up tonight," Paula Sue said. "I'm both honored and mortified."

James gave her a warm smile and wrapped some cotton pads and gauze around her hands. "This will do until you get home," he said. "I don't want to do anything with your wrist, but you should probably get it looked at. It's swelling."

"See there," Ginny said. "Do what Dr. Dreamy says."

James arched a brow, the tips of his ears turning pink. It was just about the most adorable thing I'd ever seen. James Fielding, brought to blushing by three little flirty white-haired ladies.

"You feeling okay?" James asked her. "Dizzy at all?"

"Just dizzy from her little meet-cute," Evelyn said, grinning.

"Aren't we all," Ginny muttered.

"I'm fine," Paula Sue said to James. "Thank you, sweetheart." A light rain began to fall, one of those sudden showers that can come up out of nowhere in September.

"Come on," Ginny said. "We'll take my car." She and Evelyn got on either side of Paula Sue as she stood, and the three of them walked the few yards over to Ginny's car and climbed inside. As the taillights disappeared down the road, the rain began falling harder. It was only when they were gone that I noticed the pink purse lying under the bench at James's feet.

"Shoot," I said, picking it up. "Must be Paula Sue's." I peeked inside and found a wallet with her license, car keys, and cell phone. "I'll take it to her in the morning."

"You okay?" he said.

I sat down on the bench next to James. My whole body still vibrated with the rush of adrenaline, but the mist from the rain was soothing. "That was incredibly kind of you," I said. "Also, she'll be telling everyone about how the hot, famous TV star patched her up for the rest of her life."

He turned and arched a brow. "You think I'm hot?"

"Her words," I said. My heart banged against my ribs so loudly I was sure he could hear it.

He smiled his rakish smile and his gaze dropped to my lips. "Liar."

The rain fell heavier, thunder rumbling in the distance.

"Come on," he said, glancing up at the sky. "The bottom's about to fall out."

Before I could respond, there was another clap of thunder and a flicker of lightning just over the tree line. He grabbed his first aid kit and I took the pink purse and we hurried across the lot toward James's car. The rain pelted us in big fat drops, cool against my face and hands, soaking through my jacket in no time.

Once inside the car, I raked my hands through my damp hair. I felt like I was in one of those glittery snow globes that had been shaken up. Everything I thought I'd known was upside down, and a million thoughts were whirling around me, only the tiniest bits coming into focus. It had felt that way in college, too, but I'd been too afraid to let the dust settle and wait to see the whole picture. I didn't want to make that mistake again.

"I'm sorry," I said finally.

James turned to me, puzzled.

"For that night at the party," I said. My heart was pounding now, louder than the thunder, but I couldn't hold the words inside anymore. "I know you heard that stupid thing I said to Kara about never liking you, and I've always regretted it. I was just so scared of being hurt, and I freaked out when she made it seem like it was so obvious. I panicked, and I thought the only thing I could do to protect myself was to hurt you before you had the chance to hurt me first."

"I think your exact words were *never in a million years.*" He stared at me, his eyes wide in the dim light. They were so warm, pulling me closer, and I was tired of trying to keep him at arm's length. I was tired of building a wall around myself, trying to shore it up when little bits crumbled away. I'd always needed that wall around me, but now it just felt like something else that should be dismantled. Sometimes, that wall felt so tall and so sturdy—I'd done a great job building, thank you very much—that even I didn't know how to take it down.

But now I did.

"I thought you were just pretending to like me," I told him. "I thought I was just a box you were trying to tick off, another game you wanted to win." As awful as it sounded now, that's how I'd felt back then. James Fielding had dated dozens of girls, never for very long, and when he appeared to take an interest in me, I'd thought it was just so he could reject me and humiliate me—just another way that he could topple me and make me feel gullible and small.

He shook his head. "Harper, you've got it all wrong. Like one hundred percent backwards." His lip curved in a sheepish smile.

"I was over the moon for you. You were—are—brilliant and amazing and the most astonishing person I've ever met." He sighed. "Not to mention so gorgeous you take my breath away."

I stared at him, trying to square all those thoughts with what I believed to be true about James Fielding.

"But I was afraid you'd see right through me and squash me like a bug," he said. "Because even back then, you had zero time for nonsense, and I was at least forty-five percent nonsense, fumbling along and trying to fit into a place where I felt entirely out of my element. And you were so far out of my league."

"But you dated all those other girls," I said.

"I kept hoping it might take my mind off the one girl I couldn't have." He brushed a lock of hair from my cheek and his fingers left trails of fire. "You."

My breath caught in my throat. How had he never told me this?

"I figured if competing with you was the only way to be around you, then I'd take it." He smiled. "It was completely exhausting, though. You're a force of nature, Harper. So hard to keep up with."

Before he could say anything else, I climbed over the center console and into his lap. His eyes widened as I planted my hands on his shoulders and leaned closer, my knees on either side of his thighs, our lips just inches apart.

"It just killed me that the only thing I could never win was you," he whispered, his hands resting on my hips.

I leaned down and kissed him, but had no time for gentleness. I was furious that he'd kept that from me, angry at myself for seeing only the worst in him, and thrilled that I'd been so very wrong.

His hands snaked around my waist and I kissed him harder, catching his lip in my teeth and feeling my heart pound in my ears when he did the same. His hand slid under my shirt and my skin was on fire, everywhere, and in the next thirty seconds I'd surely set this car ablaze.

When I pulled back to take a breath, he slid his hand along my arm and said, "Force of nature."

"I ran out of words."

His chest rumbled with a devilish laugh and I raked my hands through his hair—something I'd been dying to do since he first walked through the door of the inn.

"It's possible I had some feelings for you, too, way down deep," I said.

He smirked and slid his hand over my chest, just above my pounding heart. "What else you got stowed away in there, Harper?" he whispered, pulling me close as he kissed me again, his teeth pinching my lip. James Fielding wasn't a fan of being gentle, either.

Thank heaven for that.

It was a risk getting this close to him. But everything about this moment felt so right: the way his hands warmed my skin, the way he laid himself bare, the way he coaxed the same vulnerability out of me. I'd never been so close to anyone because this kind of openness always led to hurt. I wanted more of this, more of him—but I was terrified because I didn't know how to do this, to let someone in and show them all the parts of me that I kept hidden.

Part of me was still afraid that if I let him get too close, he'd hurt me in the end. But the part of me that loved feeling his hands and his lips thought it was worth it to let him make me feel good, if only for a little while.

Stop overthinking, I told myself. *You're ruining a perfectly good kiss.*

He slid his hands under my shirt, along my lower back and then his lips were on my neck, his beard stubble scratching my skin in a delightful way that made me immediately imagine how it would feel everywhere else on my body—and why on earth had I worn all these layers of clothes? I didn't know precisely what I wanted in the big picture here—I didn't do flings and this couldn't be anything but that, right?—but pulling myself away from him again wasn't an option. I just wanted to feel more of this, more of him. For as long as I could.

But then he stopped and pulled back, his brows knit together, and said the one word I did not want to hear. "Wait."

I put a finger to his lips and said, "We've waited long enough, don't you think?"

His eyes widened and his hands tightened on my hips. I leaned back down, refusing to be derailed.

"The show," he mumbled, and I pulled my lips from his neck, which smelled like an enchanting blend of cloves and woodlands that for some reason made me want to tear his shirt to ribbons and climb him like a tree.

"What about it?" I said.

He raised a brow. "Will it be weird for you, working together after this?"

With a snort, I said, "It's not like you're my boss, Fielding." As soon as I said the words, something sparked in his eyes that said he most definitely wanted to revisit that thought in a non-work setting. *Bring it*, I thought. *For the love of heaven and earth.* My whole body tingled at the thought of all the ways James Fielding might boss me around—a little zip of electric current went all the way down to my toes.

"Besides, it's just a couple of days," I said, unbuttoning his shirt. "And Tetia did say she liked our chemistry." I slid my hands along his chest and didn't care that there were still two other cars in this parking lot. I didn't even care that one little fling with James Fielding would probably mean the other shoe would drop big-time—I could likely look forward to the carriage house burning down, my car being crushed by a tree, or worse. But as long as James kept kissing me and sliding his rough hands along all of my curves, I didn't care about any of those things. Right now, he was all I wanted. Letting him make me feel this good was worth whatever complexity might come after.

He dropped his hands from my back. "A couple of days," he said flatly. His expression was hard to read.

I sat back and stared at him, confused. "I thought you wanted this, too. What am I missing?"

His brows pulled together and he swallowed hard, like I'd hit a nerve. "I'm not looking to have a fling while I'm in town," he said, his tone sharp. "Is that all this is to you?"

The way he said the words stung like a slap. He made it sound like my feeling this way, and finally acting on those feelings—was wrong. Like not overanalyzing the way I felt drawn to him was bad. Like showing him what I wanted was bad.

His words made me feel ashamed. Again.

"What did you expect this to be?" I asked him. "In a few days, you'll be gone."

His eyes looked sad. "I don't have to be."

"So, what, you'll move to Jasmine Falls so we can date? I'll leave my park job and move to Atlanta? We'll see each other on the occasional weekend when you're not filming somewhere a thousand miles away?"

His jaw tensed, but he said nothing.

This idea didn't seem simple anymore.

His gaze shifted away from me, his mouth a hard line. When he at last turned back to me, his eyes looked glassy. "I should take you home," he said, his voice strained.

I climbed off his lap and scrambled back to the passenger seat. What had I been thinking? I didn't need James to concoct come elaborate plan to humiliate me—I was doing just fine humiliating myself.

"Not necessary." I pulled Paula Sue's keys from her purse and dangled them in front of him as I opened the car door. For a moment, I'd let myself believe we wanted the same thing. But I was wrong.

"Sadie," he said, turning toward me. "Please wait."

"Let's just pretend this never happened." There was that rush of adrenaline again, but this is the one that comes when the tiger is staring you down in the jungle—the surge of adrenaline that forces you to flee from the big scary thing that's about to eat you alive.

When I scrambled out, he said, "Sadie, get back in the car. I'll drive you home."

"It's okay," I said, the rain pelting me again. I couldn't stand one more minute inside that car, and I couldn't hold the tears back much longer.

"Can we please talk about this?" he said. "Don't leave this way."

I gave him an awkward wave and shut the door, then trudged over to where Paula Sue's tan Cadillac was parked under a tree. When I climbed inside and cranked the engine, I was immediately deafened by Dolly Parton singing at about a thousand decibels. I turned the volume down to a range that wouldn't shatter glass and sat for a moment, feeling like my heart would surely burst. How could I have read everything so wrong? And why had he drawn me so close to him only to push me away?

Dolly kept singing as the rain pelted the windshield, running in little rivulets that made me think of rivers carving out canyons. What had possessed me to think that kissing James was a good idea? That being with him, even for a moment, would bring anything but hurt? As the song ended and the next one began, I looked in the rearview, half expecting to see him walking toward me in the rain.

He wasn't. But he hadn't driven away, either. His car still sat behind me, with the lights on, because James Fielding was not the kind of guy who would drive off in the night and leave a woman alone in a parking lot in the woods ten miles from town. I sighed, thinking of how right his arms had felt circled around my waist, and then shoved that thought away as hard as I could and flipped on the headlights. We didn't want the same things, and that was clear as this sky full of stars. As Dolly crooned about the one that got away from her and tore her heart in two, I steered the Cadillac out of the parking lot and onto the ribbon of road, watching as James's headlights followed in the rearview, never too far behind.

Feeling him turn me down felt just as awful as I'd imagined. There was no way I'd be able to make it through the rest of the week. It would be impossible to look him in the eye.

Chapter Fifteen

JAMES

WHEN SADIE HAD CLIMBED into my lap in that dark car, I thought two things at the same instant: one, I was the luckiest man alive on this crazy, beautiful planet, and two, I was having a heart attack. I was soaked and cold from the rain, and she was soft and warm, and the way she'd kissed me had been better than all of my dreams of her combined.

It had felt too good to be real.

When she curled her fingers in my hair and pressed her lips to mine, it was the best moment of my life. But it totally short-circuited my brain. I was like a cat that finally caught the mouse it had been chasing forever, and held it in its paw only to think, *Now what?* I'd been stunned, stupefied, and all rational thought went right out of my head as I considered what the next right move might be while simultaneously etching every detail about that moment into my memory.

And then she'd said words that cut like a hacksaw. *In a few days, you'll be gone.* And worse: *We'll just see each other on the occasional weekend when you're not filming somewhere a thousand miles away?*

It didn't sound so bad on the surface, out of context. She had no way of knowing how those words could hurt me so deeply. How could she have known that Melanie had said similar words, back when she tried to justify sleeping with someone else? *You're never here*, she'd told me, as if that excused her betrayal.

Sadie didn't know it, but she had just confirmed my worst fear: that I couldn't have both love and my career. Melanie had told me that with absolute certainty when we'd split up—and I was terrified that it was the truth. Tonight, it was as if with one glance, Sadie had peered into my heart and seen that she couldn't have a real relationship with me because it was doomed to fail.

I'd wanted her so badly that I'd tamped down all those fears about how she might leave me just like Mel did, but in an instant, that fear came rushing up like a tidal wave. *But you won't be here.* In that moment, looking into her eyes, I'd been so afraid that Melanie had been right, and that Sadie would decide the same was true for her. And I was ninety-eight percent certain I wouldn't survive that kind of heartache again. Especially coming from Sadie.

And then I thought: *that's why she was only interested in a fling.* Because she didn't see me as the kind of guy she'd have a real relationship with. Just like Melanie had said, I wasn't partner material. I was just a way to have fun in the short term. I wasn't the guy you built a life with.

All of the old hurt had come washing back over me and all I could think was *I don't want to feel that way ever again.*

So I'd panicked. I'd done the only thing I knew to do, which was push her away before I could hurt her any worse than I already had.

Sadie had looked confused, wounded, and I wanted to tell

her that the problem was me—all me. But she couldn't get out of that car fast enough. And the words died in my throat.

I'd followed her back to the inn—not in a weird stalker-y way, but because she was driving an unfamiliar car in the rain and I'm paranoid about people I love getting home safely. I thought for a minute that she might take the car back over to Paula Sue's, and then I could convince her to get back into my car, and then I'd drive her back to the inn and try to explain why I'd completely lost my mind and said the worst imaginable thing to her.

But that's not what happened. She drove straight to the inn, and I parked on the street and watched her walk down the path to the carriage house and unlock the door. When the lights came on inside, I sat for another moment, thinking maybe I should go knock on the door and just explain everything: that I was a total wreck, falling harder for her by the minute, and terrified that she'd eventually figure out she was more than I deserved.

Instead, I killed the engine and walked in the front door of the inn. It was after ten, so the great mercy was that there was no one else around. Ravi, the night owl, was probably staying up late watching a movie in the room adjacent to mine. Tetia and Ashley were likely dead asleep because they both, for some ungodly reason, woke up at dawn to go for a run, or do yoga or something equally healthy that would likely kill me if I tried it. So I slipped inside and went straight upstairs to my room, tiptoeing so I wouldn't wake anyone and have to explain why I was awake and soaked to the skin.

After taking a hot shower, I poured myself a bourbon from the small bottle I usually took with me on trips—because I often had trouble sleeping and nothing knocks me out like a couple of well-crafted bourbons—and sprawled on the bed to consider just how badly I'd ruined everything.

At last, I texted my sister Phoebe. **Hey,** I wrote. **Are you awake? I need your opinion on something.**

I'm at some godawful birthday party in a bar that has saddles for barstools, she wrote. **I've had just enough tequila to be 90-proof level honest.**

Good, because I need honesty.

My phone rang and her picture flashed on the screen.

"Hi there," I answered. "I didn't mean to interrupt the party."

"This sounds serious," she said. "And I'm happy to have a reason to go outside because the line dancing here is no joke. These people have boots with spurs, James. Spurs!"

"How'd you get roped into that?"

"Smooth," she said, the music blaring behind her. "I see why you make the big bucks now, Mister Big-Time Writer."

I snorted as I heard the squeak of a door, a flirty hello from someone, and then merciful silence.

"Okay," she said. "Now I can talk without screaming. What's going on?"

"Am I doomed to be alone?"

"I thought I was the drunk one here."

"I'm serious, Phoebe. After what happened with Mel, and after what she said, it just makes me wonder if she was right. Am I impossible to be with?"

She snorted. "First off, that woman was a shrew. A mean-spirited, cheating, black hole of a person who wanted to make everyone around her as miserable as she was. Did you spend time away from her for work? Yes. Did you deserve to be treated like garbage because of it? No. Travel was your job, James. She knew what she was signing up for."

My chest tightened. No one gave it to me straight quite like Phoebe did.

She went on. "I could say lots of things about her, but everyone's battling their own demons, and we can never know what's really in another person's heart—and I'm feeling more compassionate in my old age and adamant about getting rid of toxic thinking. But in the end, it just comes to this. She didn't help you become the best version of yourself. Being with her made you doubt yourself, and made you compromise your dreams. You don't need people like that in your life. You deserve better."

"Thanks, sis."

She sighed, and I could picture her standing outside that bar, all six feet of her, pacing the sidewalk as she talked. Phoebe was a year younger than me but had the wisdom of a person who'd lived ten lifetimes. She was determined in an angsty kind of way and didn't take crap from anyone. She was my hero.

"So no, J. You are not impossible. You are imperfectly human, just like the rest of us. And I know you're going to find that partner someday who loves you just as you are and doesn't try to squeeze you into her little man-shaped gelatin mold."

"That sounds like it came from a Hallmark movie," I said. "And maybe a little *X-Files*."

"Shut it," she said. "Sometimes Hallmark gets it right. And something tells me this is not about she-who-shall-not-be-named."

I smirked. She used to joke that Melanie was like Beetlejuice, but more earnest. You say her name only once and she appears to wreak havoc on you like a tiny, furious tornado. "I did meet someone," I said. "And then tonight I freaked out and did a really stupid thing and I'm not sure I can fix it."

She huffed. "The only thing you can do is try, J. We all make dumb moves from time to time. Usually out of fear. If she's the kind of person you need in your life, she'll understand that. Just be honest with her."

"How'd you get so smart?" I said.

"Woo-woo books and old country songs. I should probably get back to the party. I think I see the birthday girl on the mechanical bull. You feel better about all this?"

"I do. I should have asked you this question a long time ago."

"Yes, you should've. Let me know how it goes, J. I'm rootin' for you."

THERE'S some old adage that says things always look better in the morning.

It's a complete and total lie.

Now that I knew what it felt like to have Sadie Harper perched on my lap, kissing me stupid as she raked her hands through my hair and made these little purring sounds that just about stopped my heart, I couldn't concentrate on anything else. Not one single thing. When I sat down to the breakfast table with Tetia and the others, I realized that I'd put my tee shirt on inside-out and worn the same pants from yesterday. I was halfway to pouring orange juice into my coffee when Ravi said, "Dude."

When I quickly reached for the milk instead, he said, "Rough night?"

"Didn't sleep well," I said, which was true. I'd tossed and turned all night long, thinking of Sadie straddling my lap, her thighs pinned over my hips in the most delightful way, her lips hot against my neck. In my dreams, she'd done so much more, and it had felt like absolute heaven.

Waking up and finding that she in fact was *not* in my bed had been an exceptionally cruel start to the day.

Now, as Sadie greeted everyone and sat down across from me at the table, I felt my heart squeeze in my chest. Her eyes drifted to mine for a brief moment and then her expression turned stern.

As Tetia reached for a bagel, Sadie turned to her and blurted out, "Am I fired? I know we signed an agreement, but if you don't want me to finish this project, I totally understand."

Tetia, bless her, looked completely shocked. Her brows jumped almost to her hairline and her lips parted in a tiny O. "Why would you say that?" she said.

"Um, because yesterday happened," Sadie said.

I froze, coffee mug just inches from my mouth, as I imagined how this day would become an actual waking nightmare if Sadie went on to describe anything that had happened after we'd climbed into my car together.

"I was awful yesterday," Sadie said, her eyes flicking toward me. "I mean, a total dumpster fire."

Tetia frowned, chewing her bagel. "Don't be so hard on yourself. It wasn't that bad."

I glanced at Ashley and Ravi, who were busy stuffing mini quiches into their mouths and watching the conversation as if it were a ping-pong match. They were always happy to give notes on my performance, but I could tell they liked Sadie and didn't want to scare her off with their critiques. For the time being, they'd leave all notes to Tetia.

Sadie arched a brow. "I said the f-word when I dropped a cactus on my foot."

"I've heard worse," Tetia said, giving me some serious side-eye.

"If you are referring to when that donkey kicked me in the

kidney, I still say it was justified," I said, sipping my coffee. "A lesser man would have kicked him right back."

Tetia rolled her eyes at me and turned back to Sadie. "Do you want to try again?"

Sadie blinked at her, like she hadn't expected to have a choice in the matter. She glanced at me and then turned back to Tetia. "I do."

Tetia nodded like the wise mentor that she was. "Then don't worry about making mistakes. We know you're not Meryl Streep. Everybody has rough edges. We like that. You're perfectly imperfect, which is just right for this show. It makes you relatable."

Sadie let out a heavy sigh. "Thank you."

"You'll do better today," Tetia said. "I have a good feeling." She turned to me and said, "Right, James? Today's going to be great."

I swallowed hard. Was it good for the show that Sadie was staying? Absolutely. But was it good for me? Before she left me alone in the rain, I'd have said *definitely*. But now that she'd made it clear she thought I was only good for a fling and nothing serious? That made being around her the most maddening kind of torture.

This was exactly the feeling I'd been so afraid of back at Cambrick. Deep down, I'd been afraid that if the lovely Sadie Harper got to know me, she'd decide I wasn't good enough for her. And now, given everything that had happened in the past few years, she'd be right.

As it turned out, that feeling sucked even worse than I'd imagined. Worse than a donkey kick to the kidney.

"Yeah," I said. "Perfect." The way Tetia smiled, I must have been convincing.

With that settled, they all chatted through breakfast, passing the bagels and refilling their coffee like the world was not crashing down around us. As if I had not made out with my co-host in the front seat of my car like a rabid teenager, drunk on feeling her skin against mine. All I could think of was how I could possibly get through the next two days without thinking about Sadie's hands, her lips, her…everything.

This was utterly hopeless. Whatever I'd felt for her back in college had been magnified by the power of a hundred. I thought I'd gotten over her, but one look at her at the national park that day, giving her ranger program, had proven me one hundred percent wrong. She'd stood there in that little patch of woods, smiling in the golden afternoon light, talking about shorebirds and the importance of wetlands and cracked my heart wide open.

I realize how goofy that sounds, and I'm still not entirely sure where wetlands are located and why they matter so much, but I left that afternoon hoping that Sadie Harper would take a long time explaining that to me someday. Preferably after she'd stripped off my last stitch of clothing and exhausted me.

But that would almost certainly never happen now. I'd made sure of that.

"Hey," Sadie said, grabbing me by the sleeve. Tetia and the others were piling into the van, getting ready to head over to Eli's place to film the next segment. "Let's talk on the way," she said. "You drive."

It took me a moment to realize that she was leading me toward my car, telling me to drive us because there wasn't enough space for both of us in the van with the others. My brain was still apparently frozen, because Sadie was some kind of siren who could easily take control of my thoughts and all of my other parts with one smoldering kiss.

This was not going to be a good day for filming, I could tell.

She climbed into the passenger seat and as I cranked the car, I felt the weight of her on my lap again, her lips pressed against mine, and my heart was pounding like a jackhammer.

Handing me her travel mug of coffee, she said, "I think you need this more than I do."

"Thanks," I said, and it was a miracle I could utter a single syllable.

Ravi drove the van out of the parking lot and I started out after him.

"I thought we could chat before filming," Sadie said. "Obviously, I decided to stay."

"What changed your mind?"

"You," she said, and my heart inflated like a balloon. "You were right. I signed a contract. It would be wrong to back out."

"Oh," I breathed. "Right." The contract.

She glanced at me and took a sip of the coffee. "We're adults, Fielding. We're both pros. We can put one weird night behind us and do our jobs."

I concentrated on the road, trying hard not to think of her lips, rosy from the hot coffee, like they had been last night—and swollen from kissing me so hard that I saw stars. "Weird?" I said, as if it was the first time a woman had called me that.

"Awkward. Unexpected. Whatever." She flung these words around like they meant nothing. She might as well have been hurling bricks.

"Whatever?" I said, incredulous. Now I was reduced to a teenaged retort. I didn't know how many miles it was to Eli's house, but I was hoping it was enough to give me time to fix this.

She turned toward me, fixing those big gray-blue eyes on mine. They were the color of a thunderhead, and they were staring into my soul. "It was a mistake, okay? I shouldn't have kissed you. I put you in an awkward position, and I'm sorry. I don't know what came over me, but I clearly misread your signals, and I promise you it will not happen again."

I didn't care for the resigned tone in those last few words. "It wasn't awkward," I said. "I thought it was pretty damn delightful." And more than anything, I wanted her to do it again.

She blinked at me and someone honked as I veered a little too close to the center line.

"Let's just do what we agreed to do, Fielding. Be co-hosts."

"That's the coldest thing you've ever said to me."

"It's not meant to be cold. I just want to forget this misstep and move forward. I've screwed up enough lately, okay?" She sounded annoyed, hurt—but I wanted to wrap her in my arms and tell her that it was okay. More than okay. She was being so hard on herself, and I couldn't figure out why. I was the one who'd panicked and pushed her away.

"I don't think it was a misstep." Farmland whizzed past us, making me dizzy. I couldn't focus on both the road and her words, so I pulled onto the shoulder .The tires rumbled in the gravel, and a black and white cow near the fence line pricked its ears toward us.

"What are you doing?" she cried, grabbing for the dash to steady herself.

"I can't talk about this while careening down the highway. It's hurting my brain."

"Would you get back on the road? They're going to think something's wrong."

"Something *is* wrong," I said. My phone buzzed, deep in the pocket of my jeans. The car picked up the call as I answered.

"Everything okay?" Ashley said. "You need help?" The van was out of sight now, a couple of miles ahead.

I needed all kinds of help. "We're good," I told her. "Just had a little coffee spill."

Ashley snorted. "Basic multitasking really isn't your strong suit, is it?"

"Accurate," I said.

Sadie stared at me like I'd just announced I had a secret identity as a superhero.

"On our way," I told Ashley. "Right behind you."

"It's not much farther," she said. "We pulled over down here at the church. We'll wait for you."

She ended the call, and I said, "Harper, we should talk about this later, when we're not likely to cause an accident."

"We're always likely to cause an accident," she said. "Don't you see?"

"No, I don't. And hyperbole has always been your superpower."

She set those stormy eyes on me again and muttered, "Just drive, Fielding. They're waiting."

"One condition: that you have a real conversation with me about this later."

"Will it involve a comet?"

"Let's try something new."

She sighed, exasperated. "Let's just get through this day, okay? And then let's get through tomorrow, and then you never have to see me again."

"I don't like that plan." That was the absolute worst-case scenario. Why was she so eager to push me away? "I'm not driving until you agree to talk to me. Preferably in a quiet place with no moving vehicles."

She glared at me. "You're like a toddler. Or a hostage-taker. I can't quite decide."

I shrugged, turning the radio on. "Your call. It's peaceful out here. I could stay all day." She could try to freeze me out if she wanted to. She could try to outlast me, outwit me, and outmaneuver me if she liked. But I wasn't going to walk away from her again. Not like this.

She groaned, throwing her head back against the head rest. "Fine. We'll talk later for no more than the length of time it takes me to drink a beer. Can we please go now?"

I checked for traffic behind us and pulled back onto the highway. Sadie rolled her eyes so hard it made my head hurt, and I reached for the mug of coffee, taking a sip from that spot where her lips had just been. None of those words were what I wanted to hear, but clearly, I wasn't going to change her mind about anything before we got to Eli's house.

But we weren't over yet.

Chapter Sixteen

SADIE

"Sweet baby cheeses," Ashley said, her voice low. "It's like a casting call for the Thor movies in here."

Eli and Alex waved to us from the back of the forge, and when they came walking toward us with their cool swagger, I half-expected smoke to curl around them like in a music video.

Both in their early thirties, they'd been doing metal sculpture for more than ten years and had the biceps to prove it. Eli had started out as a blacksmith and quickly moved into large-scale bronze sculptures. Alex worked mostly with commissions for functional iron work like gates and railings for fancy houses, but took on the occasional outdoor sculpture. They'd both had commissions all over the Southeast—libraries, museums, even a governor's mansion. But you'd never guess that from their down-to-earth nature.

From the outside, they both looked big and intimidating—over six feet of broad shoulders and insanely muscular arms—but under all that muscle and those steely eyes, they were a couple of softies. Alex, with his bright blue eyes and wild black hair, made flannel look like the sexiest fabric on earth. Eli, with his dark brown skin and intense hazel eyes, had a rumbling voice made for the twelve-bar blues.

The two of them together was enough to knock most women off-kilter for a moment. Judging by Tetia and Ashley's stares, today was no exception.

"Sadie," Eli rumbled, pulling me into a hug. "Good to see you."

"Hi," I squeaked, as he nearly squeezed the breath out of me, lifting me off the floor. When he put me down, I glanced at James and he looked like he'd been smacked upside the head with a piece of rebar. Was that jealousy in his eyes?

After our awkward drive over, I couldn't get a read on him at all. Last night had made my head spin. First, he'd acted like he couldn't wait to get me alone, then he'd frozen when I put my hands on him, and now he was acting like he was insulted because I backed off. Probably, I'd dodged a bullet. This week had stirred up a flurry of emotions in me, and my body seemed to think that it wanted James Fielding. My brain, however, had some more complicated thoughts about the matter. The battle between them was exhausting.

The best thing I could do was put some space between us. After Saturday, that would be a few hundred miles, and James Fielding could go back to being a distant memory.

"Do we all get that kind of welcome?" Ashley whispered, her eyes wide as her gaze drifted over Eli and Alex.

"Eli and I go way back," I said. "We actually dated in high school. Even went to prom together." He'd been the first guy who seemed to really see me for who I was, and he didn't let me get away with trying to be someone else just to fit in with the crowd. He'd always have my friendship because of that.

James's brow arched and he made a noise that sounded like a growl.

So he was *growling* now?

Eli flashed his megawatt smile, then proceeded to shake hands with everyone else. They all looked dazzled, like they'd met a movie star—except for James, that is.

"Hey, Sadie," Alex said. "Glad you all could make it. We've got everything set up in the back if y'all want to check it out." When he shook Tetia's hand, he said, "We're just so glad to be a part of your show."

"And we're glad you are, too," she said. "You two are quite the sensation around here."

In addition to being incredibly talented artists, they also teamed up with the arts council for annual fundraising events and ran a mentoring program for local kids who were interested in art. They were the closest thing Jasmine Falls had to celebrities.

Eli and Alex gave us a quick tour of the space. Eli's studio was a giant barn that he'd completely renovated into a state-of-the-art forge. It was a dream setup, really—he lived in the adjacent farmhouse, on several acres of what was once farmland. Now, it was a quiet meadow ringed by forest, and felt like his nearest neighbor was miles away. Alex had his own studio, too, but they did their mentoring here, where there was more space.

"This is amazing," Ravi said, taking it all in.

"Yeah," Ashley said, "Amazing," her eyes tracking Eli as he showed us to the workstations.

James had his game face on again, but each time he looked at me, it yanked me right back to last night and made my cheeks burn with embarrassment. How had I lost control like that? I'd practically thrown myself at him.

Two more days, I thought. Two more days, and James Fielding is out of my life forever. I can let this humiliation ride out of town with him and never think of it again.

And never think of him again, either. No problem.

Eli paused, pointing out some tools we'd use in the demo. "Alex is going to show y'all how to make snakes from rebar," he said. "It's a project we do with beginner students. Pretty straightforward. We'll use a hammer and anvil, and the gas forge. We'll have gloves, safety glasses, tongs, and some smaller tools. Nothing too complicated." Alex lit the forge, about the size of a small wood stove, as Eli showed us a sample of a snake.

"Cool," James said, sounding completely distracted. The fire blazed behind him in the small forge, the heat already radiating toward us.

"I'll make one and you and Sadie can make your own right alongside me," Alex said, rolling up his sleeves to reveal forearms as solid as fenceposts. "We've got three stations set up with hammers and anvils, and we can share the forge."

"Excellent," Tetia said. "We'll shoot a little B-roll of the studio if you don't mind, and then we'll do the demos." As they chatted about the interview and where to set up the cameras, my phone buzzed in my pocket. I pulled it out and saw a text from Leah.

Got a question for you when you have a minute, it said. **Might have a job for you.**

"Everything okay?" James said.

"Sure." I turned the phone off and shoved it back into my pocket.

He looked like he didn't quite believe me.

"It's fine. Let's make some snakes."

He opened his mouth like he wanted to say more, but Tetia shouted from across the studio.

"Okay," she said, clapping her hands. "Let's get rolling."

· · ·

ALEX WALKED us through the process so we'd know what to expect while we filmed the demo. There was a solid chance I could do this without burning the building down, but there was also a decent likelihood that I could catch my pants on fire.

It was already scorching in the studio, and we'd barely started. Next to me, James wiped his brow and raked his hands through his hair, and my arms were suddenly covered in goosebumps as I thought of last night, how his hair had felt so soft in my fingers.

Focus, I thought. *Do not burn this building down.* Whatever James felt, it was obviously more complicated than I'd thought. He'd pushed me away gently, like he was trying to spare my feelings. Puzzled, I replayed that moment over and over in my mind until I realized: he must have just wanted to clarify how he'd felt back in college, because he learned he'd hurt me. He wasn't telling me he had feelings for me *now*. He'd just been trying to right a wrong.

My heart felt heavy. I'd begun to like thinking that he still wanted me, because I'd let myself want him, too. But now I needed to take all of my mixed-up feelings and burn them to ash, because nothing was happening between us.

Ravi set up a stationary camera to film the first demo and chose another area where he could move in closer as needed. Alex was all business as he plunged the rebar into the forge, then used tongs to hold the red-hot metal against the anvil and pound it with the hammer. He talked us through each step in his musical Lowcountry drawl, telling us how to hold the tools and keep ourselves safe. (Don't touch the white-hot iron was the number one rule.) Watching him work was mesmerizing—the steady thrust of the rebar into the forge, the rhythmic ping of the hammer against the metal, the careful way he bent the rod this way and that to give it a gentle curve. It didn't take long for the rod to take the shape of a snake, and every strike of the hammer caused his forearms to flex in a way that made it hard to concentrate on the iron.

"Mercy," Ashley breathed. "They don't make guys like that where I come from."

James gave me another curious look, his jaw tense. If that furrow in his brow got any deeper, it would crack his face in two.

When it was our turn to work alongside Alex, Eli handed us both a pair of heavy elbow-length gloves made of thick leather. "Safety first," he said with a wink. "Wouldn't want to have any scars after today."

James's eyes rested on mine and he arched a brow as if to say, *Too late.*

Alex did each step first, talking us through the process with each strike of the hammer. Eli stood between James and me as we followed along, stepping in to help us when necessary, and gently guiding us as we took turns heating our iron rods in the forge. It was a complicated dance with the three of us, but soon we timed our movements to keep out of each other's way.

"Just go slow," Alex said, shaping the head of the snake with his hammer. In five solid strikes, it looked real enough to me.

After what felt like fifty strikes, my snake's head was like a lopsided strawberry, but at least I'd managed to swing the ten-pound hammer without shedding any tears. My arm was already aching because I hated exercise more than anything, and this was more of a workout than I'd had in ages. No wonder Eli and Alex looked like they'd been chiseled out of marble.

"Oops," James said. "I think I broke the head off." A little chunk of iron lay at his feet.

"No problem," Alex said. "Iron is forgiving. Just heat him up and start again."

Eli walked him through the strikes and James pounded the end of the rod until it took shape again. "I think I have a hog-nosed snake," he said, holding it up proudly. This was the part of him that no doubt won audiences over—his ability to make himself seem not like a superstar, but a regular person who stumbled through new and challenging experiences, like all the rest of us.

He didn't outshine people around him—he made others shine.

Alex shifted gears, showing us quickly how to use what he called a bending fork—it looked a little like a tuning fork, held into place at the broad end of the anvil. When he stuck the red-hot rod into place, he deftly used the tongs to bend it against the wide tines of the fork, instantly creating a serpentine shape. He made it look so easy, bending the body of the snake first one way and then the opposite.

When I tried next, it felt like I was trying to tie a fisherman's knot while wearing oven mitts. I grunted as I put my full body weight into it, and Eli stopped me. "Wait," he said, his voice gentle. "Let the heat do the work." He motioned for me to heat the rod in the forge again, longer this time, until it was glowing nearly white. "Now," he said, "Not too much pressure," and as I placed the rod inside the bending fork, he gently moved my arms forward and backward in a smooth motion that put a delicate curve in the metal.

"You make this look easy," I said.

"You're getting the hang of it," he said with a smile. "Just have to tune everything else out and listen to the metal. Don't overthink it."

While I considered how exactly one might listen to metal, James huffed next to me, trying to mimic Eli's moves. There was a clatter and a grumble as James dropped his snake. Another chunk broke off and he said, "My snake just got a lot shorter."

"Just lost a bit of his tail," Eli said, stepping over to help. "No worries."

After a few more minutes, Alex was finished with the body of his snake. He showed us how to level it on the anvil, and then after laying it in the forge once more, used pliers to pinch the tip of the tail into a tiny curve. That one tiny detail made all the difference—if I'd seen that snake in the yard, I'd have thought it was real.

"Time to quench," Alex said. With his tongs, he dunked his snake in a bucket of water. "This cools it quickly so we can get on with the polishing."

James and I took one last turn in the forge, using the pliers to give our snakes a lifelike tail, and then dunked them into the bucket. When we set them all out on the big worktable, mine looked more like a kid's drawing of a snake, and James's looked like a wet noodle.

"Not bad," Eli said, with the sort of grace that's perfect for TV and for children.

"Masterpieces," James said, his tone light again. "If you need assistants, you know where to find us."

Eli laughed his good-natured laugh, and Alex grinned. James had a streak of soot across his forehead that was ridiculously endearing. When his eyes found mine, he gave me a sheepish smile that made the butterflies stir again.

Would there ever be a day when his stare didn't give me butterflies?

When they had cooled enough, Alex showed us how to polish them with a wire brush. "Just a little pressure overall will bring out a little shine," he said. Sure enough, the wire brush shined the raised pattern in the rebar, giving it a sheen that looked like actual snakeskin.

"Great," Tetia said. "You guys nailed it." She walked over to look at our little rebar snakes and said, "Let's take a break and move on to the next demo with Eli, and then we'll do the questions. Y'all are killing it today."

It was hot as blazes in that studio, and being right next to James with a big fireball between us was not helping me to focus. No matter how hard I tried to tamp all my feelings down, my mind kept drifting back to last night. How what we were doing had felt so right, and how with one question—*A fling? Is that all this is to you?*—he'd made it all seem so wrong.

Alex pointed us toward a cooler filled with ice and drinks, and I grabbed a water on my way outside. Desperate to think of anything except James and that conversation we'd had on the ride over, I pulled my phone from my pocket and turned it back on. It pinged with a missed call and text from Leah.

Hey, she wrote. **Did you hear back from Florida?**

Before my last day in the park, she'd sent me a listing for a job down in the Everglades, where she knew the supervisory ranger. I was a shoo-in, she'd said, and I had applied because it was only a few months. Winter in south Florida wouldn't be terrible, aside from the mosquitoes. It might have led to another interpretive job—but they'd emailed me back yesterday.

It's a no, I answered. **They picked someone else.**

Ted said he liked you a lot, she wrote. **They probably just snagged a local.**

Maybe, I wrote.

The interview had gone well, and Ted had sounded enthusiastic about my experience. It was a short season, though, and sometimes local hires were a safer bet for those.

Of course, it was also possible that Ted had called District

Ranger Mike for a recommendation and had gotten an earful from him that was the opposite of Leah's ringing endorsement.

The park service could be a small world. People moved a lot, and that could create inroads or brick walls in a hurry. I could go to the most remote park in Alaska and bump into the chief ranger's best friend from law enforcement training.

You have time to talk quickly? Leah wrote. **Something's opened up here.**

When I called her, she answered on the first ring.

"It's not as fun as the Everglades," Leah said, "But someone at headquarters has asked for extended leave, and it came up unexpectedly. The supervisor for this position is a good friend of mine, and she's totally immune to any BS that might bubble up from you know who."

"What's the job?" I asked her.

"It's in records," she said. "So, you know, lots of filing and not much sunlight. But there are cool people there. It'd be okay for short-term."

"How long?"

"I don't know many details," she said. "Maybe three months? But you'd be eligible to live in park housing again."

That would be a decent stopgap for me. I could stand doing anything for three months. Well. Almost anything. Filing in a basement wasn't that bad. And as Leah kept telling me, it was important not to let too much time go by without employment in the park service. Gaps looked suspicious—like you were a problem employee or not especially motivated—and if too much time went by, you might not get back in again.

"I already talked to Cheryl about it," she said. "Testing the waters and whatnot. If you're interested, she'll set up a call. They want someone to start a week from Monday, so they're only going to post the position for two days."

"Sure," I said. "Tell her I'm interested." I wasn't ready to let go of Congaree just yet—if there was a way to get back into the education side of the park, I wanted to do it. Plus, it meant I wouldn't have to keep living in the carriage house and working at the inn. I had enough money saved to keep me going for a couple of months, but the last thing I wanted was to lean on my parents for help—and working for them at the inn, even for a short time, was a slippery slope.

"Great," she said. "I really want to keep you in this park, Sadie. I know something else will open up soon. Can't tell you more than that, but I really think that if you hang on a little longer, you'll get a permanent position. One that you-know-who can't touch."

My heart lifted at her words. She always had faith in me, even when I took silly missteps. Even when I thought I was crashing and burning, she was there telling me something better was on the other side.

"Thanks, Leah. I appreciate this more than you know."

"Girl, I know how it is here. It's like a dang labyrinth half the time, but if you stick around long enough, you learn the ways, and doors start to open. I'll talk to Cheryl and text you what I know."

She ended the call and I shoved the phone back into my pocket. If this worked out, then in a little over a week, my life would be back to normal. I could get through one more day of being a co-host, a few more days of pretending to be an innkeeper, and then get myself back on track. I thought back to what Gwen had told me: *Fall down five times, stand up six.*

You got this, I thought. *You will stand up again.* If I told myself enough times, maybe I could believe it.

Chapter Seventeen

JAMES

THIS DAY WAS the absolute worst.

It was always hard to focus on anything else when Sadie was in the room, but today it was impossible.

But shooting went on whether I was distracted or not. So I tried to put on a good face and do my typical crowd-pleasing fish out of water act. To be fair, that second part was easy because I was definitely out of my element today, in a studio that felt like Vulcan's furnace. I'd been shoved into this space with two behemoths who were built like Hemsworths, complete with Hollywood bad-boy grins. And don't think I missed the way every person was eyeballing them, either, as if they just sauntered down from Mount Olympus.

I mean, they were great at what they did—okay, fine, they were wildly impressive—so it hardly seemed fair that they should have both a boatload of talent and be blessed with the chiseled features that made women's hearts beat faster than a hummingbird's.

So yes, today I was definitely a fish out of water.

It was ridiculous, of course, to be so worked up about things

I had no control over—like the cut of Eli's jaw or the way that Ashley nearly swooned when he shook her hand, or the way that Sadie lit up when he hugged her. I'd played my calming mantra in my head like a broken record and had just about pulled myself together when I heard Sadie tell Ashley that she and Eli had dated.

That single image had made my eye twitch so hard that it surely looked like I was having a stroke. The idea of Sadie dating someone else shouldn't have had that effect on me, but it did. In that split second, I realized the problem: I didn't want her dating anyone but me. Ever again. And certainly not one of the uber-charming, extra-chiseled, super talented Elis of the world.

Lord help me.

Somehow, I'd managed to go the entire morning without setting myself on fire. That in itself was a miracle because even though that iron was heated to a thousand degrees and could easily burn a hole in me, it was not at the forefront of my mind. No, my brain was focused on Sadie and how less than twelve hours ago, she'd climbed into my lap and kissed me like it was our last night on earth.

As Alex shouted out instructions, I'd pounded that rebar until it was vaguely snake-shaped, replaying last night in my head over and over as I considered how, after all this time, I could still be so stupid about Sadie Harper.

When she'd climbed inside my car, it was like a switch had flipped, and she was no longer looking at me so warily. That giant wall she'd built around herself had finally started to crumble, and she was so sweet and vulnerable and trusting that I wanted to scoop her up into my arms and tell her I'd been in love with her for ages.

After that kiss, I'd hesitated for just a moment and then blurted out words that may as well have been a shove. And then she'd hit a nerve, and I'd panicked and pushed her away. Because I wasn't interested in a fling: I wanted Sadie for real. Whether that meant moving or dating long-distance, I couldn't say. But when she'd so flippantly dismissed those ideas like they weren't even a possibility, it had gutted me.

She'd slipped out of my arms and was gone in a blink. And she probably thought I'd just been toying with her all along.

Today, she'd hardly spoken to me off-camera. Except for that horrendous car ride this morning. If I told her how I felt now, she'd probably just think I was trying to spare her feelings. She obviously didn't feel what I felt for her—so was it really fair to tell her, or was it just selfish? Part of me feared that if I did tell her, she'd bolt. And take away the last shred of hope that I clung to—the one that said maybe we just needed a little more time.

"Did you hear me?" Tetia said. "Try to wrap up by six?" She waved her hand in front of my face and said, "Are you okay, James? You don't look so great."

"Sure, fine," I said. "I think the heat just got to me."

Tetia handed me another bottle of some fruity drink with electrolytes and said, "You need to stay hydrated, champ."

"It's like an actual sauna in there," Ashley said. "My skin should look amazing after a few more hours of this." She fanned herself and tugged at the front of her tee shirt. We were sitting at a picnic table close to Eli's studio, out in the yard where there was a cool breeze. Because he had students over here, he'd set up two tables in the shade. A few yards away, Ravi and Sadie sat at the other table with Alex.

I laid back on the bench and poured the last of my cup of ice water over my head. The shock of cold made me shiver.

"I think this is the best day yet," Tetia said.

"You're just saying that because there's barbecue," I said.

She grinned. "It certainly doesn't hurt. Plus it's a nice layer of interest for the episode. These guys have that small-town, rural, we-do-everything-for-ourselves vibe that people eat up with a spoon."

"And who doesn't want to watch hot blacksmiths who can cook?" Ashley said. "This is the dream I didn't know I needed." She had her big Jackie-O sunglasses on, and even though I couldn't see her eyes, I knew they were pinned to Eli.

Several yards away, Eli stood over the smoker he'd shown us earlier (one he built himself, of course). Since we had a full day here, he and Alex had insisted on cooking lunch for us on site. Eli apparently did this all the time for the kids he mentored—I mean, I guess if you're going to have a forge blazing and flames all over the property, you might as well fire up a barbecue and go all in.

Eli seemed like an all-in kind of guy. He probably didn't push women away when they climbed into his lap. He probably knew exactly what to say to fix every blunder. Assuming he made any blunders—I had my doubts about that.

Laughter erupted from the other table, and Eli shouted, "Hey, last call. Anybody need seconds?"

The barbecue was delicious (of course, because what could these guys not do?), but now I was feeling nauseated. Partly from the heat, but mainly because we had only one more day here, and then Sadie would be out of my life again. I didn't know exactly what I expected to find when I came back to Jasmine Falls: part of me thought I might find Sadie married, or with a boyfriend, or maybe just discover that she wasn't as wonderful as I remembered. Then it would have been easy to just shoot the episode, do my job, and walk away.

But that's not what happened.

It had only taken a few days to realize that my memories of Sadie paled in comparison to this version of her. Now she was sharper, funnier, even more determined to challenge me in the best ways. And beneath all that was someone who was kind, passionate, and inspiring. She'd opened up to me more in the last few days than I'd ever expected, and I'd seen a side of her that was making it impossible to walk away from her.

I really didn't want this week to be over, but I was pretty sure that she did. The thought of leaving her was killing me—but the worst part was that she'd shut herself off from me again. I'd ruined what was building between us, and I didn't know how to fix that.

But I had to try.

AFTER WHAT SEEMED LIKE AN ETERNITY, we moved on to the last segment. I felt like I was outside my body the entire time, hearing myself as I asked questions but not really listening to the answers. The last demo we'd shoot was Eli forming a flower out of iron. Tetia wanted to show a couple of different items made from forging, but she also wanted to give equal airtime to Alex and Eli. So Eli casually chatted with Sadie and me while doing this last demo, making it seem effortless to answer my questions and forge a metal rose at the same time.

Show-off.

I wouldn't deny it was impressive, watching him repeat similar steps that we'd done earlier with the snake, forcing the iron into the forge until it was red-hot, then pounding it with an anvil to make the strip of metal thin like flower petals. He made it look so easy, bending and rolling the metal as he struck with the hammer, his big arms flexing each time he moved.

Ashley and Tetia watched him work, completely entranced. When he had the basic form of the rose, he kept heating it and teasing out the petals by bending them outward with a small set of pliers. When he'd quenched and polished it, it looked incredibly lifelike.

Okay, fine. He deserved all those *oooohs* and *ahhhhhs*.

"That's the most amazing thing I've ever seen," Ashley said.

"Keep it," Eli said, handing it to her.

Her eyes widened. "No way. Really?"

"Of course," he said, giving her his movie-star smile. "So you don't forget about us here in Jasmine Falls."

Her cheeks turned pink and she smiled. "Awesome."

My chest heaved with a huge sigh of relief. If he'd given it to Sadie, I might have burst into flames.

I'd been rattled all day, trying to think of what to say to Sadie when I finally got her alone. All I knew was that I wanted to fix what we'd broken. What happened the night before was not something I could brush off or pretend hadn't happened. The way she'd opened up to me, the way she'd kissed me—that was real, and it meant something. And even though she'd left me alone in that car, she'd never convince me it didn't mean something to her, too. We hadn't had a minute alone since we got to Eli's place today, but pretty soon we'd be stuck in my car together again, and I wanted to be ready for her.

When we'd finally finished the shoot and Ravi was satisfied that he had enough B-roll, the four of us packed everything into the van and said our goodbyes to Alex and Eli. My heart was already pounding, thinking of how I could put all of my feelings into words and not have them fly out of my head the moment Sadie set those big blue eyes on me. I had to be honest about all those feelings I'd tried to keep in check. It was now or never.

Alex handed her two more bottles of water and as she walked toward me, her expression hard to read. Before I could say anything, Tetia stepped between us.

"Hey," Tetia said. "Sadie, would you mind riding back with Ash and Ravi? I need to go over something with James."

"Sure," she said, glancing at me. Was that relief in her eyes?

"I want to get your thoughts on something," Tetia said to me, walking toward my car. "And I have an update."

"Okay," I said. As Sadie walked toward the van, I told myself *If she looks back, it's okay. You still have a chance.*

She didn't.

WHEN WE GOT BACK to the inn, Tetia climbed out of the car and said, "James, I've got a great feeling about this. I'll meet you both downstairs at six and we'll discuss everything over dinner."

"You got it," I said, swallowing hard. Unlike Tetia, I wasn't feeling hopeful. Not in the least.

"And James?" she said, leveling her big brown eyes on mine. "No spoilers."

"Of course."

When Tetia went inside the inn, I collapsed into one of the wicker sofas on the big wraparound porch. I just couldn't make myself go inside yet. The smart thing to do would be to smooth things over with Sadie before we met Tetia for dinner. But when I texted Sadie, she didn't reply. When I felt like I could breathe again, I went inside the inn, thinking she might be in the office. Since we'd brought her into she show, she'd been working in the evenings on whatever inn business she needed to catch up on.

When I went inside though, I couldn't find her anywhere. Frustrated, I tried the carriage house—but she wasn't there, either.

After checking the garden, I walked back around to the porch and texted her again. **Hey, Tetia wants to meet for dinner. Did she get in touch with you?**

I knew Tetia would have already talked to her, but I wanted Sadie to answer me. This seemed like the easiest way to do that, just a colleague confirming a working dinner.

After a few moments, she answered, **Yes. I'll be there.**

Can we talk before dinner? I wrote.

Can't, she replied.

It's important, Harper.

I'm in the middle of something, she wrote. **I'll see you later.**

My feelings would have to wait. I sighed, tossing the phone onto the sofa next to me. She could ghost me all she wanted, but it wouldn't work. She couldn't push me away so easily this time.

TWO HOURS LATER, Tetia and I sat in a booth in the dining room of the Spare Time, and I was trying desperately to stay calm. The moment Sadie had climbed across the console had been the end of one thing and the beginning of something else, and what happened in the next hour could set us on a course that I didn't know how to navigate.

"We'll bring Ashley and Ravi here tomorrow night," Tetia said. "I just wanted to talk to you and Sadie alone about this, and tonight is shrimp taco night which, as you know, is my kryptonite." She sipped from her water glass and said, "I didn't think you'd mind a working dinner."

"Not at all," I said.

We'd driven over together, but Sadie was meeting us here. According to my phone, she was three minutes late. A bad sign. For Sadie, five minutes early was right on time.

"You still feeling okay about all of this?" she asked. She

narrowed her eyes in that way that meant she was in lie-detector mode.

"Sure," I said. "I think it's the right move." Not a total lie, but I wasn't optimistic. This awful sense of dread had been gnawing at me ever since Tetia and I had talked on the way back from the forge. It was the feeling that my life was about to change in a way I wasn't ready for. I was trapped on a speeding train that was headed for a cliff, and where on earth was our server with that bourbon?

Before I could say anything more, Sadie appeared at the booth and for a moment seemed to debate about where she should sit—next to me, or next to Tetia. She'd changed out of the jeans and tee shirt she'd worn at the shoot today, and now wore skinny jeans that made her legs look a mile long and a wrap-style top that showed off all of her curves.

When I slid over to make more room, she took a deep breath and sat. I caught the faint scent of a musky perfume that made me want to slide closer.

Get it together, Fielding. Now you have to be a pro, more than ever.

"Sorry I'm late," she said. "I had an appointment that ran long."

"No problem," Tetia said. "This is casual, but I have something I wanted to discuss with you before tomorrow."

Sadie's brows pulled together with worry. She looked at me like she might pick up a hint from my face, but I said nothing. This was Tetia's meeting, and I was just here as part of the team. I was not above crossing my fingers under the table, though, because finding a path forward with her was my top priority.

When our server mercifully came back with my bourbon and a water for Sadie, Tetia ordered an appetizer of stuffed mushrooms and a bottle of red wine to share. Then she turned to Sadie and said, "How'd you feel about today?"

No beating around the bush for Tetia. Not ever.

Sadie glanced at me and said, "Good. It was a fun demo. But Alex and Eli are total pros, so I expected it to go well."

"You seemed more comfortable," Tetia said.

Sadie gave her a sheepish smile. "It was easier today, yeah."

I bit my lip, not liking the implication of that. It was easier because of what Sadie had told me in the car this morning? Easier because she'd already built another massive wall between us? Easier because she thought I was one day away from disappearing from her life forever? I took a long drink from my glass, feeling the pleasant burn of the bourbon all the way down to my toes.

"Well, I thought today was great," Tetia said. "Action, some laughs, plus a solid interview and great chemistry. It's just what we're looking for."

Sadie shrugged. "Eli and Alex are old friends. It's easy being with them and showing them off."

I didn't want to think too hard about what that meant.

"I meant the chemistry between you and James," Tetia said. "Y'all have this competitive vibe going that's fun to watch. It's not quite old friends, and not quite enemies, but it's intriguing. The kind of thing that viewers love because they sense some connection but can't quite figure it out."

Sadie glanced at me again and then back to Tetia.

Tetia smiled as our server came back with our wine and appetizers. As Tetia poured us each some wine, she said, "You can't fake that kind of thing. And it's TV gold."

Sadie tensed, leaning back in the booth.

Tetia sipped her wine and said, "I talked to James earlier, and we both agree the show's much better with you. We'd love it if you'd be co-host for the whole series."

Sadie's jaw dropped open. She looked at me, her eyes wide,

and for a moment I thought she might actually climb out of the booth and bolt. I mustered up a hint of a smile, hoping to put her at ease. Meanwhile, my heart felt like it would beat right out of my ribcage.

She shook her head for a moment, like she didn't understand, and I felt sick. If she said no, it would be the end of everything—the show, and me and Sadie. And right now, Sadie didn't look happy. In fact, her face looked a lot like it did when she'd first crashed into me in the foyer on the day I'd checked in.

I finished my bourbon, steeling myself for the inevitable. It felt like another miracle had happened—when Tetia had sent more test film to the execs, they'd fallen for Sadie, too. They agreed to offer her the job, but the sinking feeling in my gut told me she'd turn it down. Because of me.

And then we were back to Clarissa. Or maybe no show at all.

Sadie studied her wine glass, then turned back to Tetia. "Honestly, I need a minute. I thought you brought me here to fire me."

Tetia laughed, reaching for the mushrooms. "Not hardly. I want you in every episode."

Sadie's eyes flicked back to mine, and I tried my hardest to freeze the muscles in my face and hold back every thought except this one: *Just say yes.*

Chapter Eighteen

SADIE

I STARED AT TETIA, not believing my ears. Next to me, James sat perfectly still. It was unsettling how he stayed so quiet, like he could hang out on the sidelines through this conversation that was changing everything. He had to have had a say in this. He was the *talent*. And yet, he didn't seem threatened or perturbed. Or surprised, even. He was as Mr. Cool-as-Ice.

There had to be some storm of emotions rolling around in that head of his, but his expression revealed nothing. He was a better actor than I'd given him credit for.

Meanwhile, I felt like I was back inside the snow globe, my whole world being shaken around me, leaving everything a blur. How could this offer be real?

"Seriously?" I said. "The whole series?"

"Yes," Tetia said, smiling. "I've already talked to the producers, and we've got an offer drafted." She pulled a stack of papers from the satchel next to her and then slid them toward me. As I leafed through the contract, she explained how many shows they'd shoot, how long it was expected to take, and soon there were so many numbers and dates swirling in my head that I could barely keep up.

But the gist was: they wanted me.

And man, it felt good to be wanted.

Our server came back with our food, and Tetia paused to thank her. When she'd flitted away again, Tetia said, "What do you think, Sadie?"

This is amazing. This is terrifying. This is so not what I expected.

"Honestly, I'm shocked," I said. "I don't know what to say."

Tetia said, "Honestly, me too." She pointed her fork at me and said, "I thought James was crazy when he first suggested we put you in the episode, but here we are." She winked at James, and he smiled. "You're like a dang unicorn, Sadie, not to put too fine a point on it."

Never had I been called a unicorn. I felt my cheeks turning hot.

"Every now and then I have a good idea," James said, his tone light.

"Now he decides to be modest," Tetia said. She turned to him and arched a brow. "You've been around long enough to spot talent, Fielding. I never should have doubted you, even though you can be a massive pain in my ass."

"Your job would be so boring without me," he said with a smirk, and she rolled her eyes as if to say she wouldn't have it any other way.

It took a moment for all of that to sink in. James had pushed to have me in the episode, from the get-go? When I turned to him, he gave me a small shrug.

"So, as you know, tomorrow's our last full day here," Tetia said. "We're on the next location starting Monday, and then we're traveling for the next ten weeks. The tentative schedule's on the back page there. I know it's short notice, so we might be able to push things by a couple days if need be."

I flipped to the back page, still feeling like this was a dream. It was tempting of course—I mean, who doesn't want to be on TV?—but it also meant traveling all over the region with James. Seeing him every day, shooting with him for long hours, being with him nonstop and generating a constant stream of that friendly, flirty banter that was, as Tetia said, TV gold. I didn't know how I could spend that much time with him, feeling the way that I did—because despite my greatest effort, I liked James a lot more than I ever thought I would. In this last week, he'd shattered all of my thoughts about him—the old rival I'd known from school had turned into this charming guy who not only set me on fire, but also made me think that maybe I'd been too hard on myself for all these years. Maybe I should have tried more, failed more. Lived more.

I was drawn to him in a way that was confusing, and thrilling, and scary. Even though he'd drawn a line between us last night, I couldn't just flip a switch and not be attracted to him anymore. And working with him, knowing that he didn't want me the way I wanted him—that felt like too much for me to handle. Even if it was for a job that paid more than any I'd ever made.

James made it all seem so easy—like you could do whatever you wanted with your life. He made it seem like all you needed was a little faith in yourself, and the courage to take a leap now and then. And just once, I wanted to feel that sense of ease. James Fielding wasn't afraid of much, but he had fears and weaknesses just like I did—and being around him gave me the courage to step out of my comfort zone, too. If you'd told me five years ago that I'd be shooting a TV show with him, I'd have told you to go home and sleep off that crazy fever dream.

James had surprised me. And he'd made me surprise myself. I'd taken a risk this week, but it was more than that—I'd taken all the things I thought about my strengths and turned them on their head. Before this week, I'd thought the park service was my best option—the safe bet, the surest path to feeling like I had a job that was meaningful. I'd thought that if I just pushed myself to work harder, things would work out the way I wanted.

Now I wasn't so sure about that. Now I felt like maybe I'd boxed myself in one time too many. Staying with the park might be the safe bet, but was it the one that was best for my future? What if doing this show was my way of working smarter?

What Tetia (or rather, her producers) wanted to pay me was more money than I'd ever make with the park service. It was real money—money that would mean paying off my credit cards and opening a savings account. And what if this show led to something even better? All this time, I'd thought of James as being lucky. But the more likely explanation for his success was that he'd made his own luck—through moments like this. By being unafraid to take leaps that felt utterly terrifying.

My heart pounded in my ears. I took a sip of wine to calm myself and noticed my hand shaking.

"So what do you think?" Tetia asked. "You in?"

James looked at me expectantly, his head cocked to the side. I really wanted to know what he was thinking right now. Did he regret suggesting I do the first episode? Was he worried about working long hours together? Was he wishing he'd never set foot in this town?

Or was he hoping I'd say yes?

Just sitting next to him was making my heart pound harder in my chest. The warmth radiating off his skin, his faint woodsy scent, the way he fixed me with his smoldering gaze— it was all too much. Could I really keep working with him every day and not completely lose my mind? Working together would make him completely off-limits—there could be no more kissing in cars. But if I said no, would I ever see him again?

Neither of those options were super appealing.

"I'm so flattered," I said. "This is an amazing offer."

Tetia's perfectly penciled brow arched. "But?"

"Can I take some time to think about it?" I said.

"Of course," she said. "Take that home with you, and let me know if you have any questions. I'd need an answer by Sunday, though, since we're scheduled to shoot in Greenville next week."

"Absolutely," I said. "I just need to think on it."

She nodded. "Understood. But Sadie, this is the kind of chance that doesn't come around more than once." She sipped her wine and leveled her big brown eyes on me. "I think we have a good thing going here, and I'd love to see what else you can do. I know all of this has happened fast for you, but to us, this is a no-brainer. I know a great partnership when I see it. I just hope you're as interested as we are."

I nodded, feeling my heart swell. All week, I'd felt like I'd been fumbling my way through each day. To hear that Tetia saw something special in me was like a balm for the last few months, the last few years—and all those missteps I'd beat myself up over. She made me think that I could be my best self without being perfect.

But then that voice deep inside whispered, *what if the show's a flop*? I'd be a laughingstock, and it would be like the whole viral elk chase all over again. Only worse.

My failures would be made public. Forever. No matter how supportive Tetia was, I still couldn't control how the show would be received and how people would react to me. If anyone could teach me to let go of that fear, it was this crew. And I knew

Tetia was right—this wasn't the kind of opportunity that came around often.

For the rest of the meal, Tetia and James tossed around ideas for the remaining shooting schedule, and how they might extend into another season if the show did well. At last, the check came and Tetia reached for it.

"This one's on me," she said. "I'm going to head back, but you two should stay and finish that bottle. James, maybe you can answer any other questions Sadie has from the talent perspective. I'm sure a casual conversation between colleagues could be helpful." She gave him a warm smile and then eased out of the booth.

Casual colleagues. Is that what we'd be? Is that what I wanted? Something in my gut churned at the thought of tamping all these feelings down and trying to pretend we were friends and co-workers. Could I keep up *casual* with James, or would every day feel like the roller coaster that today had been?

I stood and shook her hand. "Thank you so much, Tetia," I said. "Really. I can't even say what this offer means to me."

"Of course," she said, slipping on her jacket. "I'll see you bright and early."

When she was gone, I sat back down in her place, across the table from James. He sat quietly, studying me. After a long moment, I said, "What now?" It was a genuine question, because where did we go from here?

He sipped his wine, his eyes fixed on me. "I thought you'd say yes."

"Did you want me to?"

"It doesn't matter what I want," he said, his voice friendly.

I leaned back in the booth. "This just got very complicated."

"Because of me, you mean." His eyebrows pulled together in that sad arch again, and it just about unraveled me.

Really though, it got complicated the moment I realized I felt something for him that wasn't low-level disdain. The job offer just added another level of complexity. I refilled our wine glasses, emptying the bottle. "You really think it's a good idea for me to be your co-host? For us to keep working together, traveling together, being stuck with each other all day every day."

"Yes." He didn't hesitate.

"Why is that?" I said, feeling that annoying flutter in my chest.

"Because Tetia's right. You've got this spark that's hard to find. You're good at this, and I think it'd be a shame not to see where it takes you. Working with a team like Tetia's would only help you get better." He leaned closer, his eyes wide in the dim light. "And for the completely selfish reason that I like spending time with you."

I swallowed hard, feeling the heat of his gaze all the way down to my toes. He could melt glaciers with that stare. "I have a job offer at the park," I said. "That's where I was this afternoon."

His jaw tensed. "You got your old job back?"

"No. It's a temp position in a different department."

"You don't sound thrilled about it," he mused.

I shrugged. "My friend there thinks it could lead to something bigger. Another position in education, like what I had." Problem was, I'd heard that about a thousand times before. A couple of hours earlier, Cheryl had gone over the position with me, and it had sounded dull as dishwater. Cons? I'd be in the musty basement of headquarters most of the time, and it wouldn't last longer than four months. Another position might open up, but it might not. Leah had heard rumors about a job she thought I'd be great for, and one that wasn't under

District Ranger Mike's oversight. Funding was a fickle thing, though, and all park service jobs were vulnerable to cuts. There were few guarantees. Whatever Leah heard today might be meaningless in a month.

The pros? I'd be back to a steady paycheck and not have to live in the carriage house. I wouldn't feel like I was leaning on my parents, and I'd get more service in with the park. With four more months of accrued time, I'd be eligible for permanent positions—in this park and in others. That had been my goal: to land a permanent position that wasn't so vulnerable to budget cuts and didn't require applications each year. Once you were in, you were in.

"What if this series led you to something bigger?" James said.

"TV isn't my expertise," I said. "How far do you really think I'll go? I'm like a stand-in here. I'm a nobody."

He sipped his wine. "You don't give yourself enough credit, Harper."

I sighed. "I don't expect you to understand. You're like this perfect, charming, superstar. You seem impervious to failure."

He laughed. "Mercy, Harper. You really have no idea."

"I'm not like you," I said, but even as the words came out, I knew they were only partly true. As much as James Fielding drove me nuts with his perfectionism and his competitive streak, I knew I had those things, too. The difference was that he didn't seem to have any doubt that he'd succeed. "I can't just leap without knowing there's a net below," I muttered.

He stared at me hard. "Come on," he said. "Truth time. Do you like doing the show?"

Leaning back in the booth, I crossed my arms over my chest. "Yeah. Surprisingly, I do."

"Is it more fun that filing paperwork in a basement?"

I snorted. "Obviously."

He leaned forward, elbows on the table, and stared at me like I was a puzzle he was determined to find the missing piece to. "What are you so afraid of?" he said, his voice gravelly. "This is not about a safety net."

Being humiliated on a worldwide streaming service. Failing at something else I actually liked. Falling harder for James Fielding and getting my heart crushed into pulp. All of these seemed equally likely. And all of them were a blow I didn't think I could withstand.

"Is it me?" he said. "Am I the reason you'd rather lock yourself in a basement than host a travel show?"

Every time we were in the same room together, I couldn't stop thinking about the way his lips had moved against my throat, the way his hands had slipped over my hips. If I had to keep spending eight to ten hours a day with him, I'd most certainly combust. So one hundred percent, yes.

"No," I said with a snort.

He stared at me for what felt like an eternity, those warm brown eyes seeing straight through to the hidden corners of my heart. No one on this earth made me feel as vulnerable as James Fielding. That made him way more dangerous than I could handle right now.

But he also managed to see me—like, really see me—in a way that others didn't.

"You're wrong, you know," he said at last.

"About what?"

"I've had massive failures." He sipped his wine, then looked up at me through his dark lashes. "The kind I didn't think I could come back from."

"You mean like your last pilot?" I asked quietly.

He raked his hands through his hair. "That was a big one."

"I overheard you and Tetia talking about it."

His lip lifted in a tiny smile. "See? I'm not so impervious."

"Yet here you are."

"I'm stubborn that way." His mischievous smile was back.

I stared at him, fidgeting with the wine glass.

"Tell me what you're afraid of," he said, his voice low.

The room was quiet now, the dinner rush over. We were so far in the back that we were practically alone in the place. Just two people in a corner, holding onto their secrets like they were life rafts.

"You first," I said. "Tell me about your biggest failure." Deep down I knew that everyone had failures, but part of me was just dying to know what James considered to be his most epic crash and burn. Was it wrong to be so enthralled with that idea? Yes, probably. But still, I was curious. James seemed to have everything together, living the kind of life I'd barely let myself dream of. What could he possibly be ashamed of?

"Do you *never* use the internet?" James said. "It's been pretty good at tracking all of my failures."

"I'm probably the last person on earth who doesn't read celebrity news on the internet. And besides, I'd rather hear it from you."

"That's oddly sweet," he said. "And a little unnerving."

I shrugged. "I like to get my information straight from the source."

He glanced at his empty wine glass and then shifted his gaze back to me. "You'd have to get me good and drunk to hear that story."

"Then get your jacket," I said. "This place is too nice for that, and we have to show our faces here tomorrow."

Chapter Nineteen

For real drinks, we had to go back to the Wonky Donkey. Even though it had old musty furniture and sticky tile floors, it was still my favorite place in town. The Spare Time was where you celebrated—the Donkey was that familiar place where you went to lick your wounds. Or sometimes, open them up.

Tonight, it was mostly empty. Thursdays were usually quiet there, especially during the off-season. The regulars sat at the bar, talking the ears off whoever had the misfortune of pouring drinks that night, and a few locals gathered at the tables that faced the TVs turned to whatever sport was airing. In the back, we could shoot pool and pop quarters in the old jukebox and never have to speak to another soul.

Once James got our drinks at the bar—neat bourbon for him, gin and tonic for me—he challenged me to a game of pool.

"Come on," he said, "I haven't played in years."

"Neither have I."

"Then we'll be evenly matched." He smirked as he racked the balls, rolling them along the felt of the table, getting them positioned just right. In the past week I'd noticed that James needed something to do with his hands during certain kinds of conversations—he couldn't just simply *be*. It was like the flurry of feelings was too much for his body to handle.

Sometimes I felt that way, too. Especially in moments like this, when something unspoken hung so heavy between us.

I chalked up a cue and then scattered the balls across the table with a lopsided break. "This week feels surreal," I said. "Everything's happening so fast."

"You get used to it," he said, as if I was only talking about filming.

"I need to ask you a question." There were plenty of questions I wanted to ask James Fielding. Like why, after seven years, he'd really wanted to see me again. Or why he really wanted me to keep doing this show with him. Or why he'd really broken our kiss last night in his car.

"I'm all yours." His eyes met mine as he chalked the cue and the butterflies came back like a hurricane.

I swallowed hard and went for the easy question.

"Would it be weird for you? Being co-hosts?"

"No," he said, without a whiff of hesitation. He leaned down, bracing his left hand on the table. When he lined up his shot, his gaze flicked back to me as he struck the cue ball in one fluid motion that sent the five-ball sliding easily into the corner pocket. "There's no one else I'd rather do this show with."

My heart squeezed like a fist. He wouldn't lie about something that put his career on the line—he really thought I was good at this gig. I sipped my drink, hoping the gin might help my aim, because dang if my eyes weren't tearing up a little. "Are you only saying that because Tetia asked you to?"

He smiled. "No, Harper. I mean it." He lined up his next shot, a much harder one, and missed.

As I chose my next target, he leaned against the opposite side of the table. "My turn," he said. "Why are you afraid to do this show with me?"

"I'm not," I said. "And I thought you were going to tell me about a failure."

There was that smirk again. The one that somehow managed to make him both annoying and irresistible at the same time. "Harper, you're like a bunny zigzagging across a field. Every time I ask you about the show, you deflect. What's the story?"

"I'm not a bunny." I aimed for the twelve-ball and missed. "I just don't want to waste my time on something that doesn't matter in the long run."

"Ouch," he said. "That's my profession you're stomping all over."

I sighed, wishing I could articulate these things better. "That's not what I meant, Fielding. I mean that for me, being a sidekick on a TV show doesn't seem to align with the purpose I had in mind for my life. For you, being a host aligns perfectly. To be fair, you're very good at what you do."

"That sounded like a genuine compliment."

"It did, didn't it?"

His lip quirked. "But you think this work won't make you happy with yourself."

"I think this feels like a distraction. It's not about fear." I paused. "Okay, it's a little bit about fear. TV's not the career I imagined for myself. I'm afraid I won't be as good at it as everyone thinks, and it'll just be time wasted."

He leaned against the table, looking thoughtful. "That's fair." He aimed for the three and knocked it into the side pocket, then frowned as the cue ball dropped in behind it. "I just don't want you to turn this down because of what happened last night."

I stared at him, looking for any crack in his facade. He was back to being cool, confident James—the version of himself that seemed infallible. Like a reflex, I thought of how he'd pulled me tight against him, how I'd felt his heart hammering in his chest. I felt like I'd belonged there, squeezed against him, and there was no other place I wanted to be. But I tamped those feelings way down because that was one hundred percent not what I needed to think about right now. Not his soft lips, his sturdy hands, his piercing gaze that made my insides melt into a puddle.

And I definitely shouldn't think about those parts of him if we were working together on the show.

I snorted, aiming for my next ball. "Wow. Not everything is about you, Fielding."

When the solid-colored ball sank in the corner pocket, he said, "That was mine."

I frowned, realizing my mistake as he lined up his next shot. He'd already knocked me off-kilter. Again. This was precisely why working together would be so difficult—because I always felt like being around him was like balancing on a knife blade. I couldn't help being drawn to him, no matter how much I knew that I shouldn't. It was exhausting, and letting him get too close to me would surely lead to hurt.

"This other job with the park," he said. "Is it your dream job?"

"Ugh. No." The thought of being in the basement of headquarters had not gotten any more appealing after talking to Cheryl today. "But the one I had before, doing programs like you saw, was great."

"Did you love it?" he said.

"I was good at it." At least that's what I kept telling myself. Based on the way they'd so easily let me go, though—I might have been wrong about that.

"You were fantastic." He leaned back against the table, giving me all of his attention. "But that's not what I asked you."

My heart swelled, thinking of him coming to the park that day, watching me talk about alligators and wetlands when he could have done any number of things instead. "I liked it well enough," I said. "There were good days and hard days, just like any job. I think I loved that it felt meaningful."

He sighed, leaning on the table again. "Do you really want to keep doing something that's just okay? Wouldn't you rather spend your time doing something that you love?"

"Because you think I'd love doing a travel show?"

He shrugged. "Who knows? That's the whole point. If what you're doing now isn't working for you, why not try something else? You might surprise yourself."

"Maybe I'm tired of trying and failing. Maybe I'd just like to have a low baseline for job satisfaction. Shoot for average and stop searching for a dream job that doesn't exist." And maybe not have to deal with the fallout that might happen if I did find a dream job and it didn't work out. "When I think of all the pain that comes from failing when I aim high, aiming for average sounds pretty great."

He leveled his eyes on mine, and there was that weird fluttering in my chest again. "There's nothing average about you, Harper. And you know it."

Heat rose to my cheeks as those words sank in. *Nothing average.*

He leaned closer and said, "Why are you settling?"

"Why do you care?"

"Because I get the feeling that average would bore you to tears. And you deserve so much more than that."

It was infuriating, the way he seemed to see straight into my heart. "Aren't you ever afraid of anything, Fielding? Like, so afraid that you can't breathe?"

He was quiet for a moment, his jaw tensing like I'd hit a nerve. Then he looked me dead in the eye and said calmly, "All the time."

Leaning over the table, he lined up his next shot. His forearm flexed as he sent the cue ball bouncing over a striped ball to sink his next solid into the corner. He made it look so easy I had the feeling he could have ended this game ten minutes ago if he'd wanted.

"You asked what my biggest failure was," he said, looking up at me through those thick lashes. "If you were a person who reads internet gossip, you'd know that my series pilot was an utter disaster."

"You mentioned that."

"And you'd know that before the doomed pilot, I'd done pretty well for myself as a guest co-host on a bunch of different travel shows. Really made a name for myself."

"I'm not seeing how that's a failure."

"The reason I started guest hosting was because my print career was over," he said. "And my print career was over because of what happened between me and Melanie."

"Your ex." I swallowed hard, remembering what Ashley had told me on the very first day of shooting. I'd nearly pieced it all together, and none of the pieces were good.

"You know what you should never do? Get involved with your editor. I've always been a little too efficient at certain things." He gave me a sad smile. "Destroying my writing career and my relationship at the same time might be my most efficient failure to date."

"I'm sorry, James."

"We were engaged when she was cheating on me," he said, his eyes dark. "So how's that for failure? She wanted me to take her back, but when I refused, she made it her mission to make sure no editor would ever work with me again." He sighed, as if it still hurt to think about. "She told me I brought it on myself. That I was a workaholic, obsessed with my job, and cared more about my career than I cared about her. Her exact words were that she'd realized I was the kind of person you have fun with, but not the kind you build a life with."

I felt my heart sinking to the floor.

"So she found someone who didn't work such long hours," he said. "All of that happened right before the pilot. So I was, shall we say, not at my best during filming."

"That's horrible," I said. "But you know it's not your fault, right? It's not your fault she cheated."

He shrugged, as if he didn't believe that for a second. "We weren't good for each other. I confused love with being needed." His eyes looked sad. "But for the record, my biggest fear is that she was right. That I'm not a good partner and never will be." After a pause, he said, "It's your shot."

My heart broke for him. "You can't carry that burden. Those decisions, those actions—that was all on her."

His lip lifted with a hint of a smile. "Why do you care, Harper?"

"Because it's not fair to you."

"Is that all?" He sipped his drink, his eyes burning into mine.

"You're a good person, Fielding. You don't deserve to beat yourself up over something you couldn't control."

"That might be the nicest thing you ever said to me," he said.

I tried to focus on the angle of my next shot, the chalk marks on the table, the way the light above us hummed—anything that wasn't James's piercing eyes and full lips. The jukebox had switched to something slow and bluesy, and the gin had made me less anxious and more bold, and part of me wondered if these were the last few hours we might spend together.

I wasn't entirely sure how I felt about that. My chest was still full of butterflies and I still couldn't decide what I wanted most: to jump into his arms or to walk away and never look back.

When I had two balls left on the table, James took aim at his last solid, nestled against the eight-ball. The cue ball struck them both and sent the first ball just shy of the pocket. The eight dropped into the corner pocket and he gave me a shrug. "Game over," he said, his eyes burning into mine. "You got me."

Something about the way he said those words made my heart bang against my ribs.

"Tell me why you want me to do this show so badly," I said. "The real reason."

He leaned against the table next to me, his hand nearly touching mine. "Because we make a good team, Harper. We're a perfect fit, and there's no one else I want to do it with."

"Is that the only reason?" I said, leaning closer.

His gaze dropped to my lips. "It's the relevant one."

I took a deep breath, willing myself to ask the one question that hung so heavy between us. "How do you feel about me?"

His brow furrowed. "How I feel shouldn't affect whether you take this job."

"Quit being squirrelly," I said, tapping him on the chest. "If we're going to work together, I need you to talk to me. Tell me how you feel. Why'd you push me away last night?"

"Harper." He placed his hand over mine. "I wasn't trying to push you away. You surprised me, and I said something stupid, because frankly you have that effect on me." He looked like he wanted to say more, but something was holding him back. He inched closer to me, so close that I could smell that woodsy scent again and see the flecks of amber in his eyes. "I do want to keep spending time with you," he whispered. "I'll do that however you'll let me."

His hip touched mine and I was on fire.

I closed the space between us, and put my hand on his chest. "Why is that?"

His thumb traced a line along my jaw as he leaned closer. "No one else ever came close to you, Harper. I lose myself when I'm around you. In the best way." His lips brushed against my ear and his voice turned gravelly as he said, "I shouldn't have backed away last night. But I won't make that mistake again."

My heart hammered in my chest. Were we really going to do this? It had been so long since anyone had made me feel wanted in this way, but I knew the consequences of getting too close might mean hurting each other in the end.

But what if it didn't?

"I don't think you want me to back off, Harper. I know this is scary. It is for me, too." His voice was deep and smooth, humming along my skin. When he pulled back to look at me, his gaze was full of hunger. "But the most terrifying thing of all is feeling like I might never get this chance with you again. And never is such a long damn time."

That little voice in my head squeaked with a warning, but I couldn't hear it over the hammering of my heart. I knew we were about to cross a line, but another little voice whispered, *Would that really be so bad? Isn't this what you wanted all along?*

I grabbed his shirt and pulled him against me. He grunted in surprise as his hands landed on the edge of the table, on either side of my hips, caging me in. His sexy half-smile was back, and I was dying to feel his hands on me. My gaze dropped to his lips, daring him, and that was all the invitation he needed. He kissed me, gently at first, and then there was the pinch of his teeth, the scrape of his stubbled jaw, and then the weight of his body pinning me against the table. He slid one hand along my neck and the other around my waist, and I could have stayed like that for days.

When I caught his bottom lip in my teeth, he grinned and pulled away. His eyes were blazing as he mumbled, "I meant what I said, Harper. I'm not interested in a fling." He slid his fingers along my cheek. "You're it for me, and I'll prove it to you if you let me."

My breath caught in my throat. "This could make working together tricky."

"Or better than we can imagine," he whispered. "But if you tell me to wait ten weeks until we finish shooting, I'll do it. Whatever you say."

In that moment, I didn't care how being together might make working together harder. I didn't even care that we were in a dark part of a bar where we were somewhat hidden but not quite alone. Could someone see us? Sure. Did I care? Nope. There was a solid chance he'd break my heart into pieces when all of this was over. But in this moment, he felt electrifying. All that hurt that might come in the end? Right now, it felt like it'd be worth it.

"What do you think, Harper?" he said. "Take a chance on us?" His stubbled cheek tickled my neck as his lips moved to my jaw, finding that spot that made my toes curl. I didn't know if he was asking me to take a chance on us or the show, and in that moment, they were the same. His hands tightened on my waist and I raked a hand through his hair.

Then I opened my eyes, and I nearly choked.

"James," I said, tugging his hair. When I pulled away from him, he froze, his eyes resting on mine.

"What's wrong?" he said, his voice raspy.

"Ashley and Ravi just walked in." With beers in hand, they had just walked into this back part of the room, as if looking for a table.

His eyes widened as he quickly stepped away from me, casually reaching for the cue stick as if he hadn't just lit every cell in my body on fire.

Ashley noticed me and waved, and I waved back, sipping my drink and hoping they couldn't see the way my cheeks burned. My legs felt like noodles, and I was certain the table was the only thing holding me up right now. James gave me a wicked smirk that made me tingle all over and then turned to face them.

As they crossed the room to join us, James said, "Hey, guys. What a surprise."

Ashley and Ravi exchanged a look that I couldn't quite decipher and Ravi said, "What are y'all doing here?"

"Proving she can still wipe the table with me," James said, his voice cool and even. "You two up for a game?"

"Ugh, I suck at pool," Ravi said. "Darts, though. That's another story."

"There's a board back there," James said, nodding his head toward the back wall.

"Cool," Ashley said, her gaze flicking from me to James.

As she and Ravi headed for the dart boards, James grabbed his jacket and said, "Do you think they saw us?"

"I have no idea. Are you worried?" Despite the rules that James and I might lay down for ourselves, I didn't want Ashley and Ravi to think I was getting this job because of whatever was happening between us. That thought hit me like a sucker punch. I'd either be the nobody, riding on his coattails, or I'd be the woman who got the job because she was dating the star. And I'd been around long enough to know that it could take a lifetime to shake that stigma.

James arched a brow and we headed toward the back wall, leaving plenty of room for Jesus between us. Part of me wondered if Ashley and Ravi had just saved us from making a big mistake, and another part was afraid we might never have a chance like that again.

Chapter Twenty

JAMES

Sadie was impossible to read.

She hadn't uttered a single word about what happened last night at the bar. Not through breakfast, not on the drive over to the Spare Time this morning, and not in any of the short breaks we had while filming the final segment with Chef Max.

Not that I really expected her to lay herself bare while Max Eckhart was showing us how to marinate beef tenderloins, but still. I'd expected her to have something to say about that kiss. I'd gone to bed thinking about it, woken up three times reliving some version of it in dreams that ranged from sweet to exceptionally naughty, and still had it replaying in my mind like a song on repeat. No matter how hard I tried to concentrate on Max's cooking lessons this morning, Sadie's scorching kiss was all I could think about.

Sadie had a deep furrow in her brow, as if she was also preoccupied with something weightier than locally-sourced beef.

Currently, Max was standing between us, like a big muscular wall of culinary genius. This didn't stop me from stealing glances at Sadie and trying to read her expression and determine what precisely she was thinking about me, but it did stop me from smelling the spicy scent of her perfume and accidentally brushing against her as we worked.

Probably, it was safer that way.

Last night, as I'd walked Sadie back to the inn, it was all I could do to keep my hands off her. Like a reflex, my palm kept drifting toward the small of her back, and I even caught myself reaching for her hand when we crossed the street. She'd kept her distance, though, as if that moment in the bar hadn't happened at all.

When we'd made it to the carriage house, she'd said, "James, I need to be honest. I don't know what I'm feeling right now, and I need to take a beat."

It wasn't what I wanted to hear, but I understood. As eager as I was to know how she felt about everything that was happening between us, I wouldn't force her to tell me. First, I'd pushed her away when she'd climbed into my lap, and now I was pawing at her on a pool table. I was not behaving like a man who wanted to date her for real—I was behaving like a guy who wanted to take her up on her offer of a fling. And now there was the complication of working together, and good grief—she probably thought I was coming on to her just to get her to agree to do the show. I'd put her in an impossible situation.

Could I be a bigger idiot?

We needed to clear this up, ASAP. I didn't have time for tenderloin and farm fresh vegetables. I needed to get Sadie alone and sort this out so that I could get on with loving her for the rest of my life. The only thing stopping me from doing that was Max, who towered over us like a Viking.

And Tetia, of course. And the contract for this episode.

Patience was never my strong suit.

"How are those carrots coming, James?" Max smiled at me and nodded in Sadie's direction. "And how about the onions?"

"Great," she said, blinking back tears.

Max grinned. "Yellow onions are good for soul-cleansing."

His shoulder-length blond hair was pulled back into a ponytail, and the sleeves of his chef's jacket were rolled to the elbows, exposing intricate black and gray tattoos on his forearms.

He moved around his kitchen like a machine, his movements quick and precise. "You two ready for this?" he said, his green eyes twinkling. "This is an easy dish that anyone at home can replicate."

Sadie and I had both tied on aprons to assist, but seeing as how boiling pasta properly was a stretch for me, I had my doubts that I could produce anything in a kitchen without catching something on fire—especially since being in the room with Sadie made me feel like I might combust at any moment. Whatever fantasy I'd had about leaving this place and forgetting her had gone right out the window after I'd pressed her up against that pool table and felt her lips against mine.

I really hoped she was willing to give us a chance, because I would never get over her after this week.

"Today's dish is simple and rustic," Max said. "Every couple of days our menu changes based on what's fresh at the local farmer's markets. Today we're doing beef tenderloin with roasted veggies. And we'll end with derby pie."

I pretended to be captivated as Max told us all about how he'd acquired the bowling alley. While he seasoned the beef filets, I tried desperately to remember the questions I was supposed to ask him and stop thinking about how Sadie had pulled me against her, those stormy eyes of hers full of want.

"Why a bowling alley?" Sadie asked. She'd probably heard

this story a dozen times, but she pretended like it was her first time hearing it, looking utterly enchanted while Max told us the story of how he'd bought what was once the town's beloved hangout and breathed new life into it.

Max was one of those strong quiet types who needed to be prodded into conversation, but once he got rolling, he was full of interesting details. Even though we'd given him interview questions ahead of time, his first answers were brief. Sadie, though, was great at asking him "Why?" each time he gave us an abbreviated answer, and nudging him toward those anecdotes that viewers tuned in to see. Pretty soon, she had him talking about his love of bowling while he seared the tenderloins, and that's how we learned that he'd been on a competitive bowling team in college called The Mis-splits.

"This place was a no-brainer," he said with a grin. "Now I get to combine all the things I love. And have retro '80s bowling nights."

"A man after my own heart," Sadie said. That line was in the script, but it still burned me more than it should have.

"James, why don't you toss those veggies in some olive oil," Max said. "Give 'em some love."

Sadie poured the oil into the big bowl of carrots, parsnips, and onions that we'd chopped. As I tossed them with my hands, she sprinkled on the herbs that Max had set aside in tiny dishes.

Following Max's instructions, Sadie took the bowl from me and emptied the veggies into a roasting pan while I wiped my hands off on a towel. As Max told us about the local farms around here, I fantasized about cooking with Sadie every day.

"It took a while for people to get used to the unpredictable menu," he said. "But now I think people see the value in using everything fresh and in season whenever possible, and in supporting the local farms. We try hard to let nothing go to waste." He eyed the filets, then put them onto a plate. "Okay, Sadie. Time to deglaze with the wine."

Max showed her how to deglaze the pan, then how to add in a few more ingredients and whisk it into a sauce that smelled heavenly. While she whisked, he pulled our finished tray of vegetables from the oven. "Usually twenty minutes does it, but these are done when they reach your desired tenderness," he said. He poked a carrot with a fork and then held it to Sadie's lips.

That move was not in the script. I knew it was just for the benefit of good TV, and probably they were friends because Sadie seemed to know everyone in this town. But that didn't stop my hand from squeezing the spoon I was holding so hard that my knuckles turned white.

It was ridiculous to feel so possessive of her, but I couldn't help it. I'd never felt this way about anyone. Ever.

"Perfect," she said. A tiny smile touched her lips, and suddenly I wanted to learn to cook real meals, just for her—just so I could see her make that contented face for me every single day.

"Cooking is adventure for me," Max said. "I used to think I'd never have my own restaurant because the odds felt stacked against me. All my life, I'd heard that ninety-nine percent of restaurants fail. I figured there was no way I was good enough to be in the one percent that made it."

"But here you are," Sadie said. "Beating the odds big-time."

He smiled. "I had an amazing mentor named Denise. She taught me to keep doing what I loved, and not let fear drive my decisions. She taught me to give myself time and patience—and also grace when I stumbled and failed." He stepped away for a moment and nodded toward the door to the kitchen where what looked like a torn piece of paper was held in a frame.

"I'll never forget when Denise told me that," he said. "I'd gotten a horrible review, and I was terrified that my career would be over. She was teaching me her favorite Alfredo dish, one with these rare truffles she loved." He tapped the frame and said, "She handed me this box of fettuccine and told me to read the instructions. I was puzzled, because anyone can boil pasta, but she said, *Just read it, Max.*"

Sadie looked into the frame, which I now noted was a portion of a pasta box with a large heart drawn over some of the words with a fat red marker.

"Cook to desired tenderness," Sadie read.

Max nodded. "Bring an outrageous amount of water to a boil, and that's your only instruction." He tapped the glass and went on. "She said, 'We're all just trying to find our desired level of tenderness, Max. How tender, how vulnerable, do we need to make ourselves to get what we want the most?'" He gave Sadie a soft smile and a shrug. "I thought vulnerability was a weakness until I met her. But now I know better."

"Desired tenderness," Sadie said. "I like that."

I glanced over at Tetia and Ashley, because that exchange hadn't been scripted either. Tetia had her hand over her chest and Ashley brushed a tear from her eye and I felt like the wind had been knocked out of me. Sadie really was a dang unicorn. She'd managed to pull that out of Max with less than a dozen words, and lord knows nothing raised ratings like a big cinnamon roll of a guy laying his heart out on a table in front of a beautiful woman.

The only thing that landed better ratings was a handsome dude handing out roses while wearing a tux.

Sadie's brows arched in this sad, sympathetic way and I thought for sure my heart would explode. I didn't want this to be our last day of shooting, and I didn't want this to be the last time I saw her.

She couldn't deny she was having fun with the show, and I couldn't understand how she didn't see how amazing she was at this job. I'd had to struggle to fit into this host persona, but for her, it came naturally. She just instinctively connected with people and found common ground, and encouraged them to open up and share these pieces of themselves that struck a chord in you that you didn't even think was possible.

If anything, I'd be *her* sidekick in this series. And I was perfectly fine with that. I might have the learned skills, but she had something you couldn't create with even the best script on the best day. She was charisma, and hope, and wonder all rolled into a package that was network gold. Sadie Harper needed to shine.

"So for those of us who struggle in the kitchen," I said, "what's your best advice, Max?"

"Time and patience," he said. "Anybody can cook if you have that. And a decent knife, of course. Good tools are essential." He poured the sauce over the filets and added in a serving of vegetables. When he sliced into the beef, he said, "You want to let your filets rest a few minutes to let all the loveliness happen inside before you cut into them. And then when you do, it's magic."

Time and patience. Two things I was running out of.

TETIA BELIEVED in celebrating our hard work. Tonight, that meant dinner at the Spare Time and bowling a few games. Max had insisted on hosting us and cooking those tenderloins for real—

and bringing us a bottle of Champagne to celebrate the end of our whirlwind week of shooting.

This day had been excruciating. Ever since breakfast, I'd felt like the clock was running down at the end of a basketball game and I was perched in the stands, hoping for a three-pointer and knowing that buzzer would sound any second. Sadie and I hadn't had a minute alone together, and she still hadn't said whether she was going to accept the position. In fact, she'd barely spoken to me at all when we weren't on camera.

When Sadie left the table for a moment, I turned to Tetia and said, "Has she told you anything yet?"

Tetia arched a brow. "No. You need to steel yourself for Plan B."

"You know I don't like that option."

Tetia leveled her eyes on mine. "Even if it's the only way this show gets made?"

I bit my lip. "Surely there's a Plan C."

"Not with our budget and timeframe." Her expression said she didn't like our alternative much, either. She nodded toward Sadie and said, "If anyone can sway her, it's you."

I chewed my lip as Sadie came back to her seat across from us. Tetia gave me a slight nod that meant it was time for me to go all-in and said, "Guys, I'm beat. I'm going to head back early and crash."

"We're never going to get you to bowl, are we?" Ashley said.

Tetia grinned and she stood up from the table. "One day you'll catch me in a weak moment."

"Good night," Ravi said, waving. "Thanks for dinner."

"Thanks for being the most awesome crew," Tetia said. As she headed for the door, I thought maybe Ashley and Ravi might read the room and leave Sadie and me alone. But then Ravi reached for the wine bottle and topped off our glasses.

Ashley turned to Sadie and said, "So, are you in?"

Sadie leaned back in her chair and sipped her wine. "I haven't decided yet."

Ashley's brows quirked up. "You mean we haven't utterly charmed you this week? Made you feel like this is the best job on the planet?"

Sadie smiled. "Y'all are great. It's just a hard decision." She glanced at me then, and my heart sank. His eyebrows pinched together just like they had when she'd climbed out of my lap in the car. I really didn't want to be the reason she said no to this.

"Time for the hard sell," Ashley said to Ravi. He nodded in agreement.

"What can we tell you?" Ravi said. "Tetia's gone, so you can ask us anything."

Sadie tucked her hair behind her ears—another of her nervous habits. "It's just happening so fast. I don't know anything about being a host and doing a show—not for real. I feel like an imposter."

Ravi snorted. "That just makes you human."

"You're great at this," Ashley said. "This has been one of the easiest shoots we've ever done."

Ravi nodded.

"It's true," I said, but she looked like she didn't believe me.

Sadie shook her head. "You guys are sweet, but what if this week was a fluke? I mean, I'm from Jasmine Falls—of course this week was easy for me. What if we go somewhere else and I turn out to be terrible? Then I've wasted my time, your time, Tetia's time. And then I'll have lost my chance at getting back into the park service here."

"Have you had fun this week?" Ashley said.

Sadie shrugged. "Sure. But there's more at stake than having fun." She gave me a wary look, and I couldn't help but think this was all happening because of me. Because I'd kissed her. I'd made things confusing. I knew her well enough to know that she'd compiled a list of all the pros and cons she saw with this job, and it had left her torn. (And I had a pretty good idea of where I'd landed on that list of hers.) She was the secret sauce for this show, the piece we hadn't known we'd been missing, and now she was walking away from this very good thing because I hadn't been able to rein my feelings in and act like a professional.

I'd blown it. Again.

I stood abruptly, nearly knocking the chair over, and went up to the bar for another drink. I couldn't stand listening to Sadie's excuses anymore, so downing another bourbon or two to make her voice good and fuzzy sounded like a solid plan. As the bartender set my drink in front of me, Ashley came and sat on the stool next to mine.

"You want to tell me what's happening?" she said.

I sipped the bourbon and said, "You're wasting your time. She's not doing it."

Ashley sighed. "You two have a history."

"Not in the way you think," I said.

"Something got stirred up this week, but it's pretty obvious it runs deep," she said. "I'm not asking for any details, because it's none of my business. But whatever all of this is, just be honest with her."

"I've already wrecked it, Ash. She's not coming with us, and without her the show's dead in the water."

"You don't know that," Ashley said, but her jaw had tightened, and a tiny frown line appeared in her forehead—the one that meant she was skirting the truth.

"I do," I told her. "And you do, too. Without Sadie, it's game over. End of story."

"Tetia said the backup was Cl—"

"Shhhh," I said, placing my hand on her forearm. "Don't say her name. We don't want to summon her."

Ashley frowned. "I don't like her, either. She's got bad energy."

She knew as well as I did that having Clarissa as my co-host wouldn't cut it. We could limp along, and maybe even make it through the whole season. But Clarissa Davis was the opposite of Sadie: abrasive, arrogant, and nothing but sharp edges. The show might get made, but it would be a far cry from what we'd envisioned.

"I know. The thought of having to work with that woman every day for ten weeks makes me want to die."

Ashley groaned. "Isn't there any other way?"

I shrugged. "The execs like her. She brings drama and a huge fan base, and for them that means revenue. The only reason they were willing to take a chance on Sadie was because Tetia convinced them that—in her words—our chemistry is better than conflict."

"Conflict gives me hives," Ashley said, wrinkling her nose. "I don't approve of this backup plan."

"Join the club." I knocked back the rest of my bourbon. "We're about to go up in flames."

"What's going up in flames?" Sadie's voice came from behind me and my whole body stiffened.

Ashley's eyes went wide. When I turned, Sadie was standing behind us, a puzzled expression on her face. She glanced at Ashley, then turned her focus on me. "What's going on, Fielding? And what's this backup plan?"

"My advice still stands," Ashley said to me, tapping her finger on my chest. "I'm going to go somewhere else now." She squeezed past Sadie and told her, "Let's chat again in a little while, okay?"

When Ashley was out of earshot, Sadie crossed her arms over her chest and said, "Well?" Her eyes had turned that stormy gray again, dark in the dim glow of the bar.

I sighed, motioning to the bartender for another bourbon.

"It's true," I told her. "Everything they said back there. How great you are at this, how easy the shoot was, how over the moon Tetia is—I know you can't tell because she's more cryptic than the Sphinx sometimes, but believe me, she's beside herself happy."

"Okay," Sadie said, her tone cool.

"The backup plan is what happens if you turn this down. And that plan is a horrible woman who thinks she's a comedian and is about as charming as a wolverine yanked out of its hole. She has a big social media following and looks great on paper— and on camera. But we absolutely despise each other."

Sadie arched a brow, leaning against the bar stool next to mine.

"Not like you and me," I clarified. "I mean we *actually* despise each other. It'll be an utter nightmare, and there's no way the show will work. Probably, she'll make me have an aneurysm, if she doesn't stab me first." I sighed. "But the execs like her, and she's their second choice."

"I see." She pursed her lips and stared past me like she didn't want to look me in the eye. She looked hurt, like she wanted to disappear.

I reached over and placed my hand on her arm. "You're the one everybody wants. But we always have to have a backup in case something falls through. It's not personal. Just standard practice."

Her eyes shifted to mine. "But it's more than that, isn't it?"

She put her hands on her hips and drew my eyes straight to those heavenly curves and my heart squeezed like a fist as I realized this could be the last time I'd see her.

"It's just a precaution," I said. "In case you turned us down, or in case we get out of Jasmine Falls, and you decide you don't want to do this anymore, or in case—" and I paused because I realized that the truth was about to destroy Sadie.

Her eyes were glassy with tears. She already knew what I was going to say. "In case I blow it." One tear slipped down her cheek, and I wanted to die. "In case I'm not as good as you hope." She looked to the side, wiping her face with her hand. "You think once I get out of Jasmine Falls and leave my my comfort zone, I'll be a disaster."

I slid my hand over hers and felt her tense. "Sadie, no. I don't think that at all. No one here thinks that." But I wasn't being completely honest. No one was perfect. No one. We had to have a backup plan, even though I didn't want one. I knew, with ninety-nine percent certainty, that Sadie would be everything we wanted and more. But I could see that all she was hearing was that one percent of doubt.

She shook her head, still avoiding my gaze, and gently pulled away from me. "They're expecting me to fail," she ground out. "They don't have faith in me. And neither do you."

I stood, but she was already backing away from me. When she looked at me, there were tears in her eyes, but also anger.

"How could I have ever though this would work?" she said, her voice low. "This will never work." She gestured between us. "We will never work." She shook her head and looked back toward the table where Ravi and Ashley sat sipping their drinks and pretending to ignore us, as if the whole fate of the show wasn't imploding just a few feet from them. For the first time since I got here, she looked like she'd given up.

"Please stay," I said.

She shook her head. "Your world isn't right for me, James. That's pretty clear now." When she turned again, I reached for her, wishing there was something I could say to make her stay here long enough to explain. For once, I actually didn't care about my career. I only cared about her.

"Sadie," I called.

She turned to me and said, "Checkout's at ten. See you in the morning." It wasn't her words that struck me, but the way she looked at me. She didn't look angry or hurt anymore—she looked like I'd given her exactly what she wanted.

Chapter Twenty-One

SADIE

Cleaning rooms at the inn was a great way to take my mind off of James...until it wasn't. Stripping beds and washing towels allowed my mind to wander too much. It made it too easy for me to remember the look of disappointment on Tetia's face when I'd told her I couldn't accept the position. It was too easy to replay the way Ashley and Ravi had both pulled me into a tight hug and told me they'd miss me. And it was way too easy to keep replaying the way James had glowered at me with that furrow in his brow and then walked out the front door without saying a word.

He'd looked so frustrated, with his jaw so tense he'd surely crack a tooth—but I was too hurt to talk to him. They could say this backup person was just a precaution, but I knew what that really meant: Tetia and James were hedging their bets because they didn't believe that I could really do the job they wanted me to do.

And no matter how much I felt myself falling for James, I couldn't be with someone who didn't have faith in me.

Turning them down was the right move.

So why did it hurt so much when they left?

Since only one couple was checking in this afternoon, I focused on getting the room they'd booked—Ashley's—done first. It only took an hour, so I moved on to Ravi's and then to Tetia's, leaving James's for last. When I got to his room, there was a lingering woodsy scent that was entirely James, and it made my heart do that weird flip-flop in my chest that made it hard to breathe.

That room could wait.

By mid-afternoon, I'd washed every dish, every towel, and every sheet. But every time I sat still, my stupid brain started thinking about James. I hated that we'd left things the way we had, but what else could I say to him? Whatever was happening between us had set me on fire—I'd felt like we were finally seeing each other for real, and seeing past all of those ridiculous walls we built around ourselves. He'd been so tender and sweet when he'd let himself be vulnerable, and I'd felt like I was seeing the real version of him: the one who liked stargazing and greasy burgers. The one who liked hanging out with me when I was in my pajamas, feeling sucker-punched by the world. The one who wanted to see me be adventurous and succeed—or be there to help me dust myself off when I failed and say, *No big deal. You'll get 'em next time.*

But now all of that felt like just another fantasy. Some version of him I'd made up because it was what I needed.

Annoyed with feeling sorry for myself, I pulled my phone from my pocket and texted Gwen.

Hey, I wrote. **You up for movie night tonight?**

Ooooooh, yeah, she replied. **I've had a week.**

Same.

Oh no. I thought things were going well.

They were, I wrote. **Until they weren't.**

Gah. I'll bring the cake. I tried a new flavor and need a beta tester.

I'll have the forks ready.

When my phone buzzed again, it was a text from my mother.

Hi, kid! How's the weekend look?

One check-in today, one tomorrow, I replied. I hadn't heard from my mother in days, which meant she was having a wonderful time. That also meant she had no time to spend worrying about me—which would change the second she set foot back in Jasmine Falls.

My chest tightened and I groaned, thinking I needed to find a new housing situation ASAP. Just as soon as I accepted that job in the records department.

Ugh. The thought made my stomach churn.

Super, she replied. **We'll be back tomorrow evening. You doing okay?**

Great, I wrote. But that was a total lie. **Everything's fine.**

Knew you could handle it, she answered. **You always do.**

Travel safe, I wrote. **Love you.**

Love you back!

I shoved the phone into my pocket and went in search of something else to clean. Soon my parents would be back, and then I'd be working in the basement of the headquarters building. For the first time, that actually did feel depressing. Like the opposite of what I wanted.

By the time my check-in arrived, two fifty-something sisters knocking another national park off their bucket list, I'd managed to vacuum the entire inn and make up all the rooms—except for the one that James had used.

Cleaning that room meant erasing the last traces of him, and I couldn't make myself do that yet.

As the two ladies walked upstairs to their room, the bell over the front door clanged. When I stepped out of the library and into the foyer, I saw a young guy standing by the door holding an enormous box.

"Are you Sadie?" he asked.

"Yes," I said, eyeing the box in his arms. "But I wasn't expecting any deliveries."

"Sorry." he said. "I was supposed to bring this yesterday."

"But I didn't order anything."

He pulled his phone from his pocket and scrolled for a moment. "Gift order," he said at last. "Last name Fielding. There should be a card inside." He smiled, like that explained everything.

"Oh," I said, a little breathless. "Thank you."

When he left, I stared down at the box, my heart squeezing like a fist.

By the time Gwen knocked on the door of the carriage house, it was nearly seven o'clock. She marched inside and set a small cake on the counter—she called this her demo size. The stress eater in me would demolish this thing if I were alone, but thankfully Gwen would save me from myself.

"Lemon blueberry," she said. "With some secret ingredients I'll disclose later. Wouldn't want you to make a snap judgment." She winked at me and sat down at one of the bar stools. "This was a great idea you had. I took tomorrow off to recover from this horrendous week and I plan on doing all I can to turn my brain to mush tonight. I want to forget about men and forget about clients, and if that requires an ungodly amount of carbs and wine, then so be it." She still had her hair pulled up in a short ponytail she always wore at the cafe, but she'd changed into leggings and an oversized sweater that she'd never wear when baking.

I grabbed two plates from the cabinet and said, "I fully support that plan."

Gwen sliced into the cake with a giant knife and handed me a small piece. So we'd pace ourselves, then. *Always looking out for me, Gwen.*

She groaned. "This week has been packed with a groomzilla, the worst date ever, and enough unsolicited advice from my mother to put me into therapy for another year."

"Yikes," I said, opening a bottle of dessert wine. "I'm going to need some details about that date."

She rolled her eyes. "My sister's trying to play matchmaker again. In a weak moment, I agreed to go out with this guy she works with. He was a total snob and kept texting someone else during our dinner. He couldn't even remember my name."

"Ugh."

"Yes, exactly. She's not going to like the way I repay her for that. I don't know why she and my mom think they have the solutions to all of my problems, but this should be the last evidence I need to prove them wrong."

I poured two glasses of wine and handed her one. "Here's to solving our own problems, no matter how long it takes."

"What's that?" she asked, pointing toward the big box that had been delivered earlier. I'd left it on the couch, still unopened. It was big enough to hold a large piece of luggage, but light as a feather.

"Something James sent me."

"What is it?" she said.

"No idea. Could be full of balloons for all I know." I'd considered that—a box of helium balloons that said *Congratulations! Way to Go!* Something James would have planned as a surprise after I'd agreed to do the show.

My heart hurt a little at the thought.

"Okay, spill," she said. "Why the mystery box? What happened?"

"They asked me to do the whole series with them. Co-host every episode."

Her brows shot up to her hairline. "Oh my god, that's amazing! You're going to be famous!"

"I told them no."

She frowned, confused. "You did? But I thought you liked it."

"I thought so, too." I'd given her updates all week, but I hadn't told her about the last couple of days and everything that had happened with James. Now, as I recounted the last few conversations I'd had with him (and the kissing), she leaned closer, her blue eyes wide.

Finally, she let out a low whistle and took a bite of cake. "You've had a busy week, sister."

"The worst part," I said, "is that I was really having fun doing the show. And I thought I was good at it." I sighed. "But when James told me about that other host, I just lost it. It made me feel like I'd been living in a fantasy."

"First of all, from what I saw, you were great at it." She pointed her fork at me. "Second, don't let some dude shake your confidence. Tetia offered you the job, right? So Tetia also thought you were awesome."

"Well, no one said *awesome*."

"Semantics. Clearly that's what she meant."

I smiled. "She *was* disappointed when I turned down the offer."

Gwen rolled her eyes, teasing. "Well, duh. Of course she was."

I shrugged. "Thanks, Gwen."

"I mean it. I'm not saying that as your friend. I'm saying that as someone who, one, will binge watch a good travel show until the end of time, and two, was so nervous that day and relieved that you put me at ease and made it fun for me, too." She waved her fork at me and went on. "I've been thinking of making some changes in my business and struggling with the future I want. And that day with y'all really made me look harder at it."

"You're a huge success, though. You know that, right?" Gwen had built her cafe from the ground up, all by herself. Within a year of opening, she'd made it one of the most popular spots in town.

She snorted. "Doesn't always feel that way. But the point is that the conversation we had that day really had an effect on me. I'm looking at things a bit differently now. I'm seeing what makes me happy more clearly, and it's helped me get clear on some goals. That's because of you."

My heart swelled at the idea of something so small having such a big impact. For me, that day was about having fun while interviewing a friend and showing off her skills. But for Gwen, it was clearly much more.

"And really," Gwen said, "I don't think them having another person in mind as a backup host is any reflection on you." She picked at the cake. "I know it might feel that way, in your sweet little perfectionist brain, but think of it this way. A TV show is a huge investment. What if you got four episodes in and decided you hated it, or—heaven forbid—had some emergency that meant you had to leave?"

"I'd keep working. I wouldn't quit."

"Yes, but they don't know that," she said. "They're probably used to people with a non-Sadie work ethic flaking out on them all the time."

I considered that while I had a bite of cake.

"And you said yourself, James told you she was their backup plan *if you said no*. That also tracks. If they've put all this effort into the planning, they're going to have a few contingency plans. I mean, I love you, but they're not going to scrap the show because you turned them down."

I nodded. Her logic was, as usual, infallible.

"And so what if a tiny part of them worries that a former park ranger might not be perfect as a television host? Don't you think that's reasonable? They want *you* Sadie. But you can't ask them to ignore reality. That's unfair."

This was why I loved Gwen. Because she never minced words.

"When you say it that way, it makes total sense. How did I not see that?" I slumped forward, resting my head in my hands and feeling like a fool.

She shrugged. "You were surprised. And hurt. And a little lovesick." She pointed her fork at me again. "But this doesn't mean you get to beat yourself up about it."

"Yeah, okay." She was right. On all counts.

She raised a brow. "And them needing a backup doesn't say anything about your value as a person."

I let out a heavy sigh, and it was like an incredible weight had been lifted. When I closed my eyes, all I could see was James. The way he'd looked so deflated last night, the way he'd reached for me so tenderly and tried to take my hand, even when it felt like I'd shatter into a million pieces.

"What makes you happy?" Gwen said. "I mean, aside from

wine and my amazing lemon cake." She grinned and wiggled her eyebrows.

"I used to think it was working outside and getting people excited about conservation," I said. "But I'm starting to feel like it's deeper than that."

She nodded.

"I like connecting with people. Making them curious, showing them new things." I shrugged. "Sounds kind of cheesy when I say it out loud."

"It's not, though. I think you're starting to see your superpower, and I think there are lots of ways you can use it. Maybe the park service was just one way to do that."

"It's a predictable one," I said. "I show up every day, do my job well, entertain the visitors, and move up in the ranks. Once you move out of temporary positions, it's safe."

"Is that really what you want, though? Safe? Predictable?"

I shrugged, but deep down I knew the real answer. "Steady paychecks are nice."

She raised a brow, taking another bite. "Don't hate me when I say this because I say it out of love. But you have a tendency to take low-stakes jobs, and then you tell me that you get bored easily. Maybe it's time to take a leap and do something you wouldn't normally consider."

I opened my mouth to argue, but then realized I had in fact complained to her about being bored with my job at the park—many times. It had been challenging at first, and then it wasn't anymore. But it had felt predictable and secure, until the day it had fallen apart.

"The park's a known quantity," Gwen said. "I get that. And I get that doing something that feels totally different, like a TV show, can be really scary. But what if it's just the kind of adventure you need to let yourself fly? What if you stay with the park, and then in ten years, you feel like you've settled?"

I sighed. "James said something similar. About taking a leap."

"He did?"

"He said he didn't want me to miss a good opportunity just because it was a little scary. And that I should do what I love." He'd said it while giving me that easy, reassuring smile.

I was really going to miss that smile.

She raised a brow. "He makes a good point." After a moment, she turned back to me and said, "Tell the truth, did you say no to the job just because of James?"

It was impossible to lie to Gwen. All week, I'd been telling myself that I didn't deserve this job because I didn't have the right experience, that it felt like a detour from my "real" career. And after last night, I'd told myself that it could never work with James, and that he was just being his usual charming self because he wanted me to do the show. But now all of that felt like just another story I was telling myself—one that made it easier to walk away from him.

"I think I fell for him, Gwen. I let myself believe that he felt the same way, and then it all blew up in my face and I pushed him away. And last night—" I shrugged. "I just felt like this plan-B co-host meant that he didn't believe in me like I thought he did." I sighed, feeling like a wound had opened up. "Just when I feel like I understand him, he does something like that to throw me off-balance. So yeah. I don't see how we can work together when it feels so complicated."

She sighed. "You didn't tell him any of this, did you?"

"Not exactly."

"Were you going to say yes before you found out about the other co-host?"

I bit my lip. "I wanted to. The thing is, I think I still want to." I took another bite of cake. "I feel like I've lost something and it hurts. I feel like I passed on a good opportunity for what might be a dumb reason."

She set her plate on the bar and turned toward me. "It's tough love time. I need to say this because I'm your friend and I love you."

I looked at her, feeling like she was staring right into my soul. It didn't matter how big I built those walls around myself—Gwen could always find a way through.

Her big blue eyes were pinned on mine. "Is it possible that the big problem here is fear?" she said. "That you're afraid of failing with the show, and with James?"

I reached my fork toward the cake but she dragged my plate away, leaving me stabbing at the air. She wasn't going to let me cram my feelings down any longer, and part of me was grateful for that. Holding all my feelings down was like trying to force a beach ball underwater—the harder you push, and the deeper you shove it down, the more explosive it is when it finally breaks free.

It was just hard to imagine what came after, when the big tangle of feelings were laid out to see.

"I get it, it's a big scary new thing," she went on. "But is it possible that you're pushing both things away because you're afraid of what happens if they don't work out the way you want?"

Never. Maybe. Absolutely.

Her words felt like a kick to the chest. That's how I knew they were true. "It's possible," I said, tears welling in my eyes.

Gwen gave me a tiny smile and reached for my hand. "Honey, failure is nothing to be afraid of. Or ashamed of. It's a sign of bravery. If you never let yourself try and fail, then you never get what you want." She squeezed my hand and said, "I could tell you a dozen stories about some epic failures I had. If I'd let any of them stop me, I wouldn't be living the life I have now. Yes, failure hurts sometimes, but it gets you where you need to be." She shrugged. "I mean, look at this week you've had. If the park service had the good sense to keep you, you wouldn't be about to star in a TV show."

I scoffed. "Star is a stretch."

"Not from what I saw." She sipped her wine and said, "And as for James, how do you really feel about him? Would you have regrets if you never saw him again?"

My heart squeezed at the thought. Deep down, I knew I'd been pushing him away because that was easier than taking a chance on him hurting me. It was easier than admitting that things between us could be messy and complicated and wonderful all at the same time. And that this might be just the beginning.

"How'd you get so good at this?" I asked her.

She smiled. "Told you—thanks to my mother, I've had lots of therapy. Some of it's been quite useful."

I shook my head. "Even so, I already told Tetia no."

"So call her up and tell her yes."

"And then there's James. What if I tell him how I feel and it all falls apart?"

She narrowed her eyes, waving her finger at me. "Don't do that. That's the fear, and your brain, trying to protect you. When she rises up, you need to knock her back down. Or, you just say, *Thanks, brain, but I've got this.*"

I leaned over and pulled her into a hug, feeling like something in my heart had cracked wide open.

"There's one more thing you need to handle," she said, nodding toward the box.

I'd been afraid to open it, too. Afraid of what might be inside and what it might mean.

She followed me as I grabbed a pair of scissors and cut the tape on the box. Inside was a smaller box wrapped with a ribbon. A small card from Lucinda's art gallery was attached. On the back side, it simply said,

Shine on, Harper.

    — J.

I pulled the silver ribbon from the box and opened it carefully. Inside was a giant paper star light, almost two feet from point to point, like the one that had hung above us in the booth of the Wonky Donkey. Like that one, this star had some pieces that were made from maps, but this one was also made from handmade paper filled with different bits of handwriting. I turned it in my hands, reading some of the words.

Sadie is the bravest person I know.

No one taught me to love nature quite like Sadie.

I love Sadie because she's inspiring, compassionate, and kind.

"What is this?" I said, feeling my voice catch.

Gwen smiled. "Lucinda included a note about how she made it. But the short version is that James asked a bunch of us to write down what we admired about you on some special paper that Lucinda uses for her light sculptures. And then she did her Lucinda magic, and here we are." She sniffed. "And I had to keep my mouth shut for days." She bit back a grin, resting her hand on my shoulder. "You know how hard it is for me to keep secrets, babe."

I slid my fingers over the smooth paper, but it was hard to read all the words when I was blinking back tears. "I can't believe he did this," I said. He had to have ordered it right after that night when I'd told him I felt like such a failure. Before my being a co-host was even on the table.

Gwen sighed. "For what it's worth, I think you should talk to him. And I don't think it's too late."

"I have a favor to ask," I said.

She smiled. "Name it."

Chapter Twenty-Two

JAMES

I SHOULDN'T HAVE LEFT the way I did. It was a jerk move to walk out without trying to talk to Sadie again, but I was frustrated with her and furious with myself and had no idea what to say to her anyway.

Still, I should have tried.

I could have told her that I'd completely fallen for her and couldn't stop thinking about how great we were together. That I wanted to spend every minute with her. But she'd built her big wall again and hadn't even spoken to me when we checked out this morning. She'd brushed me off so easily, and that made it clear that whatever I said to her wouldn't have made a bit of difference. So instead, I'd climbed into my car, followed the rest of the crew to Greenville, and spent the whole two-and-a-half hour drive trying not to replay the last week's events over and over in my head.

Spoiler alert: I'd failed at that.

Now, we were all sitting out on the patio of the hotel bar, pretending not to be devastated that we were continuing the show without Sadie. Tetia had booked us all single rooms at a swanky little hotel in downtown Greenville, close to where we'd be shooting for the next few days.

This was also the last night of peace I'd have before Clarissa Davis showed up. She'd check in tomorrow night, and then make my life absolute misery for the next ten weeks.

"You okay?" Tetia asked me.

"Super," I said, sipping my bourbon.

"Lies," she said.

A few feet away, Ravi and Ashley were giggling, watching a video on Ashley's phone.

"Okay," I said. "I'm annoyed. Frustrated. My fury burns hot with the fire of a thousand suns. Is that better?"

"Well, it's more honest."

"I just hate that we have to work with Clarissa. She's already stringing us along. I mean, we're sitting here waiting on her, and she hasn't even signed the contract. It's ridiculous. And typical Clarissa Davis."

Tetia sighed. "I think she's angling for another offer. She's supposed to confirm in the morning."

"She's already posting teasers on her socials, though. Heaven forbid she not tweet and tok and gram her way into every headline." I opened my phone and showed one of her feeds to Tetia. It was filled with typical unfunny jokes from Clarissa, plus a few questionable comments that were sure to ruffle some feathers. "She thinks any publicity's good publicity. She'll die on that hill."

Tetia groaned, handing the phone back to me.

"She's going to bring us the wrong kind of attention," I said.

"It'll work out," Tetia said, sipping her drink. "We'll make sure it does."

"The last time Clarissa and I were in a room together, she threw her shoe at me."

Tetia frowned. "That was childish."

"And completely on brand for her. I still have a dent on my chin," I said, pointing to a nearly invisible mark. "It was a wedge sandal that was heavy as lead. She could have killed me."

"She steps out of line again and she's out," Tetia said. "Zero tolerance. I put it in her contract."

"You did?"

"I'm not letting that woman bully you again. Or anyone else in my crew." She nudged my shoulder and said, "I got you."

"Still, this is going to be the longest ten weeks of my life." There were a lot of things I could suffer through for the sake of my career, but Clarissa Davis wasn't one of them.

Tetia stared out over the skyline. How could she be so calm about this? "Just be your charming, adorable self," she said. "And think about what you want this project to lead to. You can still make this work for you."

I sighed, savoring the pleasant burn of the bourbon. I knew where I wanted to be, and I also knew I'd ruined my chance at getting there. Sadie Harper didn't want me in her life, and she'd made that crystal clear.

"I'm going to turn in," I said, though there was zero chance of me falling asleep any time soon.

Tetia gave me a reassuring smile. "Tomorrow's a new day, Fielding. Don't kill this project before it even has a chance to breathe, okay?"

"Okay," I said, not feeling one bit better about any of this. "I'll do my best."

"You always do," she said.

Yeah. But sometimes it just wasn't good enough.

As I trudged back toward the elevator, I thought again of calling Sadie—for the thousandth time today. I even pulled my phone from my pocket and started to dial her number. But as I stepped onto the elevator, I thought better of it. There wasn't quite enough bourbon in me to make me think that calling was a good idea—and what on earth would I say to her anyway? I still scrolled through my texts though, just on the off chance that I'd missed one from her.

I hadn't.

Back in my room, I locked the door behind me and collapsed on the bed. It was a gigantic king—one big enough to sleep diagonally in. But this room felt cold and empty, not cozy like my room at the inn. I turned on the TV, hoping to find some documentary that was boring enough to put me to sleep, but my plan backfired when the show I watched about fungi proved to be completely fascinating. By the time the credits rolled, I was both desperate to talk to Sadie and to try eating a magic mushroom to see exactly what insights it might reveal about my life choices and what might lie beyond.

So not what I needed right now.

Determined to shut my brain off, I went into the enormous bathroom and turned on the faucet in the tub. It was one of those giant spa tubs, and even though they sometimes grossed me out (because how many people had been in them, and doing what?), I was broken down enough not to care. My shoulders ached from tension and I just wanted to lie back and feel those little jets hit all the tense spots that were wound so impossibly tight. While the water ran, I poured myself one more bourbon from the mini bar and stripped out of my jeans and tee shirt.

As I sank down into the water, as hot as I could stand it, I tried to convince myself that this week I would not self-destruct. It was nearly midnight on a Saturday night, and I was alone in a bathtub that was definitely big enough for two, scrolling through social media pages on my phone. Looking for any post that might distract me from thinking about how I'd once again ruined everything.

Where were all the cute puppies when you needed them most? Tired of scrolling through everyone's perfect snapshots, I opened my meditation app and put on a recording that was supposed to make me wind down. I set the phone on the floor and pressed a wet cloth over my eyes, and tried to focus on the soothing lady's voice—and not think at all about how she sounded just a little bit like Sadie.

My chest heaved with a sigh. I should have talked to her. Fought for us. I shouldn't have walked away like that and given up so easily. That was just another reason for her to be disappointed in me.

My phone buzzed from its spot on the floor. Probably Tetia or Ravi, checking in on me.

Don't worry, Tetia wrote. **We got this.**

OK, I typed. I wanted to believe her.

Breakfast meeting at 8. We'll talk strategy.

Great, I answered. **Sleep well.**

I placed the phone back on the floor. A couple of minutes later, it buzzed again with another text. When I leaned down and touched the screen, I saw Sadie's name.

Are you awake? She wrote.

I stared at the screen, suddenly dumbfounded. Simple yes or no, Fielding. Not a hard question.

Yes, I typed.

Three dots. Then nothing. My heart was a jackhammer.

I leaned back in the tub, trying to decide if I should write more. I started to type a longer reply, but then stopped. When the phone rang and her name popped up, I was so surprised I nearly dropped it.

She wanted to talk.

My heart was in my throat, but I managed to answer on the third ring.

"Harper?" I said, like the screen might lie.

"Hi." She sounded out of breath. "I know it's late."

"It's okay."

"Can you talk a minute?" she asked.

"Sure." I tried to sit up straighter, but my foot slipped and one of the jets tickled one of my tender bits, and I yelped as my elbow banged against the side of the tub and the phone slipped from my hand.

Right into the water with a *plunk.*

I yelled a whole bunch of words you shouldn't yell at top volume after midnight in a hotel as nice as this one, and scrambled to fish the phone out of the water.

The screen flickered in this weird glitchy way and the call was gone. I slammed my fist against the side of the tub—huge mistake—and then my hand was throbbing and I was biting back more very bad words and Sadie was still gone.

There was a knock on the outside door and I sighed, thinking surely this was someone with a noise complaint. Just what I needed to kick this week off. The headline would read, *Travel Show Host Wreaks Havoc in Greenville Hotel, Claims Broken Heart is to Blame.* Clarissa would likely sprain a finger with her grams and toks.

"Sorry," I yelled, "Just had a little accident, but everything's fine."

The person knocked again.

Grumbling, I stood up and sloshed water onto the floor. My head was a little fuzzy from the bourbon, but at least the tension in my neck had eased a bit. I reached for one of the big fluffy towels and quickly wrapped it around my waist. Maybe I'd get lucky and this would be the night manager, and not some ornery person who'd been dead asleep next door. That was the last thing I needed right now.

I took a deep zen breath like my calming app had taught me, and prepared to offer my best fake smile and most charming apology when I opened the door to whoever was waiting to run me through the wringer.

When I pulled the door open, my heart banged against my ribs so hard that it hurt.

Sadie stood in the doorway, her eyes drifting down to the towel, her mouth in a tiny *O*.

Chapter Twenty-Three

JAMES FIELDING, nearly naked, was enough to take my breath away. This wasn't the way I'd expected this evening to go, but then what about this last week had unfolded the way I'd planned?

He was soaking wet, clutching a towel low on his hips. Water dripped from the ends of his hair and I was mesmerized by one large droplet that fell onto his shoulder and rolled over his collarbone, then tumbled down his very cut chest and abs, then lower to where his hand was doing a meager job of securing that towel.

Lord have mercy.

His eyes were wide, pinning me there in the hallway, and every single thought fell right out of my brain.

Well. Except for one.

"You're here," he said, like he was convincing himself of this fact. "But how?"

"I thought you hung up on me," I said. For one moment that had felt both like a blink and an eternity, I'd thought he'd ended the call, cut me off, and it had been the worst feeling in the world. So bad that I'd almost turned on my heel and walked back toward the elevator and driven right back to the interstate. But I was done making assumptions and excuses. I was done letting fear hold me back. I'd come too far to not hear the words —one way or another.

"I would never," he said, looking dead serious. "I dropped my phone in the bath. Think I killed it."

"I didn't take you for the type who soaks in a bath."

"It relaxes me," he said. "Usually." His brows pinched together in confusion. "How did you know I was here?"

"Ashley told me." Right after I'd asked Gwen to cover for me at the inn, I'd texted Ashley and asked her which hotel they had booked. She'd promised not to say a word to anyone.

A door opened somewhere down the hall. "Can I come in?" I said.

He nodded, as if coming out of a trance. "Of course." He stepped backward into the room and bumped into the wall by the closet. "Give me just a minute," he said. "I need pants."

"Debatable," I mumbled, finally getting a good look at that tattoo that started just below his elbow and covered most of his biceps. I hadn't taken him for a birds-and-flowers kind of guy, either.

There was so much I wanted to learn about James.

He scooped up an armful of clothes and slipped into the bathroom while I walked over to the big windows by the bed. Outside, the streets of Greenville were quiet. My whole body had been buzzing the entire drive here, and now I felt like I might collapse. But there was no backing out now.

When James came out of the bathroom, he'd changed into a slim tee shirt and broken-in jeans. He was barefoot, and his hair was even more unruly than usual—he'd obviously toweled it off and stopped there.

Disheveled James was very distracting. *Focus, Sadie. You came here for a reason, and it was not to gawk at James and all of his perfectly chiseled parts.*

"Can I get you something?" he asked. "Water? A mini bottle of something stronger?"

"No thanks," I said, my gut twisting into a knot. "I went over everything I wanted to say during the whole drive. Over and over, and now that I'm here, I still don't know how to say it."

He sat on the foot of the king-sized bed and it was only then that I realized I'd been pacing in the space between the bed and the dresser. When I stopped and stared at him, he said, "Just spit it out, Harper. You can tell me anything." His voice was calm, tender.

"I just needed to talk to you face to face," I said. "I didn't like leaving things the way we did, and I think I've been unfair to you."

He stared at me, his brow furrowed. "I was unfair to you," he said. "I should have told you about the backup plan with Clarissa. I'm sorry that I kept that from you." He sighed, his voice gentle. "But it was important to me that you make a decision based on what you wanted, and not what you thought would help me or anyone else."

"Understandable," I said. "But I need to be able to trust you, and I can't trust you completely when I think you're hiding things from me. Even if you think you're protecting me."

He nodded. "No more secrets."

Feeling like a weight had been lifted, I sat down on the dresser across from him so we were barely two feet apart. "Also, I panicked. Of course you needed a backup person. Of course you needed a plan in case I didn't work out."

He gave me a sad smile. "It was never because I didn't believe in you."

"I see that now."

Leaning forward, he placed his elbows on his knees and looked up at me through his thick lashes. "Good. Because there's no one I believe in more than you, Harper."

My heart did that flip-flop again that left me nearly breathless. There wasn't a doubt in my mind he was telling me the truth.

After a moment, I said, "I got the paper star that you ordered. Why'd you send me that?"

His lip lifted in a tiny smile. "I knew you liked the artist. Also, I thought you might need a reminder of all the things people love about you." His brows pulled together, and that wall I'd built was crumbling to dust.

"That's one of the nicest things anyone's ever given me."

"I was just getting started."

"You've wrecked all of my plans, you know."

He looked up at me, his eyes wide in the dim light. Four floors below us, the city was quiet. But up here, my heart was pounding so hard I thought it might explode.

"I just wanted to get my old job back, get back to my ordinary life," I said. "I had no plans to get pulled into anything remotely as challenging or exciting as last week. I wasn't looking for a new career path. And I certainly didn't intend to fall for you, Fielding." I sighed, sliding my hands along my knees. My body was still buzzing and my skin felt too tight, but for the first time in a long time, I knew this was precisely the place I needed to be. My heart was hammering in my chest, but I had to keep going. I had to tell him the truths I'd been holding onto like secrets. "I don't know what's going to happen, and I don't even know what I want to happen. All I know is that I couldn't stand the thought of not seeing you again. I was afraid to tell you how I felt, and afraid you might hurt me, and Fielding, I don't want to miss out on something great because I was afraid." I sighed. "I also didn't envision spilling my guts in a strange hotel room in the middle of the night, but I drove over two hours on a total sugar high from Gwen's cake, and it's after midnight, and I guess I feel like I have nothing to lose."

He leaned closer to me, his knees nearly touching mine. "Say that part again," he said, his voice gravelly.

"That I have nothing to lose?"

"That you're falling for me."

"Fell. Hard. Past tense, Fielding." The tornado of butterflies was back. "I just don't know exactly what that means."

He moved off the bed and onto the floor in front of me. On his knees, he came closer and rested his hands on my thighs, looking up at me with that hopeful, lopsided smirk that would surely undo me for the rest of my days. "What if we took our time to figure that out together?" he said.

Take our time. I could do that. All the ways that James might take his time with me was a compelling thought to consider.

"I like that idea," I said.

When I squeezed his hand, he said, "For the record, I fell hard for you, too—ages ago—and I know exactly what it means for me." He rose then, and sat next to me on the dresser, his thigh pressing against mine. His hand cupped my cheek and he said, "It means you're the person I want to talk to at the end of the day. You're the person I want to stumble through the woods chasing comets with. You have my whole heart, Harper. And I don't want it any other way."

"What if this doesn't work?" I said.

He slid his thumb along my jawline and smiled. "Whatever comes after will be better than never giving us a chance."

"That's a little bit terrifying," I said.

He smiled and whispered, "Yeah, but in the best way." He

took my hand then, and placed it on his chest, right over his heart. I could feel the steady thumping, the pace just as fast as mine. "I was afraid I'd never see you again," he said. "I really hated that feeling."

"I've never felt this way about anyone before," I said. "I don't know how to do this."

"I don't either, Harper. But there's no one else I'd rather figure it out with." He slid one hand to the nape of my neck, and then his lips were on mine. He kissed me tenderly, taking his time.

I was going to enjoy this side of James Fielding. With any luck, for a very long time.

When he finally let me go, I said, "So I have to ask one more thing. You still up for doing the show together? Be honest."

He frowned. "I'd love to, Harper, but I think we're stuck with Clarissa. She's on her way here."

"What if there was still a way? Would it be weird for us to work together while we're—figuring all this out between us?"

His smile warmed me to my core. "You know there's no one else I'd rather do the show with. I love working with you." He slid his arm around me and mumbled, "Almost as much as I love kissing you."

I gave him a playful nudge and pulled my phone from my pocket. "Hold that thought. I'm texting Tetia. She's expecting me."

"What?" he said, looking confused. "Now?"

"I called her on the drive here because I felt so stupid for turning this down. But I needed to talk to you first, and make sure that we were okay before I committed one hundred percent."

"Are you serious?" he said, his eyes widening. He looked like he'd just learned he won the lottery.

"She told me things were still up in the air and we might be able to work something out since the other party was creating some…difficulty."

He raked his hand through his hair. "That's a nice way to put it."

I sent a quick text to Tetia: **Are you up? Too late to talk?**

Three dots. James and I stared at the screen.

Instead of responding to my text, Tetia called me. James grinned as I answered the call.

"Hi, Tetia," I said. "You're on speaker and James is here, too."

"Sadie," she said. "I'm happy to hear from you."

"Is this real?" James asked her. "Can Sadie still co-host?"

"Clarissa never confirmed," Tetia said. "So yes, we have a clause that could make that doable."

James gave me a wicked grin, slipping his arm around my back and pulling me against him.

"I'll make a phone call first thing in the morning, and we can go over details at breakfast," Tetia said. "Sadie, can I get a verbal acceptance from you now, and have you sign in the morning?"

"Of course," I said, feeling breathless. "Absolutely, I'm in."

"Wonderful," she said. "Let's say eight."

My heart fluttered in my chest—I hadn't let myself believe this could all work out until this moment. "Thank you so much, Tetia," I said. "This is amazing."

James smiled and kissed me on the cheek.

"So glad to have you aboard, Sadie," Tetia said. "I'll see you both in the morning."

She ended the call and James pulled me into his arms.

"Not so fast," I said. "I need to go book myself a room."

He cocked a brow and tightened his arms around my waist. "Why on earth would you say such a thing?"

I swatted his arm playfully. "We're taking our time, remember? And we have to be pros about this."

He kissed my jaw, in that spot that he knew drove me crazy—because James was both thorough and a quick learner. "As you wish," he mumbled.

"We'll tell Tetia everything tomorrow," I said. "We have to handle this the right way. No more secrets."

I felt him smile against my neck. "No more secrets." When he pulled me tighter against his chest, he said, "I'm so glad you want to do the show. I knew this was a good fit for you."

"We're a good fit," I corrected. "Even though you have this pesky way of making everything into a competition."

"Oh, I've got lots of ideas for competitions we can have," he said with a wicked smirk. He nudged me toward the bed, and my heart hammered against my ribs. "How about we have one before you book that room?"

Before I could answer, his eyes flashed with mischief and he tackled me onto the bed, tickling me mercilessly. I laughed and squirmed in his grasp, though there was no other place I'd rather be. Just him, just here. In this moment that was the end of one thing and the beginning of something else—something that was terrifying and thrilling, and perfectly imperfect.

Chapter Twenty-Four

SADIE

Ten Weeks Later.

"Told you we could do it," James said. He gave me his usual smirk, delighted that, once again, he'd proven me wrong.

That smirk had become one of the highlights of my day.

I'd bet him that there was no way we could finish the last episode this week, but we had. After losing a few days of shooting in October when Ravi had the flu, and then having to reschedule the last artist we'd planned to feature for the series, I was sure we'd have to extend our shooting schedule past the holidays.

But today we'd wrapped, three days before Christmas.

"Fair enough," I said. "Name your prize."

"I need to think about that for a minute." James smiled, leaning back in the deck chair and propping his feet up on the ottoman. This patio was amazing, with a gas fireplace that kept us toasty while we stared at the ocean. The outdoor chairs were nicer than most furniture I'd ever had inside my house, and I was going to miss this place. We were staying in a little bed and breakfast near Jekyll Island, Georgia, where we'd just finished filming for two days. It was chilly here, especially in the evenings, but we'd stayed plenty warm while working in a glassblowing studio down the road. For the last two days, we'd filmed with Javier and Sophie, a couple of renowned glass artists who had their art in museums all over the world. They'd been an absolute delight, and we'd managed to both, one, not break anything that cost more than our salaries combined, and two, not set ourselves on fire while making glass Christmas ornaments.

A last-minute fill in, this had been one of my favorite segments. If I'd learned anything in the past couple of months, it was that sometimes those unexpected roadblocks meant that you just ended up in a place better than you could ever imagine.

That was happening a lot lately. Traveling for this show had meant all kinds of delays, surprises, and pivots. I was learning to be more flexible with my expectations, and I didn't hate surprises quite so much anymore.

Finding Javier and Sophie, for example, had been a delightful surprise. December could be a hard time to schedule anyone—especially as a last-minute replacement, but this Hail Mary had worked out perfectly. And we never would have found Javier and Sophie if James hadn't been secretly looking for some romantic place to escape to after the holidays. We'd barely had a day off in over two months, and James had announced a couple of weeks ago that he wanted to take me someplace where we could relax and decompress—and spend some quality alone time together.

That was another delightful surprise.

After New Year's, we'd be back here, spending two weeks

doing whatever we wanted. Ten weeks of filming was an intense schedule, and we both were itching for some time off to enjoy each other in some unscripted ways.

I'd already started a bullet list.

During James's internet sleuthing, he discovered that every year Jekyll Island had this famous treasure hunt where they commissioned dozens of glass artists to make beautiful hand-blown globes that were a nod to the glass floaters that were once used in fishing nets. For decades, people had collected these glass globes when they washed up on beaches, and now the annual treasure hunt made beach combing a little more interesting. Each January and February, volunteers hid plastic dummy globes all around the island. If you found a dummy globe, you took it to the nearby visitor center and exchanged it for one of the real prizes—a hand-blown globe made from a famous artist.

Javier and Sophie had been chosen to take part this year, and they showed us the stunning globe they'd made. The glass was a midnight blue, swirling with bits of silver, violet, and copper. It looked like a galaxy you could hold in your hands. We'd been so enamored with it that they'd given us a smaller duplicate that they'd made into an ornament as a thank-you for bringing them onto the show.

"Take me to Jasmine Falls for Christmas," James said, giving me a lazy smile.

"What?" I said.

Earlier, he'd told me that he didn't have real holiday plans because his parents were headed off to Napa Valley and his sister was going to spend the week with her new boyfriend. A few weeks ago, he'd seemed perfectly content to stay at his apartment, drinking eggnog and watching off-beat holiday movies.

"That's what I'd like for my prize," he said. "Christmas with you." My heart squeezed in my chest at the thought. This was how he operated now: all of these competitions he insisted on having? When he won, he wanted something that made me happy, and I did the same. No matter the challenge, it was always win-win.

He really was the best surprise.

"Really?" I said. "You're ready to meet my family?"

His gaze settled on mine—that smoldering stare that warmed me straight to my core. "I don't want to be away from you. And I'd be delighted to meet your family."

"Deal," I said. "We could head to your house tomorrow and then drive down on Christmas Eve. I bet if we asked really nicely, we could stay in the carriage house and have some privacy."

He gave me a devilish grin. "I like the way you think, Harper."

My parents were eager to see me after being away for nearly three months, and would no doubt grill us about what it was like filming the show. My mom was obsessed with travel shows and couldn't wait to see the inn featured on TV—she was a little disappointed that I'd left town so quickly, but she loved the idea of me doing a streaming show—and finding this new job that I loved. She was also very interested in learning more about James.

"What time are we meeting everyone again?" I said.

James glanced at his phone. "Dinner at seven. We have some time." Tetia, Ashley, and Ravi were joining us for dinner to celebrate the official wrap. We'd be in post-production for a while, but so far the feedback from the dailies was promising. The streaming folks were happy, Tetia was happy, and for the first time in a long time, I was happy. Our crew felt like family, and for the first time in a long while, I felt like I belonged.

"So I have one more question," James said. "I've been thinking it over and need your opinion."

"Are you already thinking about the next season?" It wasn't definite yet, but Tetia had a strong feeling that we'd get another season—or several—and her hunches were solid. But even if we didn't, I wasn't afraid of what might come after. I was beginning to see that failures were sometimes a way to redirect us toward what we really wanted. And sometimes, late at night, I even said a little quiet thank you to Chief Ranger Mike for redirecting me in a way I couldn't ignore.

James smirked. "Let's revisit that thought after our holiday. If it's all the same to you, I'd like to not think about work for a while." He reached over and slid his hand along my arm, his fingers lacing into mine. "I have some other things on my mind."

"I like that plan."

He squeezed my hand and said, "After Christmas. After Jasmine Falls. How do you feel about Atlanta?"

"Can't say I've spent much time there," I said. "I could check it out."

His lip lifted in a tiny smile. "What I mean is, how would you feel about living in Atlanta, in my apartment?"

"Oh." I blinked at him, my heart hammering in my chest.

"My lease is up soon," he said. "Where we go after is wide open." He sat up straighter, sliding his chair closer to mine. His eyes widened with a flicker of excitement. "I know we said we'd take our time, and I'm still happy to take this as slow as you want." He wrapped my hand in his, and my pulse pounded. "But after spending all this time together, I don't want to spend a single day—or night—without you."

"I don't want to be away from you, either." I'd been thinking about this for weeks, dreading the moment that we'd be split apart. We'd kept our separate rooms during all of this travel, but he was the first person I saw each morning, and the last person I saw each night. We had our morning coffee together. We fell asleep watching movies together. We talked late into the night, sometimes on the patio of a hotel, and sometimes from our separate rooms, in those moments when we were drifting off to sleep, but still not ready to let go.

The filming was fun—one adventure after another—but James was the best part of each day and I didn't want that to end.

"So that's a yes?" he said, bringing my hand to his lips.

Heat bloomed in my chest. The thought of being with him every day—finally by ourselves and not on a stage—was intoxicating. As much as I loved working together, I was ready to have James Fielding to myself for a while. "Absolutely," I said, climbing into his lap.

In this moment, I wasn't afraid of all the things that might go wrong, and wasn't worried about how the universe might try to balance out my happiness with heartache. Until now, my life had felt like a series of events created by opposing forces—something wonderful happened, and something devastating followed. But I was beginning to see that all those stories I'd told myself about forces working against me were just that: stories. Stories that made my failures bring shame. Stories that took away my confidence to build the life I wanted. Stories that held power when they shouldn't. When we'd first started filming, I'd still felt like an imposter—a woman pretending to be a co-host. But then I began to think of it as just me being me, learning to adapt to whatever situation we landed in and finding the wonder there. And soon I wasn't an imposter anymore. I was a woman challenging herself to use moments of discomfort as a way to grow into the woman she wanted to be.

I didn't know what precisely came next, but I didn't need to. In this moment, I was content to curl up against James's chest, content to listen to that steady thumping of his heart, grounding me in the wonder of *now*.

His arms tightened around my back as he said, "I can't wait to find your new favorite places." His eyes were fixed on mine as I sat up straighter in his lap, locking my arms around his neck.

"Lucky for you," I said, "we have all the time in the world." I leaned down to kiss him and felt his hands rest on my hips.

"Yes," he said, his eyes so warm and full of love. "Lucky for me."

Join My Newsletter

Subscribe to Lucy's newsletter and be the first to learn about new releases and special offers. As a bonus, get a free Jasmine Falls novella, *You Got This, Maggie Monroe*, when you join.

Sign up at lucydayauthor.com.

Acknowledgments

There are always so many people I'd like to thank when I finish a book. It's a long process that's a lot of fun, takes a lot of work, and a lot of people help along the way. Without those people, you wouldn't be holding this book in your hands.

Thank you always to my dear friend Katie Pryal, who is always one of my first readers. You always help me through the hard parts. To Camille Pagán, I send a very special thank you for inspiring me and encouraging me when I needed it most. I am so very grateful for you. To Darci Swisher, thank you for your wonderful feedback—I'm so lucky to have found you!

Thank you to all of my friends and family, for believing in my dreams and encouraging me to keep writing, even when it's very hard. I love you all so much.

To my readers, thank you for spending your time with me. You make me excited to keep thinking of new ways to write about love, and I'm so happy and humbled that you come on these adventures with me. You keep me hopeful, and energized, and excited to write.

And finally to Andrew: the best love story is the one we write together every day.

About the Author

Born and raised in South Carolina, Lucy Day loves sweet tea, summer nights, and big-hearted love stories. She is winner of an IPPY Silver Medal for Romance (The Almost Lovebirds, 2023). She started writing in college and wrote her first novel after leaving her job at a web comic in St. Louis. Lucy is a bird nerd who can't live without strong coffee and wide open spaces. She's married to her best friend and when she isn't writing a new love story, she's out walking in the woods, dreaming up her next adventure.

To learn more, visit lucydayauthor.com.